Praise for Just Between Us

"Have you ever been in love? Like really fallen head over heels whirlwind in love? If you have, get ready to relive it. If you haven't, the world of Zach and Tosha in *Just Between Us* will pull you right in and make you fall in love with their story. The author transported me through a gambit of emotion. Anger, vulnerability, love, confusion, utter joy, laughter, even fear and uncertainty take the stage in this saga. I could not wait to move through each chapter to find out what was going to happen next. How would this love story unfold? How would everything turn out? Would they be brave enough to surrender to true love? The pages turn themselves as you search for clues as to what you would do if this were your story. I enjoyed every piece of playful banter and every twist that left me feeling uncertain as to what the next chapter held.

You must read this to find out what love looks like and how to recognize it in your life with your family, with your friends, and within you. Both Zach and Tosha take time to reflect on their individual truth and what they are willing to do to honor it. Every time I read this, I uncover a detail that I missed before. So, it becomes a new quest to reveal what else is lurking in the recesses of each scenario. It is rare that I will read a book over and over again, but this one is worthy of my annual reading list. The excitement that comes from following these characters provides me just the right level of hope and joy to ca˙

ıldra Oates, Beta Reader

D1711130

Just Betw........................... novel that delves into both the harsh and hopeful realities of a budding relationship—what it means to have baggage, what it means to finally store that baggage away, what it means to regain long forgotten trust, and most poignantly…what it means to be a family. Tosha and Zach's unexpected relationship after a blind date is surprisingly relatable, and perhaps it is because the author is able to bring so much honesty and transparency to her writing. This couple may be fictional, but they certainly are not idealized. Through the intimacy of breaking bread, à la dinner dates with a toddler in tow, the reader hopes for their love to prevail against the odds. Each detail is intentional and culminates in an exciting, fast-paced affair of honor.

Any reader who has experienced heartache, loss, and redemption in love can connect with Tosha and Zach as they struggle to overcome the roadblocks in the way of their love. "What if…?" questions will pop up into the reader's mind through each scenario, making this book a great opportunity to read alongside friends, family, and partners. Cassandra Ulrich has a wonderful touch for giving the reader a peek into the promising, the painful, the sensitive, and the sensual.

~Rachel Parsons, <u>Do What's Write: Writer's Group & Podcast</u>
co-host

Praise for Other Books by Cassandra Ulrich

A Beautiful Girl

"Few YA books involve serious musicians or the healing power of music. As a musician, I was thrilled that this one included both. I was compelled to finish this in one reading. My heart pounded in my ears at the terrifying scenes involving the evil, truly evil stepfather. I had to keep reading to learn how the situation was resolved."

Professor Gore, Co-Author of All is Assuredly Well

"I received my book on Saturday evening when I got home and four hours later, I had read the entire book. Cassandra, I truly cannot remember the last time I read an entire book in one setting. Congratulations for your gift. I can now say with conviction that "My name is Renee Rolling, and I am a beautiful girl"."

Renee Rolling, Avid Reader

Love's Intensity

"Wow, this book has a lot going on it but in a good way. What would you do if found out that the "help" had a past with the very people that you worked for? That's what Brad and Kressa face in the book. Brad's dad was best friends with Kressa's mom growing up and that [didn't] sit well with Brad's stepmom. Loved that little conflict in the book. Kept the adults interesting and not just window dressing in the book. Too often parents in YA books are forgotten about or worse, just window dressing. ~ I highly recommend Love's Intensity..."

Love, Laughter, Friendship

Billiard Buddies

"This book kept me engaged the entire time from start to finish. I was on edge waiting to see what would happen next. I would recommend this book if you like romantic novels."

Dione A. Quarles, Avid Reader

Adelle and Brandon: Friends for Life

"In *Adelle and Brandon: Friends for Life,* Cassandra Ulrich once again writes believable characters I immediately like. She draws Adelle and Brandon so perfectly that I can relate to them as I would to friends. In this short story, Ulrich masterfully handles the inner thought process for Adelle which gives the readers a chance to experience the character's inner struggle as she tries to hide her true feelings for her best friend. The sign of a good story is that it lingers in the memory for days. After reading *Adelle and Brandon: Friends for Life,* I find myself wondering how they are both doing."

Gail Priest, Author of the Annie Crow Knoll Trilogy and Eastern Short Shorts

If It Kills Me

"Jaeson is shy, awkward and I'm surprised he doesn't end up with burn marks in all the wrong places as much as he spills coffee in her presence. I'm thinking, "oh wow, what a klutz!" At the same time, I'm secretly rooting for him. He's clearly smitten with the woman from the first time he lays eyes on her. I mean, really, how can she not tell?! Part of me wanted to whack her with a newspaper driving home the message, 'obvious'! She stays with Rick despite the fact he's an all original playboy and is bound to break her heart. With every excuse he made, I wanted to wring his neck and cheer on Jae. I have to admit though, I respect Jae for doing the right thing by her and his roommate. Most men would've just taken what they wanted without care to someone else's feelings.

Mrs. Ulrich delivers a clean, sweet romance that will grab you from the beginning of the story to the end. Sorry folks, no spoilers here, buy the book!!"

~Angel Brown,

Reviews, Excerpts, and Promos

Danny R.O.S.S.

"Danny R.O.S.S. is a wonderful adventure with covert style action, an undercurrent of romance, with a dash of science fiction. The delicious tension between Danny and Dr. Zan--both gun shy from previous tragic romances--adds to the fore story of a navy seal faced with a dramatic career change caused when an Ops goes horribly wrong. Cassandra Ulrich hits all the notes with a beautiful balance of emotion and twists driven by multiple covert operations keeping the reader on their toes. The addition of the short "Battle at Kitee" was an incredible extra treat. Hooyah!"

~Suzanne Y. Snow, Author of the science fiction series "Forrorrois"

"It's a super sweet Navy SEAL novel with a touch of science fiction."

~USA Today Best-Selling Author Jennifer M. Eaton

Praise for Books by Cassandra Skelton

Real Purpose: You Are Special

"Very inspirational and spiritually uplifting."

Kiana Jones-Peoples, Avid Reader

By Cassandra Ulrich

A Beautiful Girl
a teen inspirational novella

Love's Intensity
a teen paranormal romance novel

Billiard Buddies
a New Adult romance novella

Adelle and Brandon: Friends for Life
a contemporary women's fiction short story

If It Kills Me
a New Adult contemporary romantic comedy

Danny R.O.S.S.
a teen SciFi adventure

By Cassandra Skelton

Poetic Collections

Just Between Us

by

Cassandra Ulrich

ơ

cassandraulrich.com

Collingswood, New Jersey

Just Between Us

By Cassandra Ulrich

Published by: Cassandra Ulrich
P.O. Box 492
Collingswood, NJ 08108-0492
Email: cassandra@cassandraulrich.com

Visit Cassandra Ulrich, Author Official Mobile Friendly Site

10 9 8 7 6 5 4 3 2 1

To my Kittitian siblings with love.

Acknowledgments

ය

God – for my gift of creativity.

Family – for inspiring me to keep on writing.

Friends – for reading and rereading my stories and poems.

Assaldra Oates – for being my beta reader and promising to read this story once every year.

Editor Angel Brown – for catching all the areas that didn't flow well or enhance the story.

Rachel Parsons – for proofreading; you are a master comma czar. Thank you!

Loving and devoted step and adoptive dads – who cared for a ready-made family as if they were genetically their own; you inspired Zach's character.

Bernadine – for helping me with Olivia's Kittitian dialect, for walking with me on this publishing journey from the beginning, and for falling in love with Zach and Tosha's story when I'd only read you two scenes from the first draft. I based Zach and Olivia's sibling relationship on ours. This story is my gift to you. Happy Birthday! Luv you tons.

Just Between Us

Cassandra Ulrich

ᥫᨒ

Chapter 1

Thrilled to spend a long weekend with best friends Karida and Tevin, Tosha secured her toddler Emily in one arm and grasped the handles of the stroller before she climbed up the steps into a bus. Although she had a Toyota, she didn't feel like driving.

Besides, with Chaz's car in the shop, he'll need it for groceries.

"Mommy, how long this goin' take?" Emily asked.

"Long enough for you to take a nap, baby."

"I don't want a nap."

Her little girl snuggled against Tosha's breast as she stared at the passing scenery. Tosha longed for the soft snores that never came. Every so often, Emily squirmed around, which squeezed Tosha's legs in places she'd forgotten about. Her toddler's energy never seemed to diminish until she fell asleep at night.

This is going to be a tough ride for both of us. Maybe I should have driven that car after all.

Thirty minutes into the ride with all its stops and starts, Tosha's stomach protested. She pulled a bottle of water out of her weekend satchel and took a sip. When that seemed to settle things, she swallowed another mouthful.

3

She thought back to all the times Chaz said he had everything handled. That she didn't need birth control. How he didn't need condoms. So far, Emily was the result of the one time his method didn't work.

What if it's happened again?

Tosha lived with Chaz for three years in the hopes of getting married. When she got pregnant with Emily and Chaz gave her a ring, Tosha thought marriage was imminent, that he'd commit. Yet, even after almost three years since Emily's birth, Chaz still delayed what she wanted most—security with him for a lifetime. Her naivety continued to haunt her.

Once the bus arrived at her stop, Tosha gathered up her child and belongings. She sucked in a deep breath and placed Emily in her stroller. The short walk helped to settle Tosha's stomach, but thoughts of another baby occupied her mind.

Soon after Tosha knocked, Karida, her childhood friend, opened the door and gifted her the biggest grin. "Hey, girlfriend. So glad you and Emily could stay over. Come on in."

"That was a *long* ride. Emily wouldn't sleep."

"Because I not tired," her daughter said.

Tosha placed Emily on the floor and shook her head as her daughter scampered off toward the guest bedroom. "She never stops."

"Well, you're here now. I'll help you look after her." Karida hugged Tosha and gazed at her with concern. "You look worn out. Do *you* need a nap?"

"No, I'm good. My stomach's a bit upset."

"Did you eat something crazy?"

"I don't think so."

Karida raised her eyebrows. "When's your period?"

"I haven't missed it yet."

"That's not what I asked you."

"It should come next week."

"Want to check?" Karida asked.

Tosha didn't answer. Instead, she bolted for the bathroom, flipped up the toilet seat, and released the contents of her stomach into the bowl. When she finished, she turned toward the doorway to find Karida standing there.

"After we get you cleaned up and settled, I'll head over to the pharmacy to pick up a kit for you."

Karida didn't go for a few hours, considering Tosha paid homage to the porcelain god all evening long.

I definitely should've driven my car.

***

Still in denial, Tosha tucked the pregnancy test kit into her bag the next day.

"I'll take it when I go home," she said to Karida.

"Suit yourself."

However, after a second night of nauseated misery, she pulled it back out of her bag when she woke the second morning and marched into the bathroom.

Minutes later, Tosha was still sitting on the toilet, staring at the stick.

Pregnant.

A knock on the bathroom door made Tosha sigh.

"You okay in there?" Karida asked through the door.

"Yeah. Give me a minute." Tosha tidied up, washed her hands, and opened the door. She offered a lop-sided smile. "I'm pregnant."

"Oh, Tosha, another baby. I'm so happy for you."

"What if he's upset?" Tosha asked as she stared at the test stick.

Karida's elation turned to trepidation. "Then he has only to blame himself. You've given him the best of yourself. You deserve better." Karida laid a hand on Tosha's shoulder. "Call us if he gives you a hard time. You always have a home here with Tevin and me."

Tosha hoped it wouldn't come to that. Chaz had always treated her well, and when Emily had been born, he'd taken care of her well enough. At least, that's what she tried to tell herself.

He'll be happy. It'll be different this time. Perhaps, now Chaz will say "I do."

Emily dashed between Tosha and Karida to hug Tosha's legs. "Are we going home to Daddy today, Mommy?"

"Yes, and guess what?" Tosha knelt on the floor. "You're getting a new baby brother or sister. Isn't that great?" Tosha forced a smile on her face.

"Yay. I can't wait," Emily said then ran off again to the guest room.

***

Later, about mid-afternoon, Tosha and Emily hugged Karida and Tevin goodbye.

"Come, Emily, let's go tell Daddy the good news. He should be home by now."

"Okay, Mommy."

With an umbrella stroller in one hand, Tosha held Emily in the other and got back on a bus for the return trip home. This time, Tosha's stomach behaved as her baby girl pointed at all the parks as they rode on.

"Can we go to the park, Mommy?"

"We'll see, baby girl. I want to stop at the corner store to get a few things."

By the time they arrived at their stop, Emily possessed pent up energy. Tosha's heart beat with love for her precious little girl.

"Looks like we better go to the park first," Tosha said.

"Yay!" Emily clapped her hands.

Tosha's thoughts swirled. She placed her daughter into the stroller and walked to a playground two blocks away, a small detour but worth the huge grin on that precious little face. An hour later, Tosha gathered up her daughter and buckled her into the stroller once more. After visiting the corner store to pick up a few items to help with the morning sickness, she pushed the stroller up to the door of the apartment she shared with Chaz and lifted her now napping daughter out.

All her hopes vanished when Tosha heard laughter and moaning coming from inside. Without hesitation, she turned the knob, surprised to find the door unlocked. She pushed it open and gasped. Her hand rushed to cover Emily's eyes in case she woke to this atrocity—Chaz doing *it* with a woman in the middle of the living room floor. He groaned, his behind thrusting to and fro, oblivious anyone had entered the room.

Tosha stared and mumbled, "Sugar Honey Iced Tea," into her daughter's hair. She wanted to scream, but Emily's even breathing prevented her from uttering the many profanities scratching on the edge of her mind. Her face grew hot.

"What the h——," escaped her lips. Tosha stopped herself before the word came out her mouth. Her daughter shouldn't be subjected to the string of curses lying on her tongue. Chaz stopped and pulled away from whoever it was without clothes on the floor beneath him. Tosha hissed. "How dare you!" To her dismay, Emily stirred. Tosha bit her tongue to avoid saying more words unfit for her little girl's ears.

"What Mommy?"

"Don't look," Tosha replied, redirecting Emily's head into the crook of her neck. Her daughter must not be subjected to the sight of her father doing the nasty with the tramp on the living room floor.

Leaving the front door open, Tosha stepped forward, not caring who saw Chaz and the whore naked. "Bird In The Chicken House!" Hot blood bubbled through Tosha's veins. She thought of so many things she'd like to do to this man, but none were worth being taken away from her children for life.

"Get dressed," she growled, itching to say more but not in earshot of Emily.

"What are you doing here so early, Tosha?"

She could hardly believe he had the guts to ask.

"Is this your woman?" asked ugly, sitting on the floor feebly attempting to cover her ample pale breasts. There was more that woman should have kept under wraps from someone not her own.

Tosha ignored them and rushed to the bedroom she shared with the man she now despised. She slammed the door shut and locked it before placing Emily on the floor.

"Mommy, what's wrong?"

"We're leaving. Daddy did something very bad."

"What?"

"He proved he doesn't love me, baby. We have to leave."

Tosha dashed to the closet, pulled out a suitcase, raked the zipper open, and threw in some clothes. *I need to hurry up.* She'd have to come back later for the rest of her stuff when he was out. *Where are we even gonna live? We can't stay at Karida's and Tevin's forever.*

Chaz banged on the door, yelling for her to let him in. She unlocked it and glared at him.

"Go away," Tosha said, fighting back the tears. "I can't believe you were…" She stopped herself. The next word wasn't pretty.

"What are you doing?" He filled the doorway with his bulky form.

"Leaving. It's now clear to me we're *never* getting married. I'm pawning the ring. You owe me that much. Now, move aside. I need to pack Emily's things."

"Where are you going?" he asked with a now somber tone.

"Why do you care? You can finish up with Miss Thing out there when we're gone." She zipped up her suitcase and dragged it on the floor before she grabbed Emily's hand and pushed past her ex-fiancé.

Tosha dared not look toward his plaything for fear she'd beat that trick to a bloody pulp. Once inside their little girl's room, Tosha closed the door. But it didn't stay closed long. He followed her. She pulled out an armful of clothes and threw them into an open bag with a panda painted on the front.

"I want you to stay."

"Why? So you could come home to a brainless release? How many, Chaz? How many have you been with? Is she the first?"

He frowned. "No. She's not the first." He shrugged. "I lost count."

Tosha's eyes bulged in disbelief, and her heart fell through her stomach and onto the floor for him to stomp. How could she have been so stupid? He never wanted to marry her. He used her as an excuse for a façade of stability. How could she have been so blind?

Lifting Emily up into her arms, Tosha wrapped her free hand around both sets of handles.

"How long?"

"Oh... I'm not coming back." For the sake of her daughter, Tosha hated what she knew she would say next. "You never really loved me. You put up with me because I got pregnant. You blame me for that. So, we're moving out to start a new life away from you. You are now free of us, 'cause I'm sure free of you. I don't care if you support her or not. I'm done with you."

"I'm sorry, Tosh. It just happened."

Her cheeks grew hot, and the muscles in her neck tightened. She grimaced. "So, she just happened to stop by, and you just happened to slip into her..." She bit her tongue again until it hurt. She dared not say anything like that for

Emily to hear. She took a deep breath and calmly said, "Leave me alone. I'll get out of your way."

"What will you do for money?"

"Ha," she laughed. "You've taken so much from me, and I doubt you'll give any of it back. Thank God, I still have people in my life who actually love me. My friends will help me."

"Tosha."

She brought up a palm toward him and snarled. "Stop talking. Don't say my name."

He reached out toward her, but she stood firm.

She forced, "That would be a mistake," through clenched teeth.

"Mommy, Mommy."

"Shush, baby," she said in soft tones, patting Emily on the head. Tosha returned her attention to Chaz. "You brought a slut into *our* apartment so that our daughter could walk in on *THAT!* So, before I lose my mind and my religion, move aside and let me do what I need to do, so help me God."

"I'm sorry," he said, shrugging his shoulders again and stepping aside.

"Oh… That you are, but it's too late for that. You've been building three years of sorry, and I'm done."

She glared at him until he left Emily's room. Her daughter began to cry.

"Need help?" He didn't even face her.

"No!" she said, rushing past him and out the front door into the hallway. She'd manage. Tosha turned to Chaz one last time. "You never once told our daughter you loved her. Why's that?"

Chaz jerked his head to the side and turned away from her, his final act of disrespect toward her. She'd been stupid to believe he'd ever marry her. He toyed with her love, and now her heart shattered in tiny pieces.

She struggled not to join Emily's crying before she arrived at her best friend's front door. She threw the bags into the trunk of her old Toyota and buckled Emily in the back seat. The instant a strange perfume wafted up her nose, the dam holding back Tosha's tears broke. She gritted her teeth as heat rushed to her face. *He drove that hussy here in* my *car?*

"Mommy, why you sad?"

"Daddy did something very, very bad, baby."

"Where we going?"

Two faces popped into Tosha's head. Karida and Tevin. "Friends, baby. We're going to our friends' house."

Tosha dialed a number she knew by heart.

"Kar, I need a place to stay…permanently. Chaz has some ho in our home. I'm…" Tosha sniffed. "I'm leaving him, and I'm never coming back."

<u>Chapter 2</u>

"Hey, Zach, what brings you here so late?" asked Tevin. "When Karida told me you were sitting in the living room, I thought she was sleepwalking."

"You know, Tev, I just don't understand women. I take them out to decent places, and just when I think things are going great, they find some pathetic reason to break things off with me."

"What happened with Amy? I thought she liked you."

"We have too many incompatibilities. At least that's what she said. What the heck does that mean? I thought opposites should attract."

"I'm sorry, Zach."

"That's the fourth girl in three months, and Amy lasted three weeks. I'm striking out, and I can't figure out why. I'm tired. I'm tired of the bars, the dating networks, all of it. I guess I'm just meant to be by myself," Zach said, stretching out on the sofa.

"Hey, don't give up just yet. What if Karida and I gave it a shot?"

"What? Like set me up?"

"Sure. We usually stay out of our friends' personal dating lives, but I think we might have someone who might work out. No promises, but…"

"I don't know, Tev. I think I need a break."

"All right," agreed Tevin, "you take a break for about a month. It'll give her a chance to settle in. She just found a place across town. I'll have Karida talk to her about you."

"You really think this'll go somewhere? My heart can't take any more duds."

"I can only say I don't think her heart can either. It's risky, like any relationship, but I think you two have a chance at working out together."

"Okay. I'll let you lead on this. You've never thrown me under a bus. I trust you," said Zach, and he closed his eyes.

***

For two weeks, Tosha strove to find a place she and her daughter could call home before walking into the right apartment. Fortunately, her old Toyota didn't require any repairs. She couldn't afford too many expenses on top of everything else she needed to buy.

At first, Chaz called to talk to Emily, but by the third week since she'd left him, he'd lost interest in the one person Tosha hoped had a hold on his heart. Her own heart broke as she watched her recently potty-trained child regress into messy diapers once more.

Tosha got out of the car, picked Emily up into her arms, and strolled up the walkway to her best friend's home.

"Tosh. Em. Come in. It's so good to see you. Dinner is almost ready," said Karida with a huge smile.

"Do you need any help?" asked Tosha as she placed Emily and the diaper bag on the carpeted floor.

"Not at all, but come sit on the stool while I finish the stew."

Tosha eyed Emily who by now had found the train set Karida and Tevin kept in the living room to entertain her daughter. Karida had always loved trains. How many trips had they taken across numerous states together, all via trains? Tosha returned her attention to Karida who had been speaking the whole time.

"So, Tosha, I have a surprise for you."

"I'm thinking I'm not going to like *this* surprise."

"His name is Zach, a close friend of ours. Tevin and I think you two should meet, go out, and get to know each other."

"Karida," Tosha said, exasperation evident in her tone, "I just got out of a horrible relationship. I really don't want to enter another one right now, especially not with Emily."

"Zach is different. He's really sweet and kind, a decent guy. He's good with kids. We all taught at camp a few years ago. He's amazing."

"If he's so amazing, why isn't he already on someone else's arm?"

"We're not quite sure except that he's looking for more than a fling. And so are you."

"How old is he?"

"Twenty-four."

"He's four years younger than me."

"Yep, and he knows that."

"What else have you told him?"

"I showed him your picture, and he liked what he saw. I'm afraid we don't have one of him, so you'll just have to take my word that he's hot."

"And he doesn't mind I'm so much older than he is."

"'Inconsequential' is the way he put it. The date is on."

Tosha rolled her eyes. "I can't believe you told him how old I am." She had a tough time believing that her best friends were playing matchmaker so soon after the end of her nightmare relationship.

"Girlfriend, please, give this a chance. You're not obligated to like him, but I think he'll at least make a great friend."

Tosha let an audible sigh escape her lips. "Kar, I'm afraid."

"I know. Just...take this step. I'm here to help you down whatever road you choose."

"What about Emily?"

"Taken care of. We'll watch her for the night...all night if we need to."

"Karida!"

With palms raised, Karida said, "I'm not implying you'll sleep with him, but you may want to take a break from her after a wonderful evening."

"You have high hopes, don't you?"

Karida smiled. "Tosha, you deserve some hope just about now."

"And I'm pregnant. Does he know?"

"We haven't said anything about your life. We think that's your business to divulge. Trust me. I wouldn't encourage you to do this if I thought you'd get hurt. Zach is worth the shot."

"Very well. You think it's wise to go out so soon after Chaz?"

"Yes, I think you need this even if all that happens is a good friendship."

"All right, I'll go out with him," Tosha said against her better judgment. "When is this hook up planned?"

"How about in a week?"

Chapter 3

"Sit, Tosha. I'll get Em ready for bed," said Karida, who then greeted and fussed over Emily.

Tosha wrung her hands and glanced around. Her gaze rested on fresh flowers that Karida always kept around the house. The daisies, in particular, resonated with her.

With Emily tucked away in one of the bedrooms, Tosha's heart beat hard when the doorbell rang. Tevin nodded, encouraging her to answer the door for her blind date.

"You're a much more beautiful sight than I am. He always sees my mug," Tevin joked. "I think I'll like to see him blown away by the woman he's taking out tonight."

"I'm nervous," said Tosha.

"So is he," said Karida as she reentered the room. "Just smile, and the night will take care of the rest."

Tosha placed her hand on the knob and opened the door to a tall, slender, well-built man, his well-dressed attire topped off with a black bow tie. His eyes brightened at the sight of her, and he granted her the biggest grin she'd ever seen on a first date. She gasped, smiled back in spite of herself, and had to proverbially pull herself off the floor.

"Good evening," he said with a tenor voice as smooth as butter, "I'm Zach Caldwell. You must be Tosha." He extended his hand, but it took a moment for her to register what he expected.

"Yes, Tosha Brown," she responded, realizing that she needed to shake his hand. He had a firm, yet gentle grip.

"Are you ready to go?" he asked.

She nodded and hooked his bent arm.

He waved at Karida and Tevin. "I'll have her back before midnight."

"There's no curfew. Just have fun," said Tevin.

Zach opened the passenger door and ushered her into his car. Once he'd gotten settled next to her, he pushed the key into the ignition and turned toward her.

"I've never been on a blind date before. Karida said you'd be fine wherever we went, so I figured I'd take you to my favorite steak restaurant. Is that all right?"

"Yes, that's great," she said, suddenly feeling like a schoolgirl going out for the first time. "I've never been on a blind date either. I think I'm a bag of nerves right now."

"That makes two of us, so how about we try to relax and not worry too much about pleasing our friends. I look forward to knowing you."

Tosha nodded, and he started the car.

A few minutes later, Zach broke the silence.

"I must confess I didn't come into this date quite as blind as you might think."

"I know. Karida told me you saw a photo of me."

"That picture didn't quite capture the essence of your beauty. You're gorgeous! I must tell Karida to purchase a different camera."

Warmth rushed to Tosha's cheeks. "Thank you. You had the advantage. I didn't see one of you."

"I hope you're not disappointed."

A nervous smile escaped her lips. "Not at all. You're a very good-looking man."

"You're not just saying that? I'd think you beautiful no matter what your impression of me."

"No. I mean it."

"I'm not a disappointment?"

"You're an I'm-having-trouble-breathing kind of handsome." Saying "hot" or "eye-candy" just didn't seem appropriate on a first date. With his complexion a lighter shade of milk chocolate, he was, mmm, so fine. Tosha fanned her face.

He grinned, and his cheeks flushed a reddish hue. "Thanks, Tosha, you made my day."

"You're welcome." Tosha gazed out the window. She found it difficult to look at him for fear she would pounce on him and cause an accident.

"I didn't mean to make you uncomfortable. I'm really glad you agreed to go out with me."

"I'm all right. I'm glad, too," she admitted, as much to herself as to him.

Zach grinned again. In minutes, he pulled into a parking lot.

"I'll get your door." He exited and walked around the hood with a confident businessman's swagger—back and neck straight with a casual swing of the arms.

She glanced at the steering wheel. Lexus. He had to be a white-collar worker. No way a construction guy drives a car like this.

He opened her door and offered her his hand. His touch sent electric chills to her core. Why hadn't Karida warned her that she'd found the man of her dreams? He released her hand the moment she stood, but she almost didn't let go. She matched his long-legged steps until he reached the front entrance where he opened the door. He waited until she entered before doing so himself.

Tosha had never known what it was like to be treated so special. Every second spent with him was a dream she didn't want to end.

The model-looking young woman with blue eye shadow over slanted eyes smiled as Zach approached, Tosha close on his heels.

"Good evening, Mister Caldwell. Reservation for two?"

"Yes, please. By the window, if possible."

"Of course. Just a moment."

Tosha peered into the seating area while the lady typed something into a tablet. White tablecloths, napkins folded into shells, and waiters in black ties and vests greeted her eyes. Women wore low cut formal dresses.

"I'm underdressed," Tosha said.

"Naw. You're perfect," he whispered in her ear.

Goosebumps rose on her arms. Her cheeks warmed.

"You're all set. Come with me," the girl said, breaking the spell. Her shapely bottom swayed as she stepped away from the maître d stand and led the way.

Zach grasped Tosha's hand before following.

"You must come here a lot."

He glanced back at her and grinned. "I do."

"Is this satisfactory, Mr. Caldwell?" The woman gestured toward a table with a rose candle and a single red long stem rose in a tall crystal vase.

"Yes. Thank you."

Tosha's lips parted a little, but no sound came out. Had he actually ordered a rose for her?

"I will get this out of your way," the lady leaned over and grabbed the vase, "and box it up when you're all finished."

He nodded and pulled out a chair for Tosha before seating himself on the other side of the cozy rectangular table. "Is this fine? She can find another—"

Tosha found her voice again. "It's more than fine."

The young woman smiled. "Wonderful. Here are your menus. Your waiter will be over shortly."

Once the pretty girl had reached her stand, Tosha returned her gaze to Zach. His eyes sparkled as if he'd not taken his eyes off Tosha for even one second. She glanced at the candle to halt whatever charms he sent her way. Seconds later, she looked up again, hoping she'd be able to compose herself.

Might as well start with some basic questions. "You bring all your first dates here?" *Why'd I even ask that?*

"Never. You're the first."

"But you said you ate here before."

"I bring my clients here."

"Clients." She frowned at him.

He chuckled. "Business clients. Not the other kind you're thinking about."

Good Lawd. He reads minds, too? "What do you do?"

"I work for a large accounting firm downtown."

She wrapped her hand around the water-filled stem glass to her right and took a sip. He did the same. She put the glass down before she spilled it on herself.

"Why me?"

"I wanted to impress you."

"So far, so good." She picked up the menu and gasped. "There aren't any prices."

"I wouldn't have brought you here if that mattered. Just order whatever you like, but save room for dessert, if you can."

"What are you getting?"

"The filet mignon."

"Do you recommend it?"

"I do, but not your first time."

"What? You don't think I can handle it?"

He smiled and shook his head. "Maybe, but how about I share a bite with you and see how you do. I suggest," he glanced at the menu, "the T-bone with baked sweet potato."

"You think you know me that well."

"Trust me on this."

"Hmm." She took another sip of water. *I bet it's expensive.*

"And just in case you're thinking it's the money, it's not. One bite may cost you more than cash. But we'll have to see if I'm right about you. You might be thanking me. Besides, the T is my second favorite here."

"Yes, we'll see about that. I'm sure I could handle anything put in front of me, but I'll order the T-bone. I just happen to like good steak on a bone."

Zach grinned at her and placed the order when the waiter arrived.

"Would you like to look at our wine list?"

Tosha shook her head.

"Not this evening," Zach said. "Something less spirited like…"

"Sprite or ginger ale," Tosha said.

"And I'll have a Coke."

"Very well. I'll be back momentarily with your drinks."

Zach turned his head to face Tosha. "No wine, huh?"

"I'd like to remember every detail about the evening."

"Understood."

"So, is Zach short for something?"

He smiled. "Zacharias."

"Either you're Jewish or your dad toted scripture."

"The latter. He was a proud Black man from St. Kitts."

Her interest peaked. "Wow. Have you been there?"

"Once. When I was sixteen. It's a beautiful island."

"I've seen pictures but never visited."

"You should. I think you'd enjoy it. Palm trees, sparkling sand, warm ocean water."

"Here are your drinks," the waiter said, interrupting the conversation as he placed the coasters and glasses down. "I brought you a ginger ale." Tosha nodded at him in acceptance. "Do you need anything else?"

"No, we're fine," Zach said.

Tosha waited until the waiter walked away. "Did you stay in the capital?"

"Basseterre? No. My dad's family lives in Tabernacle, so I stayed there. It's a small village where everyone knows everybody else."

"What was the most interesting thing you did while you stayed there?"

"I learned to climb the coconut tree like an island boy and used a machete to cut some down."

She leaned toward the table. "Weren't you scared you'd fall?"

"Some. The worst part was how badly I scraped up my feet and legs. There's an art to it."

She continued asking him questions about his trip, and he answered each one without hesitation. His attractive smile revealed that he didn't mind. The waiter returned with their meals after what seemed like mere moments.

"Mmm. That looks delicious," she said. Her mouth watered at the sight of his filet mignon.

"Would you like to try a bite?" Zach asked.

She shook her head. "No, I'm good." The T-bone would more than fill her up.

He cut off a piece of the filet and offered it to her from his fork. "Really, I don't mind."

"You don't care if I eat from your fork?"

"No. Why? Do you have cooties?" He grinned.

"No," she said and scrunched up her nose. "I haven't heard that word since grade school."

"I like using it from time to time. It seemed appropriate in this case." He made a circle with the piece of meat right in front of her nose. "Eat. Before it gets cold."

She leaned in, opened her mouth, and pulled off the mignon with her teeth, careful not to touch the fork.

"Be careful now," he said with a smirk.

The instant she bit down, warm juices flowed across her tongue. She placed her utensils down, palmed the table, and wrapped her thumbs underneath. Her eyes fluttered closed, and a moan escaped her lips. She kept chewing, letting the succulent meat roll around her mouth until she swallowed. Ripples of bliss swept over her from head to toe, just like an o...*my, what is happening to me*? Even her abdomen fluttered, reminding her of the baby in her womb. *But it's too early for that.* Aware again that Zach had been sitting across from her, she opened her eyes—and found his eyes opened wide with eyebrows raised—unable to prevent the warmth rushing to her cheeks.

"Yeah, it's that good." He lowered his eyebrows, an adorable quirky smile forming on his lips, but the twinkle in his eyes revealed something more.

Tosha glanced around to find others staring at her. Her gut clenched. "Was I that loud?"

This time he chuckled. "Not loud. You were...I'm trying to find the right words to describe this. You were immersed," he waved an asparagus stuck to the end of his fork at her, "in whatever was happening there. It was...a rather *moving* experience for the rest of us."

"I'm so embarrassed," she said and shielded her face with her hands.

"I think I have you beat on that one."

She peeked at him through her fingers. "How so?"

"Imagine sitting here, watching you...woo, then have everyone study me wondering what *I* did, only to find myself wishing *I* were that piece of meat. I'm the one who should be embarrassed."

Her face burned again.

"I have got to learn how to make this mignon just to see that happen again." He grinned.

"Stop. I was *not* that loud."

He shook his head.

"I was?"

Instead of answering, he cut another piece and popped it into his mouth. Closing his eyes, he chewed but didn't make a sound.

"I don't know how you ate that so quiet-like."

"What you did really wasn't so bad." He sliced off another piece and held it up. "I fell under the spell of this morsel during a meeting with a customer I'd only just met. Think of it…I'm moaning across from someone I wasn't even attracted to. How'd you suppose that looked to everyone sitting close by?" He ate, chewed, and swallowed. "They let me come back. This filet is pure ecstasy. Everyone's first time is a little boisterous."

"You knew I would do that?" She ate a piece of her own steak without the same effect. Similar melt-in-your-mouth texture but no vavoom.

"I didn't, not for sure. You could have said no to my offer," he sliced off a chunk and held the fork out to her, "Do you want another piece?"

"And embarrass myself again?"

"Now that you know it's coming, you'll handle it better. Unless, of course, you're afraid I have cooties."

"Mmm. What manner of man are you?"

He answered her with a wide grin that showed his well-formed teeth.

She opened her mouth, and he fed it to her. This time she swallowed the moan down. Oh, it was so good.

"Yeah, I definitely have to get the recipe for this. Once you have a taste of ecstasy, it's tough to eat anything else," he said.

"Next time, I'm choosing the mignon."

"So, there'll be a next time?" He winked.

"Uh."

"Don't answer that just yet. Finish your dinner. I'd like to show you something first."

"What?"

"It's a surprise. Would you like dessert?"

"I don't know. After that filet mignon, I'm afraid to try anything else."

"Nothing else will bring you to the brink like that did. You're pretty safe. You like chocolate?"

"You are trying to tempt me."

He stared at her for a moment. "I don't have to try, do I? You'd like some."

"Are we still talking about dessert?"

He chuckled. "Absolutely. We'll share." He raised a hand to get the waiter's attention.

"Is everything all right, Mr. Caldwell?"

"May we have one of what I like to call the chocolate volcano?" Zach asked.

"Of course, sir."

"But we're not even done with the main course," Tosha said.

"That's quite all right," the waiter said. "This dessert takes a bit of time to prepare. No need to rush." He nodded and walked away.

"What is this volcano?"

"You'll see."

"Is that the surprise?"

He shook his head. "No. The surprise comes later."

"Will I like the surprise?"

"How about you let me know when the time comes." He smiled. "I'd like to tell you some more about my trip to St. Kitts. We sort of got interrupted."

Her cheeks heated again. "I'm listening."

As each moment passed, Tosha failed to stop herself from falling for the charming gentleman with a little bit of a naughty humor, just the way she liked it. Why'd he have to be so perfect? What about her daughter and unborn child?

He described the home where he stayed in St. Kitts during his visit. How it stood on stilts to protect against the waters flowing downhill through the village from the dormant volcano, Mount Misery now called Mount Liamuiga, during hurricane season. How he experienced his first earthquake on the island and almost ran out of the swaying house but for fear of breaking a leg trying.

Sitting across from him, she struggled to find the right time to bring up her children. She felt like that house he'd described—shaken on an unstable foundation.

"Ready for dessert?" Zach asked, already finished with his meal. That he did so despite relaying his riveting story amazed her.

"Just about." She swallowed some potato—the last of her meal—and sipped her ginger ale.

"Great. It should be here in a few minutes. Now, it's my turn to ask the questions," he said.

"Go ahead."

"What do *you* do?"

"I'm an admin at a law firm downtown. Nothing too exciting."

"I suppose I better watch my numbers a bit closer."

"Why's that?"

"One miscalculation could lead to me showing up on your professional doorstep."

"I'm just the admin. I wouldn't be opposing you."

"Don't underestimate your value. You're privy to all their secrets."

"I never thought of it like that."

"What do you like to do for fun?" Zach asked, but the waiter returned before she could answer.

"Here's your volcano with two spoons. Enjoy."

"Wow, this is amazing," Tosha said. Dark chocolate oozed out from the top of the mound.

"I'm glad you approve. I wanted a dessert as stunning as you are."

Her cheeks warmed, but she distracted herself with a bite, praying she wouldn't moan again. The cake melted on her tongue and slipped down her throat with ease. "Delicious, too."

He smiled as he chewed. "Feel free to answer my questions between bites. We have time."

Conversation over dessert progressed better than Tosha had expected. She feared they would mull over past failed relationships and most recent breakups, but no matter what path they took, Zach only wanted to know what she liked, what she didn't, and what she dreamed about when no one else was watching. She found it easy to talk to him and hoped he felt the same.

Always the perfect gentleman, he held doors open and asked if she needed his jacket on the windy walkway. He peered at his watch.

"It's almost midnight. Are you ready to go home, or can you hang with me a bit longer?"

Tosha's heart leapt in her chest. He wanted to be with her just to talk, and admittedly she wanted to be with him, too. She hadn't realized how much she needed this—a male companion who wasn't afraid to talk about…stuff.

"I promise not to change into rag clothes at the strike of twelve," she said, and he smiled sweetly at her.

"Good. Let's walk a bit farther."

She hooked his arm as she did when he first picked her up, but this time he drew her closer to his side. Everything had been great…too great. She'd told him about her childhood and her first job at a department store. He'd told her about his summer adventure in Europe and the time he helped the victims of a tsunami in the Pacific where he had barely escaped himself. She felt drawn to him, but he lacked one thing. He didn't know about her daughter or the one on the way.

What if he doesn't like children as Karida supposes? Then this is over before it's begun.

***

"How are you with spur of the moment?" Zach asked.

"Good, I guess."

He grinned. "I want to show you something, but you have to close your eyes until we get there."

"What?"

"It's the surprise, but you have to trust me."

"We just met."

"I know, but it won't be the same if you walk up to it with your eyes open."

"Okaaay? Am I going to regret this?"

"No, I think you'll like it. At least, I hope so. Will you trust me?"

Her smile warmed him. "All right."

"Great. Close your eyes and walk with me."

"Don't let me fall."

"I won't. I'll be right next to you the whole time."

She covered her eyes with one hand while he held the other. He wrapped his free arm around her waist and guided her along the sidewalk. He spoke before each footfall, encouraging her to continue.

When they arrived at a flight of stairs, he said, "Okay, stop. We have to go down…um…like twenty steps."

"What? You know our friends will not be pleased if you hurt me."

"I'd never encourage you to do this if I couldn't take care of you. We'll go slow." He tightened his grasp on her hip. "Step with me."

She complied.

"And another."

This interaction continued until they neared the bottom before he said, "We're almost there. Just three more steps."

"Zach, this is so crazy. I can't believe I'm letting you do this." Her laughter warmed his heart, and he hoped this time things would be different.

Once they reached the last step, he said, "That's it. Just straight ahead a few paces." He led her a few feet farther and stopped. "We're here. Open your eyes."

He studied her expression as it changed from suspicion—eyebrows furrowed, lips pursed—to delight—eyebrows raised, jaw dropped—when she peered up at the crystal sculpture of intertwined swans. Her eyes twinkled.

She gasped. "They're beautiful."

His heart leapt at her appreciation. "Yeah, they are." *And so are you.*

"Thanks for this, for bringing me here. I like the surprise."

"Wow. I'm glad you like it."

"Who wouldn't?"

"Others who don't appreciate what this represents."

"I see friendship and love. What do you see, Zach?"

I finally found the woman with an outlook that matches mine. "Hope."

"I'm having a wonderful time tonight."

"I'm enjoying our time together, too." He grasped her forearm and turned her around so he could gaze on her beautiful warm-brown face with the slightly slanted brown eyes and full glossy lips. He so wanted to kiss her. He stroked her arm before leaning toward her, but she offered her cheek instead.

***

His fingertips sent shivers up her arm. Her heartbeat quickened. He'd captured her emotions, and now they began to simmer, heating up the skin on her cheeks. As much as she wanted to, she couldn't let him kiss her. Not until she'd told him about her daughter and the other child on the way.

She gazed up into his sparkling brown eyes which suddenly seemed to stare at her with amorous intensity. So dreamy, they almost coerced her into granting him her lips. But she managed to turn her head at the last moment. His breath bathed her cheek in warmth seconds before his lips touched her skin. His kiss must have held a direct link to her knees because she no longer felt them. How had she remained standing?

Zach's large, warm hands wrapped around her arms answered that question. He practically sustained her standing position. With his mouth still close to her face, he whispered, "So beautiful." His lips lightly brushed her cheek before he eased away. She gasped.

Tosha's heart danced when his arm wrapped around her waist. She didn't want the night to end. Something clawed at that happy feeling when her mind slipped to thoughts of Emily. She felt dizzy. He'd swept her off her feet.

"Would you like to sit on the bench?" Zach asked.

"No, I'm fine."

She leaned against the railing and followed his hand which pointed to a mime in the distance. She had to see if her blind date could be the one for her.

"Zach, I don't want to put you on the spot or anything, but I'd like to ask you something."

"Sure. Anything you want to know."

"Okay." She sucked in a breath. "This may seem weird, but do you want to have kids?"

Zach smiled and glanced away toward the boats chugging up and down the river. Tosha suddenly thought she'd jumped into this topic a little too quickly.

"Wow. Hmm. I do like kids, and I would like to have some, but…"

Tosha's nerves twisted. *Here it comes.*

"Well," he continued and turned to face her, "I'd like to wait a while before having them. I don't think that's something I should rush into right now."

"Oh. Okay."

"You sure?"

"Yeah, that makes sense," she said quickly, hoping nothing in her reaction betrayed how dejected she felt at that moment. She fought back tears, thinking how close she had come to connecting with the most wonderful guy she'd ever met. She rubbed her eyes, hoping to hide the fact that she wiped away a tear.

"You must be tired," he said.

"I'm all right. Really."

"I'll take you home. Where do you live?" he said.

"Oh, you can just take me to Karida's and Tevin's. I'll probably crash there tonight."

He paused and gazed into her eyes as if he attempted to read into the depths of her soul. "I don't want this night to end. Do you mind if we sit a while," he jerked his head toward a bench a few steps away, "...before I drive you back to their place? Perhaps, say, in thirty minutes?"

"That's fine." The strained tension she'd held spilled over into her voice.

She sat on the bench next to Zach and let him hold her hand. His free arm wrapped around her shoulder. Leaning back against his chest, she exhaled, not wanting the moment to end either. How could she ever tell him she's a mother?

At the end of the allotted time, Zach rose and offered Tosha his arm. She sighed inaudibly as she strolled with him toward his car.

Thoughts of revealing her being a mother plagued her as he drove back to her friends' house. She gazed at him as he spoke about his job as an accountant and searched her mind for the perfect word to describe him. Yes, "eye-candy" failed miserably. He was exquisite.

How could she tell him? He'd surely turn the other way once he knew, and she didn't want to be rejected.

Zach glanced at her briefly with creased eyebrows. He immediately returned his attention to the road.

"What's wrong, Tosha?" His concern washed over her like a gentle wave.

How could he already read her so well?

"I'm fine."

"No. Something's bugging you. Will you tell me? I know it's only our first date, but I'm a great listener."

Busted! He's intuitive, too?

She sighed and stared out her window. She couldn't tell him and ruin this terrific evening they'd spent together. She also didn't want to lie. He stopped at a red light.

"This night has been great." Tosha forced her head to turn toward him. "I am so full of happiness. Do you mind if I don't mess it up? You've been so wonderful to me. I didn't think I'd feel this good."

He glanced at her again since the light had yet to turn green and seemed to study her face.

"All right. I won't make you tell me, but understand there's hardly anything you could say about yourself that would mess things up tonight. The odds are in your favor."

She managed a smile and took a deep breath. "Thank you."

"And just to let you know, I'm pleasantly surprised at how things turned out. Blind dates scare me."

She giggled. When the light turned green, Zach accelerated the car.

Within minutes, they arrived in the driveway. Tosha glanced at the clock on the dashboard.

"You're punctual. Five minutes before midnight. Suppose my chariot won't leave me stranded by turning into a pumpkin."

"No chance." He smiled. "This ended too quickly. I'm not quite ready to say good night."

"Me either."

"Would you…do you mind if I call you? I'd hate to bother Karida again."

"I don't mind," she said, knowing she probably shouldn't give her number to him. Why would a young, attractive man like Zach want to be weighed down with a ready-made family? He'd been free to do…anything.

"So, uh, would you like to do this again? Not necessarily the same restaurant, 'cause you…"

"Will only embarrass myself again."

He chuckled. "You didn't hear that from me." He stopped smiling. "Would you?"

She squirmed. The words about her daughter and unborn child stuck in her throat. Instead, she said, "I'm afraid of jumping in too fast. I just had the worst breakup…"

He grasped her fingers. "We could take it slow."

"That would be good." She sighed.

"I really had a super time. I'm glad we did this."

"I had a marvelous time, too. You are such a wonderful person. And the swans. Thank you so much for taking me to see them."

He released her fingers, reached into a back pocket, tapped his cell a few times, and held it out to her. "Well, if you'd type in your number, I'll give you a call. Figure out what's next."

She wanted to spare him of her complicated life, but his pleading eyes refused to let her say no. She nodded. "Okay."

"Cool," he said, handing the phone to her.

Tosha typed in her name and number. She double-checked the digits before clicking "Done" then called her cell, which rang in her purse. "That way I know it's you." She handed the phone back.

"Thanks," he said and pocketed the phone.

She didn't want to end the night telling him about her children. He'd be out of there before she could say good night.

"I should go inside." Tosha reached for the latch of her door, but Zach touched her arm.

"Don't. I'll get that. Our date isn't over yet." He exited the car and sauntered around to Tosha's side. He opened the door and helped her out.

A gentleman, too. Who knew they still existed?

Standing next to the car, he reached out, grasped both of her hands, and gazed into her eyes. The most adorable smile spread across his lips and into his eyes. She found it hard to breathe and forgot how to move her feet.

"I'd really like to see you again. Tonight was amazing. I hope I didn't offend you or chase you away."

"No," she said, sounding a bit too breathy. "You were great. I had tons of fun. I can't remember the last time I enjoyed a date so much." Why'd she keep repeating herself? *He's gonna think I'm a blitherin' idiot.*

"Oh, I almost forgot." He popped open the trunk and retrieved the long box. Opening the lid, he pulled out the vase with the single rose. He handed the vase to her and lessened the distance between them.

She trembled with him standing so close. "It's my first rose."

"I'm glad your first one is from me, but you shouldn't have had to wait this long for one."

He drew closer to her. He smelled so good. Her heart never beat as hard as it did now. She wanted to tell him everything, but the words stuck in her throat. *Who am I kidding? He won't want me with two kids.* She turned her head and felt his lips against her cheeks once more. She couldn't let him kiss her on the mouth, not with the huge secret she held close, below her chest.

***

Tosha avoided yet another of his advances. Perhaps he moved too fast for her. Had he misread her? She seemed into him, too. He'd be patient—not his strong point. Who knows what she left behind in past relationships? At least she enjoyed the date.

He escorted her to the door and let go of her hand.

"You want to come in?"

"I shouldn't. It's pretty late."

"I'm sure they won't mind."

"Probably not, but if I come in, I know I won't want to leave." He reached for the doorbell.

"No need. I have a key."

He nodded and exhaled. "I'll call you soon. Not for a couple days, though. I leave on a business trip tomorrow."

"Okay."

Her shoulders relaxed as if she were relieved he was going away. He hoped he was wrong. He couldn't help glancing at the full lips she kept away from him. She wore nothing on them except for maybe some lip gloss.

Perfect!

His yearning to kiss her threatened his calm demeanor. He wanted to know her, really know her, in every way possible.

He sighed. "I don't want to say good night."

"Then don't. Just say, 'See you later.'"

He grinned and raised her hand to his lips. His heart ached for her, knowing she'd soon disappear on the other side of the front door. "See you later."

As soon as he returned to his car, he texted his sister, Olivia. *<I think I found the one.>*

<I'll be praying.>

***

Tosha found herself wishing he'd never call, like other guys who tended to wait for the woman to make the first move where phones were concerned.

She smiled at the lingering feel of his mouth on the back of her hand. "Thanks so much for tonight."

Tosha let herself in with the key Karida loaned her. With her palm flat against the wood panel, Tosha closed the door. *Why didn't I tell him?* She cried silently, leaning her forehead onto the back of the hand he'd kissed. When Zach revved the engine, she peeked through the front window to watch him drive away. She wanted him more than she thought possible. Why was this her life?

Tosha flinched when Karida spoke from somewhere behind her in the living room.

"Twelve thirty in the morning. I wondered how long I would have to wait up for you. Tell me, how was it?"

How is it even possible we talked for an extra thirty minutes after he parked the car? Tosha sniffed softly. "Oh, Kar, he's so wonderful...too wonderful." She paused briefly to catch her breath. "I totally enjoyed myself and...I like him."

"I'm so glad."

"His kiss on my cheek set all my senses on fire." Her voice quivered. "What's going to happen when we really kiss?"

"That's great, right?"

She fought to keep her voice from shaking. "It won't work."

"Why not?"

Tears streamed down Tosha's cheeks as she turned to face her friend.

"Tosha, what's wrong?" Karida asked, rising and taking steps toward her.

Tosha leaned back against the door. "He's exactly," her voice cracked, "exactly who I wanted and exactly what I need." She sobbed in her hands. "And, and I can't have him." She sucked in a breath. "I can't have him."

Karida rushed to her side. "Why are you crying? What happened?"

Tosha forced herself to gaze into her friend's concerned eyes. "It was the best date I ever had. But…I'm not good enough for that man. He's a gentleman and, oh, so fine. I don't deserve him."

"Nonsense. You're a great person. Smart. Kindhearted. Loving. Super mom."

Tosha sobbed again at those words and slid to the floor.

"Tell me what's going on? If things went so well, why are you drowning yourself in tears?"

"I'm not ready for this. I'm not ready for him. And…he's not ready to have kids."

"Really? Did you tell him about Emily…and the baby?"

"Not exactly," admitted Tosha.

"What? I don't understand. How do you know he's not ready?"

"Because I asked him a hypothetical question, and he said he'd rather wait to have kids."

"Tosha, that's not the same. What guy would say he wants kids on the first date? Any woman might run away thinking he'd impregnate her that night." Karida's tone softened. "I know Zach. He loves children, always has. He'd be good to yours."

"I don't know." Tosha wiped at her face. "If he doesn't, I won't get rid of my baby to land a man."

"You don't have to. There are plenty of guys who'd take on a ready-made family. I'm pretty sure Zach's one of them. You should have told him."

"Why? He's too good to be true. He's so perfect, but I can't have him."

"Let him sweep you off your feet."

"He's already done that." Tosha locked Karida's gaze. "I love him, Kar. I can't believe I'm saying that since we just meant, but I know what I feel. Why didn't I meet him first? Now I have so much baggage." Tosha shrugged. "I gave him my number when he asked for it, but now I don't even know if I can tell him. Maybe he won't call anyway."

"Tosha." Karida rested a gentle hand on Tosha's shoulder. "We set you up with him because he's a caring guy. Did he enjoy the date?"

"I think so. He says he'll call in two days."

"Then he will."

"Maybe not. He's going on a business trip. Perhaps he'll meet someone else and forget about me."

"He's not like that. He'll call, so you need to get your story together."

"I can't talk to him. What will he think of me when he finds out I hid the truth about my life?"

"Tosha, honey."

"No, no more matchups. I'm done. Please, Karida."

Her friend nodded. "All right, no more matchups, but he'll call. If he said he'll call, then he'll call."

Tosha eased away, letting Karida's hand drop off her shoulder. With her friend's help, Tosha stood, trudged over to the sofa, and slumped between two fluffy pillows. "How's Em?"

"She's sleeping soundly."

"Did she ask for me?"

"Well…she wanted to know if you went out to find her a new daddy."

Tosha started crying again. "I guess I failed her."

Karida pulled Tosha into an embrace. "No, you haven't. I'm sure he'll understand."

Tosha shook her head. "I won't talk to him. I can't place this on him." She stared at the ceiling. Her insides ached at being drawn to Zach. "I'm tired. I need to sleep."

"The futon is ready in the guest room with Emily."

Tosha sighed. "I better sleep here. I don't think the tears are over."

Karida released Tosha and stared at her for a moment before saying, "All right. I'll get you a sheet and a blanket. But when you're up to it, I want to hear about this date."

"Thanks," said Tosha and watched her friend head down the hallway. She hoped Karida would not press any further. After lying on the sofa, covering herself with the warm blanket Karida had given her, Tosha cried herself to sleep.

__Chapter 4__

Zach had experienced the best date of his life. Just when he'd given up on someone he could share his thoughts and adventures with, Tosha showed up with dazzling possibilities. She was sweet and adorable…and gorgeous. He'd almost forgotten how to breathe when he saw her for the first time.

He tried so hard to ensure she had a great evening and hoped he hadn't bored her to death with conversation. However, she seemed to enjoy talking to him about everything from favorite television shows to the latest blockbuster films. So, what had happened?

He'd called her every day for two weeks since that great night, but she never answered, nor had she returned his calls. His heart hurt to be away from her for so long.

When he grew anxious, he called his sister.

"Pray harder," he said. "I don't understand why she's not responding."

"Be peertient," Olivia said in a calming tone. "You doan know wha' she bin thru."

Zach had even called Karida a week following the date to find out if he'd done something to scare Tosha away.

"No, Zach. She had a great time. She really did."

"Then why does it seem like she doesn't want to talk to me?"

"She's probably just nervous," Karida had told him.

At first, he accepted that answer, but after a few days of unanswered phone calls, he tried Karida again. He tapped his desk at work while he waited for his longtime friend to pick up. He didn't have time for greetings.

"She's not answering," he snapped.

"She could be busy."

"Too busy to return my calls?"

"Do you want me to try calling?"

"I want you to tell me where she lives."

"I can't do that."

Zach sat up in the chair and pounded a fist on a stack of papers. "Come on, Karida. Does she hate me? Did I do something wrong?"

"No. It's not you."

"Then, what?" Zach asked, throwing his free palm upward.

"I can't tell you."

Zach held his temper at bay. "Do you realize how frustrating this is? I just want to talk to her. I know she had something on her mind during our date. I just want to talk to her about it."

"I'm sorry. I'll call her and encourage her to return your calls. That's the best I can do."

"Just tell me where I can see her. I won't stalk her if she's not interested."

"That's the thing. She *is* interested."

"Karida, help me."

"I'll call her and get back to you, okay?"

He sighed. He could feel the muscles in his neck relax a bit. "All right. Thanks." Before she responded, he ended the call. He could hardly concentrate on his work for the rest of the day.

He'd expected Karida to contact him with an answer by the following day. When he didn't hear from her, his patience had met its limit.

He'd given Karida's latest response a chance, but not anymore, not today. Zach regretted he had never found out where Tosha lived. Well, that would change soon enough.

Zach unlocked his cell phone and texted Tevin. *<Are you home?>*

He read the immediate response. *<Not yet, but Karida's home.>*

Zach sighed and typed. *<I need to get Tosha's address. Do you have it?>*

<No, but Karida does.>

He gritted his teeth. He'd have to pay his pal a visit. *<Mind if I head over there? I need to talk to Tosha today.>*

<Naw. Go ahead.>

<Even though you're not home?>

<It's cool, Zach. She was your friend first. I'm good.>

<Thanks, man. I just wanted to be sure.>

<Good luck with Tosha.>

Zach pulled up to the house and turned off the car. He had to convince Karida to give him Tosha's address before he lost his mind.

Zach knocked enthusiastically on the front door. The doorbell seemed too polite.

Upon opening the door, Karida said, "Zach. Hi. What brings you here?"

"May I come in?" He showed her the text conversation with Tevin.

"Sure, but I don't know if I can do as you ask." She backed away and let him pass into the living room.

"Tosha isn't returning any of my calls. I'm beginning to think she's avoiding me, but it doesn't make sense, not after the night we had. Has she said anything to you?"

Karida shrugged. "She had a good time, too."

"Then, why's she avoiding me?"

"She's…afraid."

"Of me?"

"No, but I…can't tell you."

"I need you to tell me where I can find Tosha."

"I don't think…"

"I just want to talk to her. Find out what's going on. I'm really into her. Please." He walked toward the kitchen and back again. "Would you give me her address?"

"Zach, I'm so sorry. I can't do that. I know you want to talk to her, but she needs some time."

"Is that what she told you? Because I had the feeling that she totally enjoyed herself with me. I refuse to believe I could be so off course about her."

"And you're not. She's not happy about not talking to you either. I think she misses you. She's been through a lot."

"Then, tell me where she lives, and I will get out of your space. If she tells me to back off, I will, but I want to hear it from her."

"Zach, please…"

"No. You don't get to set me up with the best date I've had and tell me I have to let go. I want to talk to her, and you're my current obstacle."

"She'll be upset if I do that."

"What about me?" He raised both hands, palms up, waist height. "You know how important this date was for me. How long I'd waited. If I'm going to be able to move on, I need to see her. Have her tell me she doesn't want this, us."

"It's complicated."

"I don't mind complicated. I mind not being able to follow through. You and Tevin got me into this, so don't think about leaving me hanging." He glided his hand over his hair from his forehead to his neck. "I'm hurting, Karida. I told you I didn't want to experience rejection, at least not this soon after the last one."

"I know, and I'm sorry."

"Prove it to me. Give me Tosha's address...please. I just need to talk to her this once. Then, I'll tear it up and never bother her again if that's what she wants. Please." His chest tightened as he waited.

"She's going to kill me."

"Karida, she may be the one I'm going to marry. I'll take your place on the chopping block if it comes to that."

His friend shook her head and squeezed her eyes shut. When she reopened them, she said, "All right. I'll do it...because I encouraged you." She went to the desk and frantically scribbled something down. Returning to him, she placed an index card in his hand.

He glanced at the address, relief washing over him. "Is she home now?"

Karida nodded. "Yes, she is. I just talked to her."

"How did she sound?"

"Sad. She's upset for not calling you back. She thinks it's too late."

"Not for me. Thanks, Karida. I'll call afterwards."

"Good luck."

Zach rushed to his car, address in hand. He stopped at a flower shop to buy a yellow rose before driving to the address on the card he held tightly between his fingers. Amazingly, he found parking on Tosha's street near her apartment building. A friendly neighbor, whom he had apparently met at a conference, even let him in when he explained his reason for being there. Stepping quickly toward Tosha's door, Zach rang the doorbell once so as not to betray his anxious emotions. A stream of sweat trickled into his sideburns.

***

Tosha finished cleaning up Emily's snack time spills when the doorbell rang. She stopped with a jolt, wondering who could be visiting her mid-afternoon. Good thing Emily finished napping earlier. Tosha tossed the washcloth into the sink and hurried to the door.

Her heart sank when she peered through the peephole, but not because she didn't want to see Zach. In fact, she couldn't stop thinking about how incredible she felt on her blind date. Everything he did expressed how much he adored her. She suddenly wished Emily had still been napping. *How am I going to explain why I didn't mention her?*

Tosha had called Karida the previous day, crying. For the first time, she had lived to see a guy keep his word and call, not just once, but numerous times over two weeks.

"Tosha, tell him about your children."

"I don't want to lose him."

"You'll lose him if you don't talk to him. I think he'll understand. Tell him. He keeps asking me how to get in touch with you...in person."

"Please promise me you won't tell him. I don't want to be rejected again."

"Tosha, you need—"

"Promise!"

Karida had huffed over the phone. "Fine. I promise," her best friend had said but clearly found it necessary to break this promise...so unlike Karida.

Tosha shrugged and opened the door. *Might as well get this over with.* Zach's face glistened with sweat, and his eyes looked sad. Tosha instantly regretted causing him such pain. Hadn't Tevin said Zach had had a tough time lately? Now she had added to that pain...and hers.

"Hi," he said, extending his hand toward her.

"Hi," she replied, accepting the yellow rose. A lump formed in her throat.

"Why didn't you return my calls?" Zach asked, his tone strained.

Tosha struggled to find the words with which to respond. Nothing seemed good enough. She almost spoke when Emily wrapped an arm around her thigh. Zach's eyes widened with surprise.

"Who is it, Mommy?"

Oh, no. Not now. I needed a little more time.

***

After Tosha opened the door, Zach stood staring at her— same gorgeous woman but without the same spunk she'd had on the blind date. No rational thought remained to calm his nerves. Then he saw her, the most precious little girl with her hair in twists like her mother's, before Tosha could answer, before he could press her for a reason. Pain flashed across Tosha's face.

Zach knew in that instant the answer to all his previous questions. Of course, they quickly became replaced by many more. No wonder she'd asked whether he wanted kids. His thoughts flashed back to the night he told her he'd like to "wait a while before having them." His gut clenched.

How I must have made her feel that night. I wish I knew about her daughter.

Feelings of remorse jabbed at Zach for the way he greeted Tosha. He began again.

"You didn't return any of my calls. I thought I may have really messed things up with you."

"No. You didn't mess anything up. I…" She shuffled nervously, the little girl still clinging to her leg. "How? How did you…find me?"

"Karida. Don't be angry with her. I refused to leave her home until she told me where you lived. I had to see you." He glanced at the little girl. "Who's this?"

"My daughter, Emily."

He squatted and, with one knee on the floor for balance, extended his hand toward Tosha's daughter. "Hello, Emily. I'm your mommy's friend."

"Hello," Emily said, still not letting go of Tosha.

"My name is Zach. You may call me Teddy if you like."

"Like a Teddy Bear?" Emily asked.

"Yeah, they're my favorite stuffed animal."

The girl glanced up at her mom for confirmation it was all right to greet him. Tosha nodded. Emily gingerly let go of Tosha's leg and eased away. The little girl stepped forward and extended her little hand toward his. He wrapped his fingers around her hand and shook twice.

"Nice to meet you, Teddy."

"It's my pleasure, Emily."

"I like pandas."

"Do you have one?" he asked.

"Not yet, but I have Teddy Bear. I show you." Emily ran off to her bedroom without looking back.

Zach stood and faced Tosha.

She shook her head. "I'm sorry. Please come in."

He stepped past Tosha and quickly noted the sofa facing the large windows overlooking the street. The blinds were open, letting the sunbeams stream into the cozy area. Toys lay beyond the sofa at the far corner of the room against cream walls. He caught sight of the kitchen off to his left. By the time he turned to face Tosha, she'd closed the door. Emily returned with the Teddy Bear, but Tosha shooed the little girl away, sending her toward the play area.

"Why didn't you tell me?" he asked, care, not malice, in his words.

She took two steps toward him. "You said you didn't want any right now. How could I tell you after what you said?"

"It's not the same. You asked me if I wanted to have kids. I meant I didn't want to make them right now. You should have told me."

"But you said you wanted to wait."

"I know, but I wish you didn't assume my answer covered every possible scenario." His tone had intensified just a bit, but softened once more when he asked, "Why didn't you tell me you had a daughter?"

"I didn't want you to reject me. I didn't want you to go away," she said. Tears escaped her glistening eyes.

"I'm not going anywhere." He swallowed to moisten his throat. "I called you for the longest two weeks of my life. If I didn't want you, I would have stopped after my second call." Despite heightening emotions, he fought to regain his composure. "Tosha, I'm okay with you having a child. I still want to see you."

"Then, I need to tell you more. Before you start making promises you won't be able to keep."

"What?"

"I'm three months pregnant."

Shock jolted his gut. He glanced at her not yet swollen belly. His usual smile refused to make an appearance just yet.

"Anything else?" he asked.

"No. I don't think so." Tosha hesitated. "Isn't that enough?"

"Enough for what?"

"For you to turn around and walk away. It's okay if you don't..."

Zach thought hard what to say next. His mind brushed past the pros and cons...of including a child in a budding romance. He stole a quick glance toward Emily before returning his gaze to Tosha. Nothing mattered more than being with Tosha and her offspring, not even the strangeness of him jumping into fatherhood.

"Those are the reasons I didn't return any of your calls. I didn't think—"

I hope I'm ready for this. "I wanted to talk to you," he began, cutting her off before she said anything to steal away the feelings he wanted to express, "to say that since we both had an absolutely wonderful time on our date the other night, we ought to schedule another one now. Of course, in light of your circumstances..." He paused, noting her frown. "...we may have to think of other arrangements that include Emily. I wouldn't mind having her along." He reached out and grasped her hand. "Tosha, I won't walk away. You stole my heart. I just want a chance to know you better. So..." He stopped his rant and waited.

Tears streamed down her cheeks. "Oh, Zach, I totally enjoyed our time together. I feared you wouldn't want me with my baggage. I'd love to go out with you again."

"Is tomorrow good? I could bring dinner."

She nodded. "Yes, that's perfect."

Tosha's beautiful face, framed by a multi-colored band wrapped around her hair, tugged at him. He ran a hand over his curly business cut hair as he watched the little girl play.

"I feel a strong urge to kiss you right now. May I? Because if you think it's too soon..."

"Not too soon. I'd like that."

Zach stepped twice toward Tosha and drew her up into his arms. Seconds after he pressed his lips against hers, the world felt like clouds and butterflies. He remained cognizant of the little girl playing in the corner, the only thing preventing him from being completely lost in the kiss. He teetered between reality and ecstasy.

She must have felt the same because when they parted slightly, she whispered, "But I can't have sex with you. I want to be a good example for her."

"I understand," he replied through jagged breath. He'd do anything she asked just to remain close to her.

He brushed his lips against hers, not wanting the sensations to end just yet, and savored her warmth for much longer than he'd intended.

"Too much?"

"Not enough."

He kissed her again, this time exploring her lips. She moaned slightly before gently pushing him away. He'd never fallen so deep into a kiss before, and he'd kissed many women. This one had swept him away completely. His heart opened wide toward her with her daughter, her unborn child, and the rest of her baggage. None of it mattered, yet all of it suddenly meant something to him. He wanted to stay in her life.

He finally reigned in his passion and released her.

"Wow. I can't think straight," he said.

He stared at her lips wondering what lay in them to seduce him so completely. He switched his gaze to her brown eyes in hopes of breaking the hold on his emotions. Her eyes seemed dreamy, and she shook her head as if in an attempt to defog her mind. She took one step backwards, her gaze still locked by his.

"I may not have any kids of my own, but I love them, and I'd like to have them. Sooner is fine." He nodded, hoping she'd understand.

She smiled and said, "How long can you stay?"

"About two hours."

"Would you like to stay for dinner? I can start it now."

He grinned. "Yes, I'd like that."

"Great," she said, now with a broad smile.

"May I help?"

"Please," she said and extended her hand, palm up, toward him.

Zach laid his hand in hers, allowing Tosha to lead the way to the small kitchen off to the side.

***

Tosha led Zach to the kitchen sink. She remained unsure why she sprayed water on his hands from the faucet before lathering them with the soap she pumped onto her own. She slid her fingers between his, careful not to miss a spot. Her chocolate complexion stood in contrast to his mocha, almost caramel, tone. Tosha mentally kicked herself for thinking of Zach as food. She dared not peer up into his eyes. The feel of his smooth hands thrilled her.

She immediately drew his hands under the flowing water to rinse off the suds. Grabbing a towel, she patted her hands dry before handing him the cloth. She tried to convince herself that she did this to ensure his hands were clean before handling the vegetables. Thankfully, without a word, he wiped his hands and hung the towel on the rack.

Tosha opened the refrigerator and pulled out two onions.

"Would you like to take care of the cutting?"

"Sure."

"Chop one and a half. Slice the remaining half for the salad."

After he took the onions from her, she grabbed a sharp knife and laid it gently on the counter. She peered into his eyes and couldn't glance away. He grinned, his teeth gleaming, and kissed her forehead. She wondered if she'd be able to concentrate enough to cook a meal that he'd like. Perhaps her invitation had been premature. Stepping back toward some chicken she'd set out earlier on the counter to defrost, she patted the section of the apron lying against her thigh before opening the sealed package.

***

Zach finished chopping the first onion when he stole a glance toward Tosha. She'd remained quiet since she cut the chicken into pieces and placed them in a bowl. He decided to pose his questions to her when she shook one of many seasonings she had lined up on the counter.

"Where's Emily's father?"

"About an hour's drive away from here."

"And the baby's?"

"Same father as Emily."

"Why did you leave him?"

"I caught him with another woman." She banged the saltshaker onto the counter. "He didn't love me, and he didn't want children. He blames me for getting pregnant with Emily. I couldn't go through that again."

"Are you…? I know what Karida told me, but I have to make sure. You're not married, right?"

She stopped and faced him. "That's right. I've never been. Chaz and I were engaged for three years. I wanted to get married, but he kept putting it off."

He exhaled relief, not wanting to deal with a messy divorce. "How is Emily dealing with all this?" He poured the chopped onion into a small dish and began slicing the remaining half.

"Emily hasn't seen him in over two months. He stopped calling three weeks after we moved out. She doesn't ask for him much anymore."

"Do you think he'll come for her?"

"I doubt it. He'd never hugged her or kissed her good night." Tears trekked down her cheeks.

"I'm sorry."

"Thanks," Tosha said before returning to the chicken.

"Onions are done. Do you have anything else for me to cut?"

"The green peppers."

A couple minutes later, he said, "Anything else?"

"No. I've got it from here. Thanks."

Zach washed his hands and placed the containers of cut vegetables next to Tosha. When he had nothing left to do except dote on her every move, he said, "Do you mind if I play with Emily?"

"Not at all."

He strolled over to the little girl and sat on the floor next to her playhouse.

"Tea?" Emily offered.

He thanked her and drank the pretend tea.

"Mmmm. Very delicious." He rubbed his belly, smiling.

"Here's my Teddy Bear."

Zach accepted the stuffed toy and bounced it around in the air. "Very handsome. Do you have a pony?"

"No."

"Hmmm. Every little girl should have a pony. I'll see what I can do about that."

"I have lion."

"Can you roar?"

"Rawr," she said. "Your turn. Be a bear."

"Grrrrr," he growled.

Emily giggled and touched his face. "You're brown. I like your color. It's darker than mine, but lighter than Mommy's." She placed her hand on his wrist. "My daddy was brown, too, just not so much." Gradually, her smile turned into a frown.

Zach picked up the little girl into his arms and hugged her tight. His heart hurt that Emily had experienced such pain at her age. He made a silent promise to make things better.

***

Zach helped Tosha into her chair after she got Emily settled in the booster seat.

"Thanks."

"Anytime," he replied and sat in the chair next to Tosha.

"What do we say before we eat, Emily?"

"We are grateful for our food, our family, and our friends. Amen."

"Thanks, baby."

Zach took a few bites and said, "Tosha, this is delicious."

"Thanks. I'm glad you like it."

Tosha studied Zach for a few seconds before taking another forkful. She chewed slowly and swallowed, amazed that this beautiful man sat only a few inches away.

"I have to know. When did you realize you wanted to ask me out again?" Tosha said.

"The moment I saw your reaction to the swans."

"Really? Why's that?"

"Because I've taken other dates there."

"And how did they respond?"

"She'd open her eyes and say 'What?' Just like that and glance around like the swans didn't exist. But you saw the beauty in the sculpture right away. Tears welled up on your lids. I knew then that I'd found who I've been looking for."

Moments later, Zach finished his second serving and seemed thoughtful.

"You look as if you want to say something," Tosha said.

He nodded and sipped some water. "I'm racking my brain trying to figure out how not to offend you."

"Just say it."

He inhaled deeply and reached out for her hand. "You thinking I wouldn't accept you with children really hurt. You made assumptions about me that misrepresented who I am. I'd like…I hope in the future you could be straight with me. No more hypothetical questions. I don't want any misunderstandings about my feelings for you." He gently squeezed her hand.

Tosha thought she'd cry right then. She hated that she hurt him and didn't want to think about life without him.

"All right. I'm sorry. I'm sorry for that and for not answering the phone or returning your calls. It won't happen again."

"Thanks, Tosha," he said and kissed her hand, sending shivers up her arm.

***

After dinner, Emily ran off to play with her toys. Tosha grew apprehensive at the thought of Zach leaving. She rather enjoyed his company and didn't mind staring at his good-looking features.

"I suppose you need to leave now," she said.

He glanced at his phone. "Actually, I can hang out here for a few more minutes. Mind if we sit and talk some more?"

"I don't mind."

Tosha settled next to Zach on the sofa. He smiled at her and reached over to grab her hand. Her heart fluttered at his touch.

"Did you think I'd stop calling, the same as your ex?"

Her gut clenched. "Yeah, I guess."

"I'm not him, Tosha. I will do everything I can to prove that to you. I really missed you."

"I missed you, too."

"You've been kind enough to tell me your story. Ready to hear mine?" asked Zach.

"Sure."

Tosha listened to Zach talk about his last girlfriend whom he'd hoped would be the one to free him from his solo lifestyle. He mentioned how he had enough of the dating scene but decided to give it one more try for Karida and Tevin.

"I'm glad I did. No regrets," Zach said.

Tosha sighed, and he drew her hand to his lips. His kiss sent nervous energy up her arm.

"I must go. I have to finish a presentation due first thing in the morning. Are you still okay with me bringing dinner here tomorrow?"

"Of course," she replied.

"Is Chinese good?"

"I like it, but I'm not so sure about Emily. She'll eat rice, though."

"Good. I'll be here around six, if that works for you."

"Yes, that's fine."

Zach stood, raising her up by the hand he still held. "Who watched her for you when we went out?"

"Tevin and Karida."

Zach nodded and headed to the door. "I should've guessed." Zach gazed past Tosha. "Bye, Emily. See you tomorrow."

"Bye, bye, Teddy," Emily said, waving.

He waved back before turning the knob. He'd barely pulled the door open before suddenly turning to face Tosha. He leaned toward her and pecked her lips—well, slightly longer than a peck.

"See you at six. I hope you have a big appetite."

Tosha smiled and stared at a grinning Zach until he closed the door. Her legs remained frozen in place until Emily tugged at her dress.

"I like him, Mommy."

Tosha peered down at her daughter. "Me too. Where's my phone? I need to call Aunt Karida."

She smiled, watching Emily rush back to play pretend with her toys, and wondered if Zach could be the one for whom she'd been hoping. Tosha grabbed her phone and pressed the button to speed-dial her best friend. Karida barely said hello when Tosha began to speak.

"I've fallen in love. He's taken with Emily. She seems to like him. I'm so scared."

"So, you're not angry with me for telling him where you live?"

"I should be, but no. Thanks, Karida."

"And don't be scared. He's a good man, Tosha. One of the best." Karida paused for a breath. "I better go. He's calling. I'll call you later. I want to hear everything."

"All right. Bye," Tosha said and ended the call, her heart so full she thought it would burst out her chest. She loved him even when she thought she'd need more time. He had her heart.

Chapter 5

Zach arrived the next evening with bags containing dishes of food. He had Tosha sit while he prepared the table.

"I thought you were ordering out," Tosha said. "Did you repackage everything?"

"Order out? I never said I was ordering out." He smiled.

"Are you telling me you cooked all this?"

"Yep. Chinese food is my specialty. I did something different with the chicken for Emily. I hope she likes what I've invented for her. I watered down the sauce a bit."

"I'm impressed, but don't feel bad if she doesn't like it. She hardly likes new food if she even bothers to try them."

"I understand. I won't be disappointed."

Zach had spent the better part of the afternoon preparing a five-course dinner, including dessert for Tosha and her daughter. He'd made a quick call to Karida, thanking her for taking a chance telling him where Tosha lived, before starting the stir fry.

He unpacked the candles, making sure to tell Emily not to touch the pretty flames on the table. Once everything had been laid out, Zach seated the two new ladies in his life.

"Emily, I made some special chicken for you, and I hope you like it. Would you taste and let me know what you think?"

Emily glanced at her mom.

"It's all right, Em. Try some."

Emily surprised Zach when she opened her mouth wide, inviting him to place a piece of chicken on her tongue. When she finished chewing and swallowed, she licked her lips.

"More please."

"Great, Emily, I'm glad you approve," he said.

"Wow, what else do you cook?" asked Tosha.

"Why don't I surprise you?"

"I'd like that, but I get to cook for you, too."

"Of course. I really enjoyed the meal you prepared yesterday. I'd like to do that again…cook with you."

Tosha's cheeks flushed. "I'd like that, too, but next time, I'll do it alone."

Conversing with Tosha and Emily over dinner came easy, like this was always his life. He liked how he always managed to make Tosha laugh when she seemed on the verge of holding back. When Emily had chewed the last morsel, Tosha stood and began to clear off the table. He grabbed a few dishes and beat her to the kitchen.

"Mommy, can I go play?"

"Yes, baby. I'll get you when it's time for bed."

"Okay, Mommy."

"Play in your bedroom."

"Okay," said the little girl as she ran off.

Tosha turned to him. "Let me pack up the food for you."

"Keep it," he said, leaning against the counter.

"You sure? There's a lot here."

"Yeah. I can always make more. Besides, Emily really liked the chicken."

"Okay. I'll transfer everything and wash out your containers."

"No need. I can always get them later."

She paused and glanced back and forth between him and the containers.

He grinned. "I'm eager to get out of this kitchen. Let's put them in the fridge and go sit on the couch."

She returned his grin when he handed her the first of four containers. He handed her another each time she'd placed one in the refrigerator. She stood and closed the door. He reached out, grabbed her forearm, and turned her to face him. He closed the gap between them and leaned forward to press his lips against hers. He'd waited all night to do this.

A slight moan escaped him when he eased away. "Come with me." He led the way to the sofa. With Emily in her room, a renewed freedom washed over him. The second Tosha settled next to him, his lips landed on hers. He slid his hand around her neck. This time *she* moaned.

"I wish I could spend the night," he whispered and kissed her again.

She broke it off and said, "The couch is very comfortable. I'll bring out sheets for you." His hand still on her neck limited her movements. "Zach."

"Share it with me."

"On this little thing? No way we both fit."

"I can make sure we both fit," he said and smirked.

"I'm sure you could." She reached behind her neck to pull his hand away, but not before he snuck in another kiss.

"Mommy?"

Tosha scooted away from him and turned her head toward the girl. "What baby?"

"I'm ti...red," Emily said amidst a yawn.

"All right, I'll tuck you in." Tosha stood and stepped toward the girl.

"Teddy come, too?"

"Sure, after I get you in bed. C'mon." Tosha took Emily's hand and led her back into the girl's bedroom.

The heat coursing under his skin refused to dissipate. Just being near Tosha thrilled him, yet she refused to cross that invisible line to be with him. He leaned back into the couch pillows and waited.

"She's ready," Tosha said from the bedroom a few minutes later.

He sucked in a deep breath and strolled to the room. "Hey, little one. You have sweet dreams, okay?"

"Okay, Teddy. You too."

"Thanks," he said and kissed her forehead.

Tosha turned off the light and followed him out the bedroom. She closed the door.

"Where were we?" Without waiting for an answer, he drew her to him for another kiss. He stepped backwards until they reached the sofa. Coaxing Tosha down, he pushed her against the pillows. His cell buzzed in his pocket. *What now?*

"You going to get that?"

Ugh. I really don't want to. "Yeah." He pulled it out and looked at the message. "Shoot!"

"What's wrong?"

He peered into her eyes. "I have to fly out in the morning."

"When?"

"Five a.m." He groaned. "I can't stay."

She giggled. "You changing your mind?"

"I want to stay with you, but I totally forgot about this. I didn't pack or anything." He leaned toward her. The warmth of her full lips pressed back. "I'm sorry. Rain check?"

"I'll be here."

"Tell Emily I'm so sorry I couldn't say goodbye in the morning." He stood, felt his pockets for his wallet and keys, and then turned to the door. He reached for the knob when Tosha touched his shoulder. She embraced him the moment he faced her. "I'm really sorry. I'm usually not this disorganized."

"Yeah, we had a busy weekend."

He smiled. "Yes, we did." He kissed her again and pulled away. "If I don't leave now, I'll never catch that flight. I'll call you while I'm there."

"Okay. Bye."

He pulled open the door and slipped outside. "Bye." He rushed down the hall.

***

Tosha's cell phone rang the moment she fell back onto the bed. Those had been some kisses. She regretted him having to leave. *It was for the best. Who knows what would've happened if he stayed?*

Karida. She swiped to answer.

"What did you do to him?" her best friend asked.

"Nothing."

"You sure?"

"We kissed. That's all."

"Well, your kisses must be potent."

"Tell me, what's going on?"

"This is the first time he's forgotten a business trip."

"He called you?"

"No. Tevin. I overheard what he said and put two and two together."

"There's nothing special about my kisses."

"Mmmhmm."

"*His* on the other hand." Tosha giggled.

"I knew you two would work out."

Tosha frowned. "He's too good to be true, Karida."

"What're you talking about?"

"What's he doing getting stuck with a woman pregnant with another man's baby?"

"That doesn't matter to him. He's taken by you."

"I'm scared I'll give him my heart, and then he'll hurt me."

"I think he already has your heart, but you got nothing to worry about. You calling him?"

"He said he'll call me."

"When has that stopped you? Surprise him."

"What if he's busy?"

"He'll answer or send you a quick text."

"All right. I'll call him around lunch tomorrow."

"That's my girl."

***

Zach paid the taxi and entered the glass skyscraper through the right half of the main double doors—his third meeting of the day, and it was only noon. *Man, how I wish Tosha were here.* He nodded at the security guard and climbed the spiral staircase to the second-floor loft. A bouquet of flowers sat on the receptionist's desk. *I'll send some to her.*

"Please have a seat, Zach. He's in a meeting at the moment."

"Not a problem. I'm a bit early."

The woman nodded and smiled.

Zach studied the framed portrait on the wall behind her— Mr. Charles Chambers shaking the mayor's hand—before he settled on the black leather sofa and removed a folder from his briefcase.

"So, how've you been?" Zach asked.

"Just peachy. It's never as exciting as when you're here, though."

"Hm. Why's that?"

"Everyone flitters around, making sure things are in place for your arrival."

He'd just opened a printed ledger when his phone vibrated against his chest. Removing the buzzing cell phone from a pocket, he peered at the screen. *Tosha.* He glanced up toward the administrator at the table "Give me a sec." He swiped to answer. "Hi, beautiful."

"Did I catch you at a bad time?" Tosha asked. "I didn't mean to interrupt."

"Not at all."

"Zach?" the admin asked. "Mr. Chambers wants you in his office when your call is over."

"Sure thing, Honey."

"Who you calling honey?" Tension permeated Tosha's tone.

He chuckled. "It's her actual name. Honey Johnson."

"You're joking."

"Not at all. I wouldn't joke like that with you." He paused. "I'm glad you called."

"Really? Why?"

"You've been on my mind all day, and just when I want to call, someone calls me into another conference. I miss you."

"I miss you, too. I wanted to surprise you."

"Thanks. Consider me pleasantly surprised," he said.

"So, our friends are blaming me for you almost missing your flight."

He chuckled again. "I don't blame you. It's just that...everything else disappeared from my mind since I've met you. I...I'm glad we met, and I want there to be an us. Do you understand?"

"I think so. Even with all my stuff?"

"Yes, with everything you are and have. Are you able to put up with mine?"

"That's funny. There's nothing wrong with you."

"Ha! Give it time."

"Zach?" Honey said.

"You have to go?" Tosha asked.

"Yeah." He glanced up and said, "Give me a minute." After the woman nodded and left, he continued. "You're not still jealous, are you?"

"Me? Jealous? I wasn't jealous."

"Your tone sure fooled me."

"Well, maybe a little."

"Good, 'cause I'd be jealous if you called some guy 'honey.'"

"I'll keep that in mind. Good luck."

"Thank you. It's going well so far, but a little luck couldn't hurt. I'll call you tonight."

"Okay. Em would enjoy hearing your voice."

"I'd like to hear hers, too. Talk to you later."

"Bye."

He smiled as he swiped the smartphone off.

***

That evening, the phone rang four times before Tosha answered.

"Hi Zach. Just got Emily out the bath." She huffed into the phone.

"You want me to call back?"

"No, no. She'd have a fit if we hung up now. Hold on."

Muffled sounds of hurried conversation reached his ears before the sweetest little voice said, "Hi, Teddy. When you coming home?"

"Soon, little one. You being good for Mommy?"

"Yes. She's sad you're not here."

"She is? You know what?"

"What?"

"I'm sad I'm not there, too. I miss you both."

"Miss you."

"Sweet dreams."

"Nite nite," she said, followed by more muffled sounds.

A couple minutes later, Tosha returned to the phone a bit winded. "Sorry about that, making you wait."

"I don't mind. Is she in bed?"

"Yes, finally."

"Good. Now I have you all to myself."

Tosha giggled. "I'm heading to my room."

"Wish I were there."

"I bet you do." She paused. "All right. I'm all settled. How did it go today?"

"We not only kept our main account, we got a new one with a subsidiary company. Looks like they still love me."

"Honey, too?" she asked.

"Her name bugs you, doesn't it?"

"Why would her parents even *call* her that?"

He chuckled. "I have no idea. I never asked." He blew out a breath. "Emily said you were sad."

"She says too much. I guess I didn't hide missing you as much as I thought." A few seconds ticked by before Tosha continued. "I need to ask you something."

"Go on."

"Have you ever gone out with her? Honey?"

"No."

"Have you ever asked her out?"

"No. I think she's wanted to ask me, though. But now it's too late."

"Why's that?"

"My heart belongs to the woman I'm talking to now."

"Oh, Zach, please don't say things you don't mean." She sniffled.

"Tosha, I'm your guy. I know we've just met, but I'm crazy about you." He paused to swallow in an attempt to wet his suddenly dry throat. "Do you feel the same?"

"Yes." She sniffled some more. "Please don't break my heart." She sighed. "I can't believe I just said that."

"It's okay. I won't. I was going to wait until I saw you in a few days, but…"

"But what?"

"I love you, Tosha, with all my heart."

"Oh, my. I love you, too, Zach."

He let the words settle deep. He grinned and imagined his arms wrapping around her just then. "Would you like to meet at my place on Friday? Emily is also welcome."

"I don't know. A new place?"

"She'll be fine."

"Really?"

"Really. I'll toddler-proof everything before you come over."

"All right. What time?"

"Six good?"

"Yes."

"Perfect. I'll text you the address. I can't wait to see you again."

With a heart overflowing with gratitude, Zach called his sister and grinned when she answered.

"How you doin'?" Olivia asked.

"Much better than last time. You were right about not knowing what she'd been through. She's a mom of the most beautiful little girl with one on the way. I told her I love her, and she said she loves me too."

"Wow. Ready made famly. You betta kip you choclate zipped up in you pants."

"Aw, c'mon, sis. I'm not as old-fashioned as you."

"I'm just sayin' tek you time. Wait on de Lawd so he can bless dis relationship lang term if it's da best for both ah you."

Zach sighed. "Olivia."

"You hear me?"

"Yes."

"You gon listen?"

He shrugged. "No promises if she's willing."

"I see. 'Member Daddy's teachings."

"Love you."

"Luv you tons, beerbee brudder. Give de little gal da playhouse I hav in storage."

He ended the call, no longer floating high on euphoric emotions.

Chapter 6

A few quick knocks reached Tosha's ears. *Zach?* She hadn't expected to see him until Friday. She hurried, checked the peephole, and pulled open the door, unable to wait a second longer than necessary. *I'm not complaining about seeing him a day early.* Zach's handsome smiling face melted the shield around her heart and threatened to diminish her resolve to wait.

His lips met hers in a rush, and his arms wrapped around her waist. Oh, how good he smelled. Not perfumed. Just natural. He kissed her cheek, her neck, her temple, repeating "I love you" between each time his mouth touched her skin.

She rested a palm on his cheek. "I love you, Zach."

He eased away and gazed at her with dreamy eyes. "I missed you so much."

"Me too. Thanks for the flowers."

He pressed against her, partially lifting her back into the apartment. His midsection brushed her hip. She gasped.

"Sorry about that." He closed the door behind him.

She understood his excitement. The way his lips caressed her skin had her sweating.

"Teddy! Teddy! Teddy!"

A blur of afro trotted toward Zach. Emily wrapped her arms around his leg. He swept her daughter up into his arms and kissed her little forehead.

"Missed you," Emily said.

"I missed you, too."

He hugged them both and didn't let go for a few moments.

"Will you stay?" Emily asked.

"Not tonight. I need to clean up and get some rest. I work in the morning."

The girl frowned.

"But I can come back on Saturday in two days and spend more time with you."

"Can Mommy and me come over tomorrow?"

"To my place?" He glanced at Tosha who gave him the I-may-have-let-something-slip look. He smiled. "Sure. Anything you want."

"Yay!"

"I can bring food," Tosha said.

"No need. I'll cook," he said.

"Go play for a bit, okay, Em?"

Her daughter nodded and ran off the instant her feet landed on the carpet.

His eyes looked weary.

"You're about to fall over. We already ate, but I left food for you. Come."

He lowered himself into a chair at the table while she filled his plate. She spread a napkin, utensils, and his plate on the placement mat and eased into the chair across from him.

"Mm. This is great, Tosha."

"I'm glad you like it." She reached for his hand. "I'm happy you're here."

"I wish I didn't have to leave."

"I know." Her heart raced as she longed for him to stay, but she dared not confess her feelings aloud. She sucked in a breath and exhaled while she willed herself to be careful, take it slow, even though her entire body ached for him.

Emily rushed over and clambered into his lap.

"No, baby girl. He's—"

"It's all right. I'm back to normal."

Tosha understood what he meant and relaxed her shoulders, doubting she'd ever be normal without him. He pretended to be Emily's stuffed lion, speaking in a gruff voice which made her precious little girl giggle. He snuck in a few last bites to finish off his dinner as he interacted with Emily.

"Thanks for this. I better get going."

"The sofa is super comfortable."

He grinned. "If I stay, I'll never make it in for work." He kissed Emily's forehead and sent her toward her toys. He turned to Tosha. "I don't even know how or if I'll sleep. I can't stop thinking about you."

She stepped toward him and buried herself in his embrace. "Oh, Zach."

He released her and, with one last kiss on her lips, walked to the door. Tears sprung from her eyes as he disappeared.

***

The chime of the doorbell still vibrated by the time Zach reached his front door. He smoothed down his shirt then opened the door. "Hey there. Come on in." Zach gestured with a backward jerk of his head. "Emily, I have something for you."

The little girl's eyes and mouth opened wide as she accepted the stuffed pony.

"What do you say, Emily?" Tosha asked.

"Tank you. I love him, Teddy."

"He loves you, too," Zach said.

Emily glanced past him and toward the playhouse in the corner.

"Can I play with that house?"

"Yes, go ahead. You may play until it's time to eat."

The little girl toddled off toward the dollhouse.

"You're spoiling her."

"Just for today. She needs toys here, too."

"Did you buy that big house for her?"

"No. It was my sister's. Olivia let me have it when I told her about Emily. She had it in storage."

"Where's your sister now?"

"On a mission trip in Burkina Faso, Africa. I don't get to talk to her much, but I did after our first date."

Tosha sighed.

He smiled, kissed Tosha's cheek, and whispered, "How about helping me in the kitchen?" in her ear.

She leaned into him. "Why is it so hard to resist you?"

He eased back. "Is that what you want?"

She shook her head. "No. I just wish I could think clearer around you."

He chuckled. "Then, I'd be all alone in my love-fog. I'm not thinking so clearly either, but I don't want to if it means you're not with me."

She nibbled her lower lip then tilted up her head for a kiss.

He pulled her close. "We better put the food out or Emily's sure to go hungry."

"Lead the way."

He grasped her hand then strolled to the kitchen.

***

Zach took the last dish from Tosha and placed it in the dishwasher. Dropping a pod into the soap compartment, he closed the door and pressed the start button.

"I had a great time, Zach."

"Me too."

"Come here, Emily."

The little girl yawned. "Pony."

"I have him," Tosha said. She picked Emily up and swung a bag over her shoulder.

"Good night," Zach said, wanting to kiss Tosha, but unsure how to do so with Emily in her arms. He kissed her cheek instead.

"I'm sorry," she said, apparently noticing his predicament.

"I'll walk you outside."

He followed and held the bag while Tosha buckled in the girl. When she straightened and stood inches away, he leaned toward her. Their lips met. Yes, it was clouds and butterflies again. He shivered with expectation. Tosha eased away.

"When can I see you again?" he asked.

"Tomorrow."

He gazed at her. "Really? You aren't teasing me."

"Not teasing."

"Good, because…"

"What?"

"I want to hang out with you as much as possible."

"I feel the same way," she said.

"And I told Emily I'd come over." He grinned.

"Mommy, where's pony?"

"Right here, baby."

She grabbed the pony from the bag still slung over Zach's arm and handed it to her little, sleepy girl.

"If you want…I don't mind…I'd really like you to stay over," he said. "That way Emily could fall asleep, and we wouldn't have to end the evening so soon."

"I don't know."

"You and Emily can have my room, or she can sleep in the spare bedroom. Please, just think it over."

She kissed him lightly on the lips. "All right. We'll stay next time. I better get going."

"Good night."

"Thanks for a great evening." Her smile tugged at his heart.

He helped her into the car and waited outside until her car disappeared around the corner. Tomorrow couldn't come fast enough.

Chapter 7

"What's the matter?" Zach asked.

"I'm having trouble breathing," Tosha admitted.

He chuckled. "Me too."

"These feelings. What I feel for you is awfully strong. I want things I shouldn't."

"If Emily wasn't chaperoning us tonight, I'd find it difficult to keep my promise."

Tosha exhaled in jagged puffs. The intensity of what she felt for this wonderful man scared her. "I love you so much."

He kissed her again, and she shivered.

"We should sit," he said.

She nodded, unable to speak.

He only sat for five seconds before standing again. "It's hot in here. I'll be right back." Zach returned with two tall glasses and offered one to her. "This should cool us down."

She gulped down the cold water, hoping to quench the thirst she had for the man sitting too close.

"I don't fully understand what's happening here, but it's some strong chemistry," he said.

"Maybe we need a sobering conversation."

"Okay. What should we talk about?"

"Do you have any faults?"

He smiled. "Yep, that'll do it." He leaned back into the pillows.

"It's just that everything's been perfect. I've never felt like this in all my life, and I keep thinking the world will disappear from under me. I feel like I've brought my mess to the table, but you...you're perfect." She peered into his eyes. Fear gripped her as she questioned whether she'd ever be good enough for him.

"Just to make it clear, from where I sit, you're pretty perfect, too, even with your so-called mess," began Zach. Her cheeks grew warm. "As for me, one of my many faults is—"

"Many?"

Zach's smirk lit up the room. "Sure. I'm extremely impatient. You bring out the best in me, Tosha. I don't know how, but you are changing me into a patient man. I just hope it lasts."

"Will you stay over? Emily asked if you could tuck her in tonight."

"I'd love that. Yeah, I'll stay."

"Sofa good?"

He nodded. "Sofa's just fine."

Her daughter ran over. "Mommy, I need a change."

"Oh, baby." Tosha stood and faced Zach. "I'll be right back. Did you have lunch?"

"Not really. I slept longer than I expected and rushed over so I could spend the afternoon with Emily like I promised."

"Help yourself to anything in the kitchen. It's a few hours 'til dinner."

***

Zach strolled into the kitchen and opened the fridge. Lunch meats, sliced wheat bread, and mayo. *That'll do.* He made a sandwich and opened her cabinets as he chewed. *Might as well learn where everything is.* Pots, dry foods, silverware, and mugs. A few minutes later, Tosha and Emily emerged from a room in the back.

"Teddy, play toys, please."

"He's eating, Em."

He got down on one knee. "I'm just about done, then I'll wash up before we play, okay?"

"Yay! I go wait for you."

"All right." He grinned, surprising himself of how much he'd wanted a family.

"You didn't bring any bags with you. Do you need a toothbrush for tonight? I think I have a spare."

"Naw, I'm set. I fly out late tomorrow morning. I put my bags in the car trunk so I wouldn't have to rush home like the last time."

"You have to go away again?" Tosha frowned.

"Yeah."

Her shoulders slumped. "How often do you go away?"

"A lot. I travel all over the country. It's why I took the job." He grasped her hand. "If you want, I'll take you and Emily along sometimes. I'm usually free after four and on weekends."

"It's just that Emily misses you when you're gone."

He smirked. "Just Emily?"

She leaned into him. "No, I miss you, too."

"Doing anything special this week?"

"Just baby doctor stuff."

"I'll call you every day."

"Me too."

He pressed his lips to hers, wishing he didn't have to leave her so soon.

***

Zach sighed the instant the plane touched down on the tarmac in Seattle. He missed Tosha. Not merely that he-longed-for-her-company kind of missing her, but the he-was-having-trouble-breathing-without-her sort. Switching his cell phone off airplane mode, he stared out of the window at the moving landscape and sighed again.

He texted *<Hey, Beautiful. Just landed.>*

<Good. When do you check in?>

<Around six.>

<Okay for me to call then?>

<Yeah.>

<♥>

Zach waited for a break in the disembarking passengers before standing to grab his carry-on. He made his way down the aisle toward the front exit, being sure to say a quick "thank you" to the pilot first. While brushing past rolling suitcases, wandering children, and dazed adults who'd been away from home for too long, Zach mulled over how much his life had changed since he'd met Tosha with her precious little Emily and unborn child. He'd never change a thing and hoped she felt the same.

He smiled at how he already thought of Emily as his little girl. He'd do anything for her. She made being a father rather easy. However, doubts plagued his mind as to whether he was also ready to be a dad to a new baby. He sighed. Besides…would Tosha ever let him…think him good enough?

He rushed down the stairs in search of the rental car zone. Three meetings in eight hours seemed too long a time to wait to hear her voice. In fact, he couldn't wait to see her.

<u>Chapter 8</u>

Tosha opened the door and welcomed Zach into her open arms.

"I missed you so much, Tosha."

She moaned into his neck. *Thursday couldn't come fast enough.*

He eased away, studied her for a moment, and then pressed his lips to hers.

"Teddy!"

Two arms wrapped around his knees. He released Tosha and bent over to pick up the little girl. He pulled Tosha close with his free arm and kissed both their cheeks.

The little girl's smile warmed his heart. "I'm glad you here."

"Me too. Can you go play for a bit so I can talk to Mommy?"

Emily nodded.

The moment he placed the little girl on the floor, she toddled back to her toys.

"Come in so I can close this door," she said. "All the neighbors are gonna start talking."

"You mean they haven't yet?"

She returned his smile.

He reached out and grasped her fingers. "I have a question for you, and I hope it's not too soon...to say..." He paused, still gazing at her.

Tosha stopped smiling and peered up into his eyes. "What is it? Tell me."

"Considering we professed our love for each other, may I tell our friends you're my girlfriend?"

The way she bit her lower lip sent warmth through him. "Yes. I'd like that."

"Great." He smiled then kissed her again.

"Are you staying for dinner?"

"Not this time. I'm beat, but I had to see you. You're still coming over my place tomorrow, right?"

"Yes, we'll be there."

"Great." He grinned. "Bring extra clothes."

***

Over at his apartment the next day, Zach opened the door within seconds of the ringing bell.

"Hey, come on in."

He lifted Emily, pecked her on the forehead, and whispered, "There's a surprise for you by the toys," in her ear.

With a huge grin on her face, she ran in the direction he pointed the instant her toes reached the floor.

He smiled and turned to Tosha. Pulling her close, he pressed his lips to hers and relished each movement. He eased away, shut the door, and guided Tosha's back toward the wall in the foyer. The moment his lips met hers, she turned away.

"She'll see you."

"Not yet. I kept her busy. New toy."

"You're spoiling her."

"For a few seconds of this? So worth it."

He closed the distance and explored her mouth. She moaned and explored his.

"Teddy!"

Zach eased away and smiled. "Time's up."

"Can I take home?" Emily hugged the stuffed puppy to her cheek.

"Of course, or leave here for your next visit."

"Yay. Tank you." She hugged Zach's leg and tugged on his hand, so he knelt on one knee beside her.

Emily pecked his cheek and wrapped an arm around his neck under his chin.

"I love you."

"I love you, too, baby bear."

Emily jerked away. "Mommy, look!"

Tosha smiled and said, "He's beautiful, baby. Now, go play." Seconds later, Tosha frowned.

Zach stood and asked, "What's the matter?"

"I'm scared for her. She adores you."

"The feelings are mutual. No matter what happens, I want to remain in her life. She's the most precious little girl I ever met, and I want to be a father to her…if you let me." He reached for Tosha's chin and lifted it, so his gaze locked hers. "But I want us to work out. I'm in love with you. I'd be a broken-hearted man if you weren't in my life. I'm in deep."

"She's not used to all the attention." She paused and searched his face. "Neither am I."

"Then, he's a fool."

"I gave too many years to that man. I don't want to make the same mistakes."

"Tosha, I'm not that guy."

She chewed on her lower lip. "I know, but I've been wrong before."

"What do you think of me now?"

Tosha's eyes sparkled. "That you're devoted, passionate, the marrying kind…" She trailed off.

"You're not wrong. I'm those characteristics and more. I want to be with you for the long haul. Let me love you for the rest of my life."

She nodded and leaned in for another kiss. This time he savored her lips a bit longer before touching his forehead to hers. He exhaled out of his mouth to release whatever this was that was building up inside. "Let's eat."

***

As Tosha leaned back against Zach on the sofa after dinner, she watched Emily play pretend with her toys. This was what she always wanted—a happy child and a man who paid attention to them both.

He caressed her fingers. "You good?"

"Mmhmm."

"Need anything?"

She nestled her head in the crook of this neck. "I have everything I need right now."

He kissed the top of her head. "I meant what I said earlier."

"About?"

"Being her father."

"I know. You already are."

"But it's more than just shelter, hugs, and making her laugh. It's discipline and security. I need to know you'll let me when the time comes."

She eased off his chest. "You talking 'bout punishment?"

"Not primarily. Discipline isn't the same as punishment, but sometimes punishment is needed."

Tosha frowned.

Zach shifted to sit on the edge of the sofa. "Look, I'm not trying to take over. I just want to be included. I want to be your partner in keeping her on track. That's all."

"Oh. Okay."

His smile tugged at her heart. "You say that now, but I've seen women put up a wall between their kids and the man who takes care of them. I just don't want that to happen to us."

"I get it. It's going to be tough. Her dad left everything up to me."

"Then, we'll talk through everything until we achieve our vibe, okay?"

She nodded.

"I don't want to lose you over this," Zach said.

"I know." She reached for his hand. "Neither do I."

He glanced over to Emily. "She's yawning. Mind if I tuck her in after you give her a bath?"

"I don't mind. She'll like that."

Tosha got Emily bathed, changed, and teeth brushed before bringing her back out to Zach. He was sitting on the sofa with a book on his lap.

"Hey, baby bear, want me to read you a story?"

"Yes, please." Emily climbed up into his lap.

He placed the book in front of her daughter and began to read. The words flowed off his tongue like butter as he switched voices for each character. Emily leaned back against him, her eyes drooping.

"The end," he said. "Time for bed."

"You take me, Teddy," Emily said with a yawn.

"You got it." He stood and cradled the girl in his arms. "Give Mommy a kiss first."

Tosha hugged and kissed Emily and continued observing them as he disappeared into the second bedroom. His voice traveled to her as he said a prayer and "nite-nite" to Emily. He returned a few moments later.

"You ready for me to tuck *you* in? There're clean sheets on the bed."

Tosha's face warmed. "I...I thought I'd sleep on the couch."

"No way. I'm taking the couch. You can sleep in my bed."

"But you sleep on the couch at my place, too."

"So? It's what a gentleman does no matter where he is."

"I'm just not used to this."

"I'm trying to spoil you, too."

"It's working. Don't stop."

"Come on. We had a long day."

"Will you read me a story?"

"If I do, will you let me leave the room?"

"Perhaps it's better I tuck myself in." She giggled, and he chuckled along with her.

"Just let me get my things before you settle in. There's a private bathroom. Give a yell if you need anything."

He grabbed a few items and kissed her before shutting the door behind him.

Oh, how I love that man.

***

Early the next morning, Zach filled up a tray with a glass of orange juice and a plate of French toast, bacon, and eggs. He strolled up to the bedroom and balanced the tray on one hand before knocking on the door.

"Tosha. You up?"

"Barely." Her sleep-infused voice wafted through the door.

"I made you breakfast. You decent?"

"Yeah. Come in."

He turned the knob, shocked at finding it unlocked. Had that been an invitation the previous night? He dared not ask her. He pushed at the door. Tosha had her hair wrapped up in a black cloth, the way his grandmother used to. She wore maroon silk pajamas, but her face, even with no makeup, took his breath away.

"Good morning, beautiful."

"Shut up." She, with an incredulous expression, held a palm up to stop him.

"I'm serious. I'm honored to have such a gorgeous woman in my bed." An image of him lying next to her flashed through his mind.

"You say that to all the girls?"

"Honestly, you're the first woman to sleep in that bed. The others never came over. Preferred that I stayed at their place." He took a few steps. "Breakfast in bed for Miss Tosha."

"Stop. Don't come any closer. I have to brush my teeth first."

"Why bother? You're only going to brush again afterwards. I don't mind."

With a hand clasped over her mouth and eyes wide, she lunged from under the covers and rushed to the bathroom.

Barf noises reached his ears. He stared at the breakfast and set it on the dresser. He may just have to wrap it up.

Entering the bathroom, he grabbed a washcloth from the cabinet and dampened it with cool water from the facet. He glanced over at Tosha, her face over the toilet bowl. He reached for a towel which he swung over his shoulder and joined her on the floor.

"Morning sickness?" he asked as he applied the cool cloth to the back of her neck.

She nodded and chucked again.

His empty stomach churned. Good thing *he* hadn't eaten yet.

***

When Tosha's stomach settled down, she straightened only to find Zach sitting behind her, a welcomed backrest. *I thought I was past all this.* She leaned into him, and he wrapped an arm around her middle. The other hand wiped at her mouth with a damp cloth.

"Thank you. I didn't want you to see me like this."

"What? Praying before the porcelain god?"

She giggled. "Yes. That. I'm a mess, sitting on this floor."

"Not at all. I spent a few hours scrubbing the toilet and floors yesterday before you came. I didn't even use it after. Went to the one off the hallway."

"You're kidding."

"Wouldn't kid the most beautiful woman in the world. Gorgeous, I might add, even though she just puked at the sight of my masterpiece."

"Ugh. I'm so sorry."

"I'll put it away when you're able to stand."

"No. I'll be fine. I can eat. I need to eat. I should clean up first."

"Well, now you'll definitely need to brush those teeth, but that's it. I scrubbed the floors, remember? C'mon. Let's get up."

He stood first and helped her up, too.

"Mommy!"

"I'll get her," he said.

"I should do that. She'll be a mess."

"I've got this."

"No. I'll change her," she said, her tone a bit sterner than she intended.

"I'll bring her and the bag, then," he said through clenched teeth. "You stay and clean up." He spun his back to her and left the room without glancing her way.

She flushed the toilet, washed her hands, then topped her toothbrush with toothpaste and stuck it in her mouth. He returned a few moments later. She rinsed and wiped her face.

"Mommy."

Zach handed Emily over. Tosha didn't miss a slight frown on his handsome features.

"Hey, baby. Let Mommy change you," Tosha said.

When she finished, Zach said, "Why don't you eat? I'll get her dressed."

"You don't need to, Zach." She grabbed for the clothes, but he didn't release them.

"Tosha, look at me."

She complied.

"Let me help you." He leaned closer to her ear but still locked her gaze. "I want to be a father to her, but you need to give me a chance to show you I'm not that guy. She's safe with me."

Tosha nodded and let go of the cloth. *He's right.* "Okay." Climbing back into bed, she sat and pulled the comforter up to her waist.

He brought the tray over and set it on its legs over her lap. Everything looked delicious.

"Let me know if you need anything warmed up."

She took a bite of the French toast. "No, it's fine. Thanks for this."

"You're welcome." He turned to Emily. "Come, baby bear. Let's get you ready for the day."

"Where we going?"

"The park. Would you like that?"

"Yes, Teddy. I like da park."

"Good. Now, reach your hands through the two armholes."

Emily did as he said so he could slide her blouse over her head.

Not even a mumble from this girl. Shock and nerves muddled together in Tosha's gut. She scrutinized every movement he made with her daughter. How he held out Emily's pants and waited with patience until her little girl got both legs in.

"Let's go brush your teeth." He stepped into the bathroom's doorway then paused. He glanced over at Tosha. "Is her toothbrush and paste in here?"

Tosha nodded and said, "Yes, there's a pink pouch."

He rummaged around the bag for a few seconds and lifted out what he needed. "Ah. Got it."

Emily followed him into the adjoining bathroom.

Zach praised Emily as she brushed her teeth. "All right. Let me give it a once over to make sure we got all the germs, okay?"

"Okay."

By the time they returned to the bedroom, Tosha had finished her food. *Now, it's my turn to get ready to go to the park.*

***

Tosha leaned back against the bench while Zach took Emily to the sandbox where two other children played. He handed her daughter a shovel and a bucket, showing her how to shovel and pour. He even brought over two handfuls of water from a nearby fountain to dampen some sand and make a bucket-shaped castle. He stood and retreated a few steps to let Emily play and mingle. He seldom ever took his eyes off the girl. As he returned to the bench where Tosha sat, he glanced over his shoulder toward Emily every other step.

His swagger distracted Tosha from checking on Emily. The way his waist moved in conjunction with his torso trapped her gaze. Even when he stopped short and peered off to the right, she didn't follow his gaze as her eyes continued to focus on his midsection. His butt sure did fill out his jeans just right. She blinked to break the spell only to find he'd already moved and slid onto the bench next to her.

"You're good with her," Tosha said, willing her body to cool down.

"She makes it easy." He glanced at Tosha. "You're a great mom." He returned to his watchful vigil over Emily.

How could this man whom she'd just met care so much about her little girl?

"I wish you were my baby's father," she blurted out. She bit her lip and berated herself. She hadn't meant to let that slip out.

He stared at Tosha a bit longer this time. "I'd like to be. Do you think he'll let me adopt them?"

Tears welled up in her eyes. "He doesn't know about the baby. I never got to tell him I'm pregnant."

"Why not?"

"The day I found out, I went home with Emily and found that man romping on the floor with some woman."

"Wow." He checked on Emily and placed two fingers against his lips. "Did she see?"

"No. She woke up, but I covered her eyes."

"That stinks. Come here," he said and gestured for her to snuggle under his arm. "Are you going to tell him?"

"I'm *never* tellin' him. I wish he'd release Emily."

"Has he called for her?"

"Not for a few weeks now. Would you really adopt her?"

"Yes, of course."

"Teddy, come!" Emily stood and reached toward him with dirty hands.

He kissed Tosha's cheek and jogged over to the girl. He brushed off her hands and swept her up into his arms. He glanced off to where he did before, but when Tosha looked, she didn't see anyone.

"Ready to go? I think baby bear's ready for a nap."

Her little girl's head bobbed on his shoulder.

"Sure." Tosha stood. "Your arms are going to be tired."

"You bet."

"We should have brought the stroller."

"We don't need it. Besides, if I can't carry her now, how am I going to be fit to carry her and her issues when she's older? I need to do this."

"You are a rare man, Zach Caldwell."

"I sure hope so. Want something to drink?"

"A smoothie would be great."

"We'll stop at the café on the way back."

I don't ever want to lose him.

***

Tosha walked into Zach's apartment first when he unlocked the door. She opened her mouth the second she realized he was heading for the second bedroom.

"Where are you taking her?"

"I'm putting her to bed."

"With all that dirt on her?"

"Why not?"

"What if we spend the night?"

"You serious?"

"I brought another outfit just in case. Is that okay?"

"Sure, but why didn't you say something before?"

"I didn't want you to see me in the morning, you know. I was nervous about spending one night, let alone two."

"And now?"

"I'm okay with it, besides I really wanted you to tuck me in, not anything more, just want to know what that's like."

"Is that why you left the door unlocked?"

She nodded, and her cheeks heated.

He chuckled. "I can stop at tucking you in. You sure that's all you want?"

"Yes, I'm sure. I can't…I'm not ready…not after…"

"I get it now." He embraced her. "I'm glad you're spending another night. We can always change the sheets."

"She'll be fine on the floor."

He pursed his lips before saying, "Oh, all right."

Zach grabbed a comforter from the closet, and Tosha helped him spread it out on the floor near the toys.

"Can we sit while she naps?" Tosha asked.

"Just sit." His eyes twinkled.

"Well, maybe a little more than sit."

"I'm in."

***

That night, Tosha placed Emily in the tub for a bath while Zach stayed in the kitchen to wash the dishes. She dipped the washcloth in the water, squeezed it, and rubbed it down her daughter's back, but images of Zach filled her mind.

"I like Teddy, Mommy."

"Yes, baby." Her tone had a dreamy edge to it. What was this man doing to her?

She finished cleaning Emily and let her play a bit longer before lifting the little girl out to dry her off.

"Will he read me a story, Mommy?"

Tosha led her daughter, all wrapped in a towel, to the second bedroom. "You want him to?"

"Yes, please."

"Don't you want me to read you one anymore?"

"Of course, but you read me one every other night. I don't see him much."

Tosha kissed Emily's forehead and pulled a ruffled nighty over her daughter's head.

"You stay here. I'll go see if he's done cleaning up."

"Okay, Mommy."

Tosha strolled to the kitchen but stopped short when his alluring gaze met hers. His smile warmed her all over. She bit her lower lip, reminding herself why she'd come out here in the first place.

"Emily's ready for a story."

"Coming." He folded and hung the towel on the oven handle then sauntered over to her, leaning in for a couple seconds without even brushing her skin with lips. He eased away and continued walking toward the room where Emily waited.

Tosha let out a breath she didn't even know she was holding. Heat washed over her, and she fanned herself.

Minutes later, with the story finished and nite-nite kisses given, Zach grasped Tosha's hand and led her into the hallway. He closed the door and said, "Your turn."

"My turn?"

"I remember a certain mature female asking to be tucked in. Tonight's your night." His smirk did not escape her notice.

"Just a story, right?"

"That's the plan." He stopped outside his bedroom. "Let me know when you're ready for me." He grinned, bit his lower lip, and backed away.

She shut the door and leaned her forehead against it.

What am I doing in this man's house? He'll have me asking him to sleep with me before too long.

Tosha brushed her teeth, showered, and dressed in rose-covered silk pajamas. She peeked out the door and found him lounging on the sofa.

"I'm ready."

Without delay, he sprung up and stepped toward her, picture book in hand. He followed her to the bed and placed the book on the side table before pulling the comforter aside so she could get in bed. He covered her up. She scooted over some, giving him room to sit beside her.

She didn't even hear the details of the story. Only his tenor tone resonated in her ears as she closed her eyes. She moaned when he pressed his lips to hers.

"Hey, sleepy head. Want me to read another one?"

"Naw, that was good. Real good. Thanks."

"Anytime. I'll get my things and leave you to slumber in peace."

"Okay," she said, not hearing whether he'd even left the room.

***

Zach blinked open his eyes. An image of a sleeping Tosha greeted his mind. He grabbed the edge of the sofa to make sure he hadn't sleep-walked back into the room.

He'd lingered in the bedroom many minutes after she'd fallen asleep, the urge to climb in next to her increasing the longer he remained seated on the bed. Her soft snores brought him comfort. She'd trusted him, and he dared not betray that trust at her most vulnerable moment. No. She'd have to be awake telling him to get in that bed with her before he'd do such a thing.

Careful not to jostle her, he'd stood up, gathered a change of clothes, and exited the room, closing the door behind him.

He smiled at the thought of having a gorgeous woman sleeping in his room. He didn't want to mess that up.

After showering and getting dressed, he went to the kitchen and whipped up some batter for pancakes. Once finished cooking up a dozen, he knocked on the door, crackers in hand for Tosha's morning sickness.

"Come in. I'm awake," a drowsy sounding Tosha said from beyond the door.

He peeked in. "I thought you might like some crackers before…"

"Yes. Please. Bring them here."

He strode in and handed them to her. "I made pancakes, so whenever…"

She nodded, mouth already filled with two crackers to help settle her stomach.

He smiled. "Let me know if you need anything." He left the room, closed the door, and waited for Tosha and Emily to arrive in the kitchen ready for breakfast.

The little girl stuffed her mouth with bite-sized pieces of pancake as fast as she could swallow, surprising Zach by eating the equivalent of two regular-sized ones.

"Somebody was hungry this morning," he said.

"Thanks, Teddy. They were yummy."

"Let's wipe that syrup off your mouth." Tosha pulled out a wipe and swiped it across Emily's lips. "We've got to get going soon."

"No, Mommy. I want to stay here."

"We're not going to stay. We need to get home."

"No," Emily said, beginning to cry.

"Hey." Zach knelt on the floor beside the little girl. "What's this, baby bear?"

"I want to stay with you." A tear streamed down one cheek.

"Well, you're in luck because after you go home, I'm going to join you. It's my turn to hang out at your place."

"Promise?" Emily pouted.

"Yes. I promise. I just need to clean up a bit first, okay?"

"Okay," Emily said and wrapped both arms around his neck.

Zach stood, lifting the little girl up in his arms, and kissed her forehead.

"You all packed, Tosha?"

"Yes. I just need to grab the poopy pull-up. I left it in the bathroom off the hall."

"No, I got that. I'll walk you down to the car and help you strap Emily in."

"You're amazing, Zach."

"I do try," he said with a grin.

***

Sunday evening, with dinner dishes cleaned and Emily playing with her toys, Tosha snuggled into Zach on the sofa. He wrapped his arms around her and nibbled at her ear. She giggled. He kissed her temple then leaned his head against hers. She stared at her daughter for a few minutes of bliss from the warmth of his embrace. No doubt her mind had to recall the most unfortunate detail from a previous conversation.

"You said you have baggage. What did you mean?" Tosha asked.

"You really want to get into that now?"

"Maybe not, but I am curious about something."

"What's that?"

She shifted a bit to peer up into his face. "How many women have you been with, and why didn't they last?"

He raised his brows, his eyes opened wide. "Wow!" He shrugged. "It's the same question said a different way."

"Oh." She folded her arms. "Will you answer?"

He nodded. "Looks like I better." He leaned back against the sofa. "I've gone out with five women but only seriously dated two. One lasted three months, the other a year."

"So, you only slept with two of them?"

"That's right."

"How long ago?"

"Five months."

"Not even a one-night stand?"

"I don't do one-night stands."

She paused and sucked in a huge breath, studying him. *Five months and no one else. Was it love?* "What happened?"

"We weren't compatible."

"In bed?"

"Mmm. That wasn't the reason."

"Did you break things off with them?"

"Yes."

"Why?"

"I wanted to get married and have kids. They didn't."

"Oh." His words surprised her.

"Are we good?"

Tosha unfolded her arms when a lump formed in her throat. "Emily's dad cheated on me. I don't want to go through that again. That's why I asked what I did. I have to make sure."

"I'd never cheat on you. You've got my word on that."

"We were engaged, Zach. Engaged. And I find out…he told me…she wasn't the only one. My world crashed that day. I swore I'd never love another man."

"And now?"

"I can't imagine a world where my love for you doesn't exist. I just want to be sure."

"I am totally in love with you, Tosha. No joke. I can't think about anything without your face filling my thoughts. I want you and me to be together for the long haul."

"Even with my kids. You said you wanted to wait."

"I know, but I want you and your children to be my family. Do you understand?"

"Are you sure?"

"More than anything. Besides, in a way, I'll be waiting."

"How?"

"I'll give you time to adjust to our new lives before adding to our number."

She tilted her head and giggled. "You're too funny."

"I'm thinking two more?"

She smiled. "Why don't we wait until this one is born before figuring out how many more kids I'm going to have?"

"Fair enough. We good?"

"Yeah. We good." Tosha stood. "You hungry?"

Zach's eyes glazed over with a lover boy gaze. "Very."

"Well, I'm not on the menu tonight. You want food?"

He chuckled. "Love some. Need help?"

"No. Dinner'd never get done." She swished around the sofa's edge and took two steps.

"Mm, sexy mama," he whispered, but the words reached her ears.

Her cheeks burned. She covered her behind—as if that would help—turned and glanced toward her daughter who continued playing with her toys. Relief flowed over Tosha until she caught sight of the smirk painted on Zach's gorgeous face. With no quip response, she swiveled on her heel and walked toward the kitchen.

She'd just unwrapped the chicken breast when firm hands slid around her waist. A jagged breath escaped her lips. He kissed her ear and leaned his head to hers.

She laid the chicken in the stainless-steel bowl to avoid dropping it on the floor. "I thought I told you to stay in the living room." Her words came out with each panting breath.

"Not exactly."

He wasn't wrong. "Fine. Why don't you go play toys with Emily? She missed you a lot."

"I'll do that later. Right now, I need to do something that'll help me refocus. Only helping you cook will do that. I can't stop thinking about you sitting out there."

"But you'll do that in here?" She laughed. "Remember the last time you helped me cook..."

"I do. That was something, all right." He eased away, his hands sliding off her hips, and side-stepped to the sink. Rolling up his sleeves, he said, "I'll wash my own hands *this* time."

She guffawed, and he joined her with his ever so sweet chuckle.

He dried his lower arms and hands. "What do you want me to do?"

"Chop that onion and the celery. Then, throw them in the pan. It won't take me long to chop and season this chicken."

"You got it, sweetie."

Oh, how she loved the way he talked to her.

Zach chopped like one of those chefs on TV, his hands guiding that knife back and forth over the vegetables. A few minutes later, he poured the onion and celery into the pan. He washed and wiped his hands again. "Be back in a moment. The bathroom's down the hall, right?"

She nodded, her thoughts straying to what he might be doing in there. When he returned in a couple minutes, she mentally slapped herself for letting her mind stray to places she'd just about die over if he ever found out.

Strolling straight toward Emily, Zach plopped down on the floor and began talking and playing. Tosha's heart tugged out of her chest and landed in his. His gentle interaction with her daughter showed her that he adored her little girl. Why didn't her own father pay this much attention?

Before long, Tosha's eyes slipped down to his crotch. She turned away, her face and neck all heated, just as he glanced up at her. Lawdy, she must tamp down the wildness in her veins or she'd repeat the same mess all over again.

She turned away to turn on the stove. The light sizzle coming from the pan helped to keep her mind off her topsy-turvy emotions. She loved him. She wanted him. She mustn't give in.

Pulling in a deep breath, she gave the food one more stir then turned off the stove. She poured the stir fry into a serving dish and walked it out to the dining table. "Dinner's ready."

"Yay," said her daughter, little feet already hurrying toward the table.

"Wait up. What do you need to do first?"

139

"Wash hands," the girl said.

"That's right." Tosha extended her hand, but her baby girl shook her head.

"Can Teddy help me? He needs to wash hands too?"

Tosha peered up at Zach's sparkling eyes.

He smiled at her. "I got this."

Tosha nodded and said, "Thanks." An unfamiliar sensation passed over her. Emily was already treating him like a father. What if things didn't work out? Would he even still want to see her little girl?

Emily returned a few minutes later. "All clean, Mommy."

"Good, baby girl. Let's get you seated."

Tosha lifted Emily into her booster seat and had her buckled in the moment Zach returned.

"I can't believe how tired I am. I better head home right after I eat."

"Why don't you stay the night? The couch is quite comfortable."

"Naw. It's best if I head back." He sat next to Emily.

"You sure? I don't want you getting into an accident."

"I'll be fine. Really." He grabbed the spoon from beside the serving dish, plopped some food on Emily's plate, and faced the little girl. "Is that enough?"

"Yes. Tank you, Teddy."

"All right. You just be sure to call me when you get there," Tosha said.

He nodded. "Now sit and eat before I die of starvation as well as sleep."

She obliged without a word.

"How much?" he asked.

"Two spoons."

Tosha paid attention to every nuance. The way he talked and smiled. How attentive he remained to her and her daughter. Once finished, he even cleared the table for her.

He embraced Tosha and whispered, "I love you," in her ear.

"I love you," she responded.

With a brief kiss good night for her and Emily, he headed home. She hated seeing him go. He called a half hour later, but those thirty minutes seemed like a lifetime.

"Just walked through the door."

"Good," she said. "Now get some sleep."

"I don't know if I can."

"Why not?"

"I can't stop thinking about you."

"Me either."

His chuckle tugged at her, threatening to pull her through the phone and into his arms. "See you soon."

"You better," she said and sighed when the call ended.

<u>Chapter 9</u>

Tosha opened her eyes and grabbed her buzzing phone off the coffee table. Too tired to make it to her bedroom upon arriving home from work, she'd sent Emily to her room for an afternoon nap then sprawled out on the sofa and fell asleep. Zach's lingering scent on the pillows engulfed her. Perhaps that's what relaxed her so much.

Karida's name and picture filled the phone's display. Tosha tapped the answer button.

"Hey, girl, it's great hearing from you."

"I hope so, considering my best friend hasn't had time to call me since she got a man."

Tosha giggled. Her cheeks warmed. "And I'm very grateful that you set us up on that blind date."

"That's good to hear. How's it going? Things working out between you two?"

"Oh, Karida, it's better than working out. He's a dream. Perfect even. And smells nice."

Karida laughed. "And with Emily?"

"He's wonderful with her. Protective, but not overbearing. She adores him."

"Why do I feel a 'but' coming on?"

"I'm afraid I'm going to do something to mess things up."

"Why's that?"

"Seems too good to be true."

"I get you, but he's the real deal, Tosha. I wouldn't have encouraged this otherwise. By the way…"

"What?"

"Why are you home so early? I called your job, and they said you left a few hours ago."

"Oh, well, I saw some spotting in the restroom at work and thought I should go see the doctor."

"And?"

"Nothing to worry about. Heartbeat's strong. Baby's moving around. I just gotta keep an eye on it."

"You and Zach haven't been…"

"Karida! No!"

"Don't bite my head off. I'm just trying to figure out why I haven't heard from you."

"Well, he's been over almost every night. When he's not here, we go over to his place."

"You spend the night?"

"Yes, but he always stays on the couch."

"Not that I'm pushing you or anything, especially since I waited until marriage, but why's that?"

"I don't know. I can't stop thinking about how much I want to be with him, but…"

"Spill it. You can be real with me."

"I know. I think I want to wait."

"But you didn't with Chaz."

"Right, and I ended up with a world of hurt."

"But Zach's different than him."

"And Zach keeps reminding me of that. I just don't want to mess this up, you know?"

"Yeah. I understand."

"But what if Zach wants to before I'm ready?"

"Tell him. Explain things to him. He'll wait until you are."

"I hope so."

"I'm glad he and Emily are getting along. I know you were really nervous about her with him."

"I still am a little. What if we don't make it?"

"Tosha, stop."

"Okay. Fine."

"He'll be a good father for Emily."

"He already is."

"Not to bring up a sore subject, but how is Emily's dad?"

"Ugh. That man hasn't called her in weeks."

"Does she ask for him?"

"Not anymore. Not since Zach's been spending so much time with her. He plays pretend with her, Karida. Gets down on the floor and interacts with her toys. She loves it."

Karida laughed again.

"After a while, Emily won't remember Chaz anymore." Tosha's phone buzzed against her ear. She stole a quick glance at the screen and sat up. "Speak of the devil."

"Chaz? You better go talk to him. See what his deal is. I'll catch you later."

"Okay. Bye, girl." Tosha clicked over to the new call. "Yeah?"

"Hey. Just checking in."

"Why? I figured you'd been too busy."

"I was."

"What? She left you?"

"Naw. I threw her out."

"Ahh. Got a dose of your own medicine, huh? Well, don't expect me to come back."

"Why? You found someone?"

"That's none of your concern."

"That's not why I'm calling."

"Why, then."

"How's Emily?"

"She's good. Happy. Well-behaved at school."

"Cool."

"She should be up from her nap by now. I'll go get—"

"No need to bother her. I'm just checking up."

"It's fine. Really. She'd like to hear from you."

"Not today, Tosha. I'm kinda busy."

Tosha's blood ran hot across the back of her neck. "Then why bother calling if you don't have time to talk to her."

"I didn't call to have a fight with you."

"What did you think was going to happen when you won't talk to your daughter?"

"I'm done with you."

"Fine, 'cause I'm done with you, too." The call fell silent.

He'd hung up on her.

Tosha turned to find Emily leaning against her bedroom's doorpost and peering up with the saddest eyes.

"Oh, baby. How long were you there? Did you hear me talking?"

"Yes, Mommy."

"Do you know who it was?"

Her daughter nodded while tears streamed down her little cheeks.

"Come, baby, Mommy hold you," Tosha said, but Emily shrugged away and went to sit with her toys.

Her darling baby girl sat sobbing for the man who cared about other things and women more than he did about his own child. Emily reached out and grabbed her pony by the tail and pressed the stuffed toy close to her chest.

"Mommy," Emily said a few minutes later.

Tosha drew close to her daughter and knelt beside her. "Yes?"

"Call Teddy please."

"He's at work, baby."

Emily's face contorted from the pain tearing at her little heart. "Please... Mommy... Call," she managed between sobs.

"Okay, baby." A couple presses later, Tosha tapped on Zach's speed dial number. His recorded message began when he didn't answer. "He's not there, Em. We can call back—"

Emily stood, the pony still in her grasp. "Leave message, Mommy."

The tone marked the end of the greeting. "Hi, Zach. Sorry to bother you. Emily asked me to call."

"Let me, Mommy," her daughter said, one arm extended toward the phone.

Tosha nodded. "She wants to leave a message."

Emily started talking before the phone touched her ear. "Teddy, I want you. Please come. Please…" The rest of the words came out as a garbled sob.

"Oh, baby." Tosha took the phone, but by the time she glanced at the screen, the call had ended. Emily must have hit the end button in her despair. Tosha wrapped both arms around her little girl. *What's that man gonna think of us now?*

***

Zach pulled the vibrating phone out of his pocket the minute he left the conference room. Someone left a message. He'd been in front of his team when the phone first shook in his pocket. A half hour of questions later, he finally had the chance to listen.

He smiled as he glanced at the name. *Tosha.* He never ceased in longing to hear her voice. However, his smile faded as he continued to listen. His baby bear needed him. He pressed the callback button as he hurried to his desk.

"Zach." Tosha's voice sounded strained, and Emily's crying reached his ears.

"What's wrong with Emily?"

"She overheard a hard conversation."

"Her father?"

"Yeah."

"You called?"

"No, he did, but..."

Tosha let the rest hang. She didn't need to finish. He now understood Emily's tears.

"Let me speak to her."

"You sure? If you're busy..."

"I'm sure. Work can wait. She's important to me."

"Okay. Here she is."

"Teddy?" Emily's voice quivered her special name for him.

"Hey, baby bear. I'm so sorry you're hurting. How can I help?"

"Come here. Are you coming over after work?"

"I can do that."

"And stay?"

"You mean sleep at your place?"

"Yes, please."

"Sure. I need to go to my apartment first to pack a few things, okay?"

Emily's jagged breathing forced its way to his heart. "Uh...oh...kay."

"Love you, baby bear. I'll see you tonight."

"Tank you. Bye."

Tosha's sigh preceded her words. "She's so sad. I came to my room so she can't hear me."

"Why did he call?"

"To check in, he said. But then when I started to get Emily, he didn't want to talk to her. He just wanted to know if I found someone. The jerk. Sorry."

"Don't be. He *is* a jerk for hurting Emily like that."

"So, you coming over?"

"Yeah, I'll pack clothes for work tomorrow then head over."

"And you were just here yesterday."

"It's fine. I don't mind at all."

"Thanks, Zach. I really appreciate you doing this. She's been clutching that pony you gave her ever since his call."

"Anything for my girls. I love you."

"I love you, too."

Zach laid the phone down on his desk and clenched his fists. *Her ex better hope I never meet him.*

***

Zach rang the doorbell and hurried into the apartment the second Tosha opened the door. He'd just dropped his bag on the floor when Emily sped toward him, calling his name. Stealing a quick kiss from Tosha, he knelt, arms open, to welcome the little girl into a bear hug. Standing, he tightened his embrace in response to her firm grasp on his collar and her nose snuggled into the crook of his neck.

"I missed you," Emily said.

"Me too," he replied and kissed her cheek.

"Teddy?"

"Yes, baby bear?"

"My daddy don't talk to me anymore. Can you be my daddy?"

He sucked in a breath and tears welled up on his lids. He placed a palm on the back of Emily's head and leaned into her. He glanced at Tosha, but her dropped jaw, wide eyes, and hands clasped over her mouth broadcasted her surprise. He eased his head away from the girl's and peered into her eyes.

"Yes. Of course. I'd be honored to be your daddy." He paused to take in the upturn of the corners of her mouth. "What if your other daddy wants to talk to you again?"

"*You* my daddy now. I only want you. Not him." She snuggled into his neck again. "I love you, Daddy."

"I love you, baby bear. Thanks for asking me to be your dad." He didn't fight back the tears any longer even as he felt the girl's tears tracking a path down his neck.

He lost track of how long he stood in the foyer with little Emily wrapped up in his arms.

***

Zach left Emily to play alone with her toys two hours after he'd first stepped through the door. He found Tosha dropping sliced vegetables into a pot.

"I didn't know she was going to ask you that," she said without looking at him. "I'll talk to her later and explain… Sorry about that."

"Don't be." He placed a hand on her shoulder. "I want this. I count being her dad a privilege. She's a great kid with a huge heart. I'm elated she asked me."

"You sure?"

"Absolutely. How are you feeling about it?"

"Okay, I guess. I just don't want her to be hurt if…"

He reached up to touch her chin and turned her face toward him. "I already told you, I'll be here for her no matter what happens between us. But I'm going to fight for this to work. Are you with me?"

She nodded.

"In the spirit of being transparent, you're not the only one who's scared. This is all new for me, and I don't want to mess it up, not with her, and certainly not with you. I love you with all my heart."

Tosha shook as she cried with the knife in her hands. He gently undid her death grip on the hilt and folded her between his arms.

"You have a huge heart, too," she said and sobbed into his shoulder. "I hate him for hurting her like that. Who does that to a child? To your own child. He's the only man I've ever been with. Why'd he treat us like this?"

Zach had no words to comfort her. He held her close until her crying had stopped.

"What are you making?"

"Chicken soup."

"Why don't I finish this for you? Go lie down until it's done."

"But you worked all day."

"And you've never cooked this late. I got this. I'm sure Emily could use some play time with Mommy if you're up to it."

"Yeah, I'll do that. Thanks, Zach."

"Anytime, sweetie."

Zach chopped up the carrots with quick movements.

***

After Zach left the next morning, Tosha called Karida.

"How's it going?" Karida asked.

"I'm not sure."

"What do you mean? Did Chaz say something?"

"It's what he didn't say that's the problem, but he's not why I called you."

"Spill it, sister."

"I have fallen totally in love with Zach. He's everything I want, everything I need. When we kiss, it's like magic or something."

"So, what's wrong with that?"

"It's all so fast. I'm scared. Last night, Emily asked him to be her daddy. I don't want her to get hurt. *I* don't want to get hurt."

"He won't, Tosh. He's crazy about you and Emily. That's so cool she called him Daddy."

"But is he safe? I mean…with Emily."

"Tosha, we would never have introduced you if he wasn't. You can trust him with her."

"But is it too fast?"

"What do you want out of this relationship, Tosha?"

"You know. Marriage."

"Then stop fighting. He's won your heart. Now, he has to tread carefully to win your mind. Open your eyes. Pay attention. I think he wants the same thing you do."

Chapter 10

Thursday afternoon, Tosha stood in her living room, staring at her phone.

"The baby's father is missing out on hearing the heartbeat," the doctor had said at Tosha's emergency prenatal appointment to check on the spotting issue. "You really should bring him to the next visit."

Tears welled up in Tosha's eyes as she pushed the call button on her cell phone. Karida didn't answer.

Tosha paced the floor as she recalled her conversation with Karida the previous day to see if her best friend wanted to accompany her to the doctor. Tosha stopped pacing and stared at her phone again.

"Call him."

Karida's words echoed in her mind, but this scared her more than anything. What if Zach rejected her because she pushed him too fast?

"He'll be fine. You'll see," her friend had said.

How'd Karida know him so well?

Tosha dialed the only other number she could think of. She rethought the wisdom of that after Zach said, "Hello."

"I'm sorry to call you at work," she said, her voice quivering slightly.

"Don't be. I'm glad you did. The meeting can wait. What's the matter?"

She exhaled and placed a hand against her mouth, forcing back the wave of sorrow that climbed up her throat. She inhaled before answering, "I have an appointment with the OB tomorrow. She said I could bring the father. I don't know why her saying that hurt so much."

"Would you like company?" he asked.

"What?"

"I don't mind tagging along."

"But you're not..."

"The father? I know, but I'd like to be...if you let me. I don't mind joining you for the appointment. Whatever a father would do, I'd appreciate the chance at it."

His response shocked her.

"You don't have to do this," she said.

"I know, but I want to be there for you, with you. What time is the appointment?"

"Don't you have work?"

"I can take off a few hours."

"This isn't your problem."

"I fail to see how going to a prenatal appointment is a problem. As for work, my schedule's pretty flexible. I'll return afterwards and work a bit late. I'm not just a pretty boy to hang on your arm."

A hearty laugh escaped her.

"I want to do this," he continued, "for me as much as for you. All right?"

Fighting him on this would be futile, especially because she really wanted him there. "The appointment is at one o'clock."

"Great. I'll tell my boss. See you at dinner. I love you."

"I love you, too."

She ended the call and sighed. Now tears of joy streamed down her cheeks.

***

The next day, Tosha promised herself that she wouldn't cry when Zach picked her up, but stubborn emotions continued to bubble up her throat. She'd run out of saliva if she kept this up the entire time it took to get to the doctor's.

She gathered her wits and glanced his way.

"I was such a mess when she said I could invite the father. I'm so sorry I dragged you into this appointment."

"You didn't drag me. I volunteered. As far as I'm concerned, Emily is my daughter now. We've adopted each other. It would make sense I be her little brother's or sister's dad, too."

"Zach. What if we don't…?"

"I want to do this. No matter what happens between us, I want to be in their lives. Will you let me?"

She hesitated long enough to let his words sink in this time. "Okay. Yes. Thanks."

"Good. Let's get in there before they give someone else your spot."

Tosha signed in and nodded to two seats nearby. Zach settled next to her and thumbed through a few magazines while they waited. Was he nervous?

When the assistant called Tosha's name, she stood, and Zach followed suit.

"Come on back," the young woman said.

Tosha peered up at Zach when he grasped her hand. She smiled, and, with a comforting wave washing over her, Tosha followed the young assistant into a square room with two chairs and an elevated examination bed. A periodic gentle squeeze from his fingers reassured her.

Once Tosha's weight and blood pressure had been typed into a handheld tablet, the young woman excused herself. In just a few moments, the doctor entered the room.

"You must be the father."

"Actually, I'm not the baby's biological father. I'm Tosha's boyfriend, and I intend on being the baby's father in every other capacity."

The word "boyfriend" startled her. Although they'd seen each other practically every day since he found her apartment, and he'd referred to her as his girlfriend, she'd never referred to him as such. She wondered why that affected her more than his desire to be her baby's dad.

Zach held Tosha's hand while the doctor pushed up her blouse so she could slather the gooey gel on Tosha's belly.

"Oooo."

"You all right?" Zach asked.

"Yes. It's just cold."

The OB moved the doppler back and forth until the sound of fast tiny horse hoofs emitted over the speaker. A wide grin formed on Zach's face.

"Wow! That's amazing."

He met Tosha's gaze with love in those adorable brown eyes. Her breath caught.

"Strong and healthy," said the OB while wiping the gel off Tosha's abdomen. "I look forward to seeing you both in two weeks."

Tosha and Zach returned to the front desk where she paid the copay. After taking a few steps outside, she turned to face him.

"What you said in there. Did you really mean it?" Tosha asked.

He peered into her eyes. "I may joke about my appearance, but I'm dead serious about being your boyfriend and the baby's father. I'd never tease you about those things. I want you, Emily, and this baby to be a part of my life."

"But it's a lot to take on."

"I didn't say I thought this would be easy. You're not the only one who's scared. But I really want to do this. I love you."

He raised his hand to twirl a stray twist of her hair before sliding his fingers down her jawline. Zach leaned toward her and pressed his lips against hers. Heat flooded every inch of her skin. She could barely stand straight. He eased away, helped her off the curb, and guided her to his car.

"Why? How could you care this much for me when we've only just met?"

"I don't know, but I have no regrets." He walked her to the passenger door.

She tilted her head up toward his for another taste. He obliged before unlocking the door and helping her in.

After settling in the driver's seat, he said, "Did you want me to get Emily before I take you home?"

"No. I need a nap first. I'll get her later." A few minutes into the drive, she said, "Thank you, Zach, for everything."

"You're welcome."

"When will you be back from work?"

"Pretty late. I'm presenting a job to a client tomorrow. Emily will probably be in bed by then."

"Oh."

"But I'll call around dinner so I can talk to her."

"She'll like that."

He reached out and again twirled a twist between his fingers. She liked the way his playfulness thrilled her.

"I know this is taboo, but I can't resist," he said. "I hope you don't mind."

Unlike other women of African descent who drew the line at allowing a male to put his hand in their hair, Tosha enjoyed when Zach played with her twists.

"I don't mind. I like when you do that."

His smile sent an electrical current through her, then he kissed her before exiting the car to get her door.

***

Soon after Zach entered Tosha's apartment the next day, Emily rushed toward him yelling, "Daddy, Daddy, Daddy," and stared at his hands.

"Did you bring a pwesent?"

He knelt on one knee. "Not this time. Is a big hug enough?"

The girl nodded and lunged at him, wrapping her tiny arms around his neck. He embraced her, stood, and swung her around.

"Want to play?" Emily asked him.

"Of course." He pecked Tosha on the lips, not exactly what he had in mind after not seeing her since the appointment. *Family life.* He strode over to Emily's play area, Tosha not far behind, and set her down on the plush carpet.

The girl picked up a stuffed animal and held it out to him. "Pony likes tickles."

Zach used his fingers to walk over to Pony before tickling it all over. "What about you, Emily? Do you like tickles, too?"

"Yes, Daddy. Tickle me."

Zach moved his fingers quickly at her sides. The little girl rolled from one side to the other, giggling from her gut. He loved hearing her laugh.

"Mommy's turn!" Emily squealed.

"Oh no, not me," Tosha objected.

"Pleeeaase? Mommy's turn," pleaded the little girl.

He couldn't deny this adorable creation. He reached over and pressed his fingers against Tosha's side. She flinched. He had her. He didn't let up, and the most glorious deep-throated chortle emitted from her lips. The sound thrilled him. Emily joined in, but Tosha focused on his hands, pushing them away. She couldn't keep him at bay for long.

"Stop," Tosha managed during a giggle. "Please."

He pulled his hands away immediately.

"Now, your turn, Daddy," said Emily.

"You'll never find it." He glanced toward Tosha's raised eyebrows. "It's in a…safe place, but you'll never find it."

"We'll see about that," Tosha said and prodded along his spine while Emily worked on his lower legs.

"Is it your feet?" Emily asked. "Take off your shoes."

"It's not my feet," he admitted.

Just then, Tosha's fingers brushed against his ears. He lurched forward.

"Your ears?" Tosha said. She reached for him again, and he couldn't help the guffaw that followed. Her touch somehow held the magic that worked all too well. He locked her gaze. Suddenly, she stopped.

"I should go fix dinner." She seemed nervous.

"Need help?" he asked.

"No. You play with Em."

A couple minutes later, he peered into the kitchen. Tosha stood still, facing the cabinet over the sink. She didn't move even after a few seconds.

"I'm going to help Mommy. Okay, Emily?"

"Okay, Daddy." After a quick hug, she returned to her toys.

Zach strolled into the kitchen and leaned against the counter, facing Tosha. Her eyes glistened. He didn't want to impose, but she seemed worried.

"Tosha? I meant what I said before. I'm not going anywhere."

"I know what you said, but…"

He had guessed her thoughts. She feared he would leave after he got tired of all this, her children and the work needed to care for everyone, but he loved her from the depths of his soul. He couldn't hear her breathing.

"I'm not him, Tosha. I promise you. You can exhale now. I'm here to stay."

And she did exhale with tears lingering on her lids.

He wiped her cheek with his fingertips and said, "What can I get you? What do you need?"

"Salt," she said softly, "I need salt."

"Coming right up." He handed it to her and touched his forehead to her temple. "How about we go out? Just the two of us."

"I'd like that."

"You think Karida will watch Emily like she did for our first date?"

"Of course. Emily loves Karida and enjoys staying over."

"Cool. You mind if I set things up?"

Tosha shook her head. "Not at all. All night?"

"No, just for a few hours our first time out without her. Movie then dinner."

"Okay." She sucked in a breath then sprinkled some salt into a bowl.

***

Tosha lay in bed thinking about Zach and the brief good night kiss that still lingered on her lips. He enthralled her, and she so wanted to believe his words, the promises her ex had never kept. Sure, Emily's dad never left her, but he'd never devoted himself to her and Emily the way Zach had in such a short time.

She didn't want to let her heart fall into a place she'd later have to climb out of. She must be bewitched by his good looks and charm. There's no way a man would take on a woman, two kids, not push her to have sex, and be an angel. He'd said he didn't want a day to go by without seeing her. She felt any minute without him near brought heartache. She couldn't have that and expect him to remain celibate.

Tosha drew courage to love from his strength and easy disposition. She needed input, so she picked up the phone.

"Hello."

"It's me, Karida."

"I know. What's wrong? It's late," she said with a yawn.

"I can't sleep. He's too good to be true."

"That's why we introduced you to each other. I'm pretty sure he feels the same way."

"I'm scared, Karida."

"Don't be. He won't hurt you. Not like…"

"That's what *he* said."

"He's not a liar."

"He's so good with Emily. I don't want her to get hurt if this doesn't work."

"Tosha, you love him."

"Yes, and that's the problem. I've got it bad. I can't stop thinking about him."

Her friend laughed. "Guuurrrlll, stop inventing problems. He's great for you. Enjoy this time. Don't let past hurts prevent you from relishing the joy of true love."

"But…"

"Listen, Tosha, if Zach messes with you, Tevin will beat him up. Okay?"

Tosha smiled then. "All right. I trust you."

"Now, let me get to sleep before I lose my mind."

"Good night and thanks for this."

"No problem. Good night, girlfriend."

Chapter 11

Tosha's hands slid from his shoulders to his chest. She held them there. His pulse raced like hers, pounding against her palms. If they weren't cuddling on a park bench...

"I'm so glad we got to go out alone," she said then pressed into him.

She hadn't expected a romantic comedy. Zach never ceased to surprise her.

He nuzzled her temple. "Did you like the food at the deli?"

"I did. I'm stuffed."

"Good. I would've taken you to a restaurant, but the one I wanted was catering a party. We'll go next time."

She stared at his mouth and touched them with her own without conscious thought. They kissed, but he soon eased away. Zach's brows furrowed with concern.

"What's wrong?" Tosha asked. Her gut clenched when he sighed.

"My job is going to break our flawless streak. I'll have to travel."

"Now?"

"Not immediately, but soon." He caressed her cheek. "I don't think I'll fare too well not seeing your face every day."

She fit her face into the crook of his neck and sighed, too. He tightened his embrace.

"What do you need from me?" Zach asked.

"To not hurt Emily. She looks up to you as a father, and I fear what will happen if you leave us. I don't want her heart to break anymore."

"Easily done. I have no intention of leaving. What else? For yourself?"

"For you to be available whenever I need you. To be tuned in to us, to me."

"More challenging, but I'll do my best," he promised.

"What about you?" she asked. "What do you need from me?"

"I need you to believe me when I say I love you with my whole being, that I want to spend a lifetime with you and that there aren't any exes waiting at my heart's door. I just need you to believe that. There's no one else for me. Can you do that?"

"Yes. I can do that."

"Good. 'Cause I don't say those words lightly." He kissed her temple. "Would you like to sit quietly for a bit? I'd like to relish this moment with you."

"I'd like that."

***

Zach sat for an hour with his arms around Tosha's shoulder. Placing an index finger under her chin, he swiveled her head so she'd face him. He kissed her long and deep then stared at the crescent moon sitting high in the sky.

"Do you still love Emily's father?"

"No. Why would you ask that? I left him."

"He broke your heart, but that doesn't mean you stopped loving him."

"I don't love him. Not anymore. You don't need to worry about him. I might hurt him if he crossed my path."

Zach chuckled. "A woman's scorn."

"What?"

"Just that I'd do well never to mess things up with you."

"I have another question," she said and paused a couple seconds. "Why do you want my baby? I guess I don't understand why you would want to be the father for someone else's child?"

"Tosha, can't you grasp what this is? What we are?"

She shook her head.

"We are family now—self-made. I want you, *and* I want these children. He knows about Emily, and I won't stand in his way if he wants a healthy relationship with her. But if he ever messes with you or her, he'll have to deal with me."

She smiled. "I got you."

He leaned in for another kiss. "Thanks for being straight with me."

"Anytime."

"Ready?"

"Yeah."

"Let's go get our girl."

When Zach extended his arm toward Tosha, she grasped his hand and stood. She placed a palm on her forehead as if feeling for a fever.

"You okay?" he asked.

"I'm fine. Just a little warm."

He raised his brows.

She smiled. "Don't give yourself too much credit. It's probably just the baby fluttering around that's causing this heat." She turned and began walking.

He studied her for a moment before following. He liked the way her hips' movements caused her dress to sway from side to side, accentuating her firm calves. He reached for her elbow and turned her around to face him. He bent forward and touched his lips to hers.

She jerked away and placed both palms on his chest, but the brief respite led to her wrapping both arms around him and pulling him close. He tightened his embrace and satisfied his craving for her lips. Too soon, she pulled away with a gasp and drew a hand to her mouth.

He said nothing, but gazed into her eyes, so full of hunger for him.

She leaned toward him and stopped, easing away again, as if fighting his magnetic pull on her. Why did she resist?

"We should probably get going," he said, freeing her from her struggle.

"Yes, let's," she said, taking his hand for the return trip to his car.

***

Emily lay quietly in bed, asleep.

Zach's intoxicating good night kiss left Tosha gasping for air. Why did this keep happening to her? His lips must contain a magical aphrodisiac. She had to remain vigilant with him.

He eased away. "I should go," he whispered.

She nodded, still unable to speak.

He hesitated but continued to release her waist though not her eyes. She longed for him but immediately glanced away.

She shouldn't.

She couldn't. Not tonight.

He stepped away slowly and smiled.

"May I stop by tomorrow?"

She exhaled, not knowing how she'd manage to resist him.

"Yes," she said before her better sense stepped in. She convinced herself that Emily would be upset if he didn't show.

As if reading her mind, he mouthed, "I don't want to leave."

And the words, "I don't want you to go," slipped out of hers.

He smirked and stepped toward her. She placed a palm on his chest. He covered her hand with his. She shook her head and leaned against the doorframe. He squeezed his eyes shut for a second, dropped his hand, and moved back.

"Good night. I'll be back tomorrow."

"All right," she said softly and hugged herself as he walked away. *There's no way he stays with me if I don't give him what he wants. What am I going to do with Emily when that happens?*

***

Zach arrived at his door, shoved a key into the lock, and rotated his wrist. Turning the knob, he pushed the door open and sighed. He wanted Tosha and to know the feel of her skin next to his.

"Wait on de Lawd."

He flopped onto the sofa and pulled out his cell phone. With two taps, ringing commenced.

"Hey," Tevin answered.

Zach toed off his shoes and swung both feet onto the cushions. "I'm finding it hard to resist her."

"Isn't that the point?"

"She wants to wait and I...I'm having a tough time with this. What do I do?"

"Do you love her?"

"Of course."

"Enough to commit?"

He didn't need to think about the answer. "Absolutely. She's captured my heart. I see only her in my future, but I don't want to scare her away."

"You won't, but she's been hurt, so tread carefully."

"Great. That doesn't help."

"I know. All I can say is that she feels strongly about you, too."

Zach had already sensed this. The way she kissed him— *rocked his core.*

"Let me say this another way. Please be straight with me, Tevin."

"I'll do my best."

"She wants to go slow. Do I just pop the question?"

Tevin sighed audibly over the phone. "I can only say that you should follow your gut. Slow in one way doesn't mean slow in another. She's cautious. She wants to be sure."

"But I've told her my intentions."

"She's been told those things before. Now, seeing is believing. The sooner, the better."

"Okay. Thanks."

"Anytime, man."

Zach ended the call and closed his eyes. *How am I going to do this?*

***

The next day, Tosha's heart leapt at the sound of a knock on the door.

"It's me, sweetie."

"Teddy!" screamed Emily. "Open da door, Mommy." Emily wrapped her arms around Zach's leg seconds after Tosha turned the knob and pulled.

"Hey there. I missed you, too," he said, picking Emily up to give her a peck on the cheek. Cradling her gleeful daughter, he stepped over the threshold and said, "Can you do something for me?"

"What, Daddy?" Emily said, eyes wide.

"Would you play alone for a bit longer? I need to talk to Mommy."

Tosha's gut clenched.

Emily nodded and ran to her play corner the moment her feet hit the floor. He smiled at Tosha then and drew her close for an affectionate hug. He kissed her lightly on the cheek before gesturing toward the sofa. He began speaking before he settled beside her.

"I wanted to talk about last night. That kiss…" He trailed off and stroked her cheek. Zach sighed and glanced toward Emily then locked Tosha's gaze. She feared the worst. "I've never felt quite such powerful emotions like that, and…"

"You want to go slow?"

"No," he said, taking hold of her hand.

Her gut clenched.

"I don't. I can't even fathom a day when I don't get to see you. It's just, I wondered how hard fast is your request we not sleep together."

Tosha drew her hand back. "You think I should because I already have kids?"

He took back her hand again, stroking it this time. "Not at all. What I felt was more than I ever have experienced, and I want to know where we stand so I can manage my response better. I almost didn't leave last night. Is your request firm?"

This time, Tosha stood, and he followed suit. She couldn't look at him. "I…I wanted you, too, but I can't be with you like that. I've done it before, and I just end up being hurt. I need to wait…to be sure. But if you can't do this, I understand…"

He placed a finger on her lips. "I'm not going anywhere, Tosha," he said, as if capable of reading her thoughts. "I love you. I'm here for the long haul."

"I've been told that before." She felt as if she would cry.

"Then, I'll prove it to you. Just let me know if you change your mind. The way I feel when you're around…I've never felt that for anyone. I hope I'm strong enough."

"It scares me how much I feel for you," she admitted.

"Me too," he said and kissed her.

Her mind grew cloudy, and her arm muscles relaxed in his grasp. He pulled away and studied her face.

"All right, I will do my best." He drew her close.

"Thanks, Zach. I love you, too."

"Daddy Teddy, come play with me," said Emily from the corner of the room.

Zach released Tosha and smiled.

"Go, we'll have more time alone later," Tosha promised.

"I'd like you to play, too," he said to her.

She smiled and shook her head.

"Please, it'll be fun."

Tosha nodded once.

"I'm on my way, baby bear," he said to Emily.

***

"Daddy?"

Zach's eyes fluttered open. *Am I dreaming?*

"Teddy? Get up," said a small voice.

He stared at the cushions. *Tosha's sofa. I'm not dreaming.* He rolled onto his back and stared up into Emily's angelic face.

"What is it, baby bear?"

"Please change pull-up," she said, holding wipes and a new pull-up in her tiny hands.

"Where's Mommy?"

"Sleeping."

He sat up and rubbed his eyes. "How'd you get out of your crib?"

"I climbed out."

"Does Mommy know you can do that?"

"No."

Zach choked off a chuckle. *Time for a toddler bed.* He stared at the pull-up. Tosha almost flipped-out on him the last time he'd offered. How'd she respond now that they've known each other a bit longer?

"Hurry, Daddy. It feels yucky."

Emily's trusting me to make things right. I'm not making her wait for Tosha to pull herself out of bed when she needs her rest. This is what dads do, so I might as well start now.

"All right, come with me." He grabbed a plastic bag from the kitchen and the changing pad from Emily's room then placed them on the carpet in the living room before motioning to the little girl to lie on the pad. Seconds after she lay down, Zach sucked in a breath in preparation for the onslaught. He ripped the sides of Emily's pull-up and almost gagged. "Whew, Emily! It stinks!"

"Yes. That's why I need change."

He grabbed a wet wipe and carefully cleaned her from front to back, the way an elderly woman at a daycare taught him before they stopped the male teachers from changing diapers. He thought he'd bring up what he'd eaten the night before. "What did you eat? This mess needed to go straight into the toilet."

"Are you mad?"

He so wanted to hold his breath, but the conversation with her prevented that. "No, I'm not mad...I'm not angry, but it's time you didn't go into the pull-ups anymore." With one more wipe, he said, "There, I think I got everything."

He didn't mind cleaning Emily, but Tosha's lack of trust placed him in an awkward position. He knew he'd never hurt her little girl or any other child, but his changing the pull-up may not result in a grateful girlfriend. He picked up the clean pull-up.

"Stand up and step into this." With a clean one in hand, he helped the little girl to her feet and pulled it up in place. She hugged his neck soon after being redressed.

"I'm sorry," Emily said.

"It's okay. Just try to go potty next time."

"I try."

She released him and ran off to play while he stuffed the toxic smelly pull-up into the plastic bag and tied it with a knot. He placed the bag in the bathroom's trash can and washed his hands. Although he preferred not to do this again without Tosha's approval, he knew he'd do it again for the little girl who'd stricken his heart. He longed to be a father to her in every way.

***

Tosha woke up and swung her legs over the side of the bed. She stood, stretched toward the ceiling, and opened her bedroom door.

Her daughter sat playing toys in the far corner of the living room.

"Come, Emily. Let me change your pull-up."

Zach spoke from the kitchen. "She's good for now. I changed a poopy one about a half hour ago."

Tosha's gut clenched. She stomped toward him. "You should have woke me. You're not her father."

He frowned. "Now, here lies the problem. How is she ever going to listen to me if you keep bringing up that my body didn't have a part in making hers? My heart doesn't care. Neither does hers. She knows who her biological dad is, and she still chose me. No matter what happens, I want to be a dad to her."

Tosha gasped. She'd always wanted this, and now that she heard the words, said like this, they burned a hole in her gut. Was he already planning for things not to work out with her? "What are you saying?"

"I'm saying I am crazy in love with you and that little girl. I'm not doing all this—coming over often, having you over, cooking you meals, playing toys—because I just want to pass the time. I'm invested. I want this to work with you. I am deep in and covered over with you as my family. In my heart, I'm already yours. But if you don't want me, I'll back off. My heart would break in a million pieces, but I'll do whatever you want me to." His voice cracked at the end, and his eyes glistened.

She never meant to hurt him. "Don't leave me. Please don't leave me. I'm sorry."

He reached out for her and pulled her into his arms. "You drive me crazy."

"I drive myself crazy. Please be patient. This is all new for me."

"For me, too." He eased away and gazed into her eyes. "Stop pushing me away. Trust me, and I'll prove to you I'm worthy. I want to be here with you *and* with her."

She nodded seconds before he pressed his lips to hers.

Chapter 12

Zach parked the car in the third spot from the mall's front door. Tosha unbuckled and placed her hand on the handle.

"Not letting me get your door today, huh?"

"No need."

"Fine, then I'll get Emily."

He stood, opened the rear door, and leaned in.

"Where we going, Daddy?"

"Inside that big building, baby bear. It's a mall. Lots to see." He lifted her out and straightened before shutting the door and setting the alarm. "You stay close to us, all right? Easy to get lost with so many people."

"Okay, Daddy."

Zach held Emily against his side with one arm and grasped Tosha's hand the other. Once inside, they walked past a clothing store for tots.

"Let's go in there," Tosha said. "I'd like to see if they have anything cute for Emily."

Zach released Tosha's hand and glanced around as Tosha browsed the clothing racks.

"Put her down so I can see how this looks."

He complied and waited while Tosha held up the dress with puppy patterns to Emily's chest.

"Do you like this one?" Tosha asked.

"Yes, Mommy. Can I have it?"

"Sure thing. Let me see if there's another style I like."

A movement to the right stole away Zach's attention for just a moment. Some guy in a green-camouflaged baseball cap shuffled past two clothing racks over. Zach couldn't make out his face, but the cap and gait seemed familiar.

The park.

When Zach turned toward Tosha, the little girl was nowhere to be seen.

"Hey, Tosh. Where's Emily?"

"She was right here." Tosha turned around, her eyes wide. "No."

"She can't have gone far. Emily?"

He called for the girl, his chest closing in on itself. *Breathe. She's all right.* He glanced toward the nearest exit. Nothing. Tosha also called for Emily. He stooped and peaked under the clothes. Still nothing. He glanced to the left and then right. Two little feet poked out from under the clothes.

"Found her."

"Where?"

He didn't answer but gestured with his head the newfound hiding place. Kneeling, he sat back on his heels.

"Come on out, baby bear."

Giggles reached his ears. He extended a hand.

"Come on. Mommy and I want to see your face."

Emily grasped two fingers and stepped out.

"Girl! What were you—"

Zach raised his palm toward Tosha, cutting her short. He didn't want Emily to retreat. This had to turn into a teaching moment. How many times had he done the same as a child? He remembered the switch all too well. Perhaps a little explanation might work better.

"So, why were you hiding?"

"I don't know." Emily's lower lip pushed out a bit.

How many times had he done the same to his mom? He almost chuckled at the memory. He recentered his thoughts and continued.

"Well, Mommy and I were very concerned when we couldn't find you. Why didn't you come out when we called your name?"

"I don't know." The girl shrugged.

"Didn't you hear us?"

"Yes, Daddy."

"Then, you should have answered."

"You gon punish me?"

"Not this time. I want you to agree to come to us whenever we call you. Can you do that?"

"Yes, Daddy."

"And only hide in a place like this if someone is trying to hurt you. Smash his foot real hard and run to hide. Understand?"

"Yes, Daddy. Near da giraffe."

"What giraffe?"

The girl pointed to a giraffe painted on the base of a door.

"Yes, that works. I will come looking for you if that ever happens. You stay put until I do, okay?"

Emily nodded.

"So, what are you going to do from now on?"

"Don't hide in da store unless someone is trying to hurt me."

"Good job. Now come here."

She fell into his open arms, and he lifted her up as he stood.

"What should you say to Mommy?"

"I'm sorry, Mommy."

Tosha stared at him, eyebrows raised, then kissed the girl's cheek. "I forgive you, baby. I got scared when I didn't know where you'd gone. Stay close, okay?"

"Okay, Mommy." She faced him once more. "Daddy?"

"What, baby bear?"

"I have to go potty."

"Mommy'll take you." He turned to Tosha. "Got everything you wanted?"

Tosha grabbed the two dresses she'd dropped on top of a rack during the search. "Yes, let's go."

***

Once at home, Emily ran toward her toys. Tosha grabbed a pair of scissors and sat on the sofa to cut the tags off the new clothes. Zach settled next to her, and she glanced at his pensive features.

"What's on your mind?" Tosha asked.

"Wondering about something."

"Like what?"

He pursed his full lips and frowned. "You have a picture of your ex?"

"Huh?" Tosha cut the second tag and placed the scissors on the coffee table. She faced him. "Why would you ask that?"

"I…uh…I saw this guy at the mall. I may have seen him before…at the park…when Emily played in the sandbox. It can't just be coincidence, so I'm wondering if he's her father."

"Oh." Tosha fumbled in her purse for her cell phone. "I kept some he took with Emily. I deleted the rest." She swiped until she found one with a good view of his face. She rotated the phone toward Zach. "Was it him?"

Zach took the phone and enlarged the picture on Chaz's face. Zach shook his head. "No, it's not the guy I saw." He handed her back the phone.

"What did he look like?"

"Light skinned. Slender build. My height. He was in the store where Emily hid from us. At first, I thought he might have grabbed her. I don't ever want to feel like that again."

"Me either." Her phone rang. Her ex. "Sugar Honey Iced Tea! It's Em's father."

"Did you just cuss?" Zach asked.

Her eyes widened. "How?"

He guffawed. "My mother's mom used to say things like that. Didn't take me long to figure out what she was *really* saying."

She frowned. "I have to get this." She scooted to the edge of the sofa to stand.

"You stay." Zach patted a cushion. "I'll go play with Emily."

Tosha swiped to answer. "What you want?"

"Bad day?" Chaz asked.

"Not until you called. What...do...you...want?"

"How's Emily?"

"She's fine."

"Can I talk to her?"

Tosha sighed. "She's playing toys. I don't know if she'll even talk to you. She overheard me the *last* time you called. She knows you didn't want to then."

"Ask her."

"Fine." Tosha stood and walked over to the corner where Emily played pretend with Zach. "Hey, baby, your father wants to talk to you."

Emily looked up at Tosha and then at Zach. She shook her head. When Tosha offered her daughter the phone, the little girl dropped her pony, rushed into Zach, and wrapped her arms around his neck. No doubt Emily meant no.

"She doesn't want to talk to you."

Chaz cussed. "You turned her against me."

Tosha stomped away from Zach and Emily. "I'd *never* do that. She waited and waited for you to reach out to her. To see her. To play toys with her. You never did *any* of those things."

"But your new man does?"

"What? How would you know anything about *any* new man?"

"Don't lie to me, Tosha. I know you wouldn't last long without someone to lie down with."

"I'm done with you. Don't *ever* call back, you hear me? You have the gall to judge what I do with my life when you…you brought some woman to our place so our little girl could see. How could you? Bye, Chaz. I'm done." She ended the call, not waiting for him to respond.

Warm hands grasped her elbows. "Tosh?"

She threw the phone onto the sofa, faced Zach, and snuggled between his arms. Silent, hot tears streamed down her cheeks.

"Mommy okay?"

"She'll be fine, baby bear. Go play. I'll come over in a little bit." He guided Tosha to the sofa where they sat with her leaning into him. He sighed. "I'm sorry you're hurting."

"Yeah. I was so stupid staying with him." She closed her eyes for a moment, squeezing more tears onto her already drenched cheeks. "Can you stay tonight?"

"Oh, sweetie, I wish I could, but…"

She eased away. "Tell me."

"I got a text while you were on the phone. I have to leave at four in the morning for a two-day trip. I'm so sorry. The timing stinks."

She heaved in a breath and pulled out from his embrace. "I'll be all right. You'll call me?"

"Of course." He reached up and wiped her face with his thumb. "I love you," he said and kissed her.

She let the passion from the touch of his mouth wash over her until the pain of her talk with Chaz seemed like a distant memory. "I love you," she whispered.

Zach smiled. "How about I cook dinner after I play with Emily for another ten minutes?"

"Sounds good."

"I'll have to leave right after we eat, but I'll call you when I get home from here."

She nodded and let him embrace her. "You'll be back in time for the appointment?"

"Wouldn't miss it. Kind of the reason I'm leaving tomorrow. I told my boss I wanted to return for that. You're important to me, and I want to be there from now on."

"Thanks."

"We'll spend some time together, just you and me, when I get back." He kissed her forehead.

Loneliness swept over her the second he stood to go entertain her daughter…their daughter for just a few minutes.

Chapter 13

At Tevin's and Karida's, Zach swooped Emily up in an embrace. "Mommy and I are going out for a while tonight, okay?" He'd spent the last two days planning this date down to the tiniest detail.

"Then, we go to your house?"

Zach kissed her little forehead. He so enjoyed playing pretend with the little girl who'd adopted him as her father, but he needed to grow what he started with her mother, too. "Not this time, baby bear. You'll be sleeping here tonight, but we'll come back for you in the morning."

Emily frowned.

"You'll be good for Aunt Karida and Uncle Tevin, right?"

"Yes, Daddy."

His new name continued to thrill him. He looked forward to the day the baby would say the same. For now, the racing beat of Tosha's unborn child's heart warmed his own. At the last visit, two days ago, the doctor mentioned only a two week wait until the day he'd be able to feel the baby kick. He could hardly wait.

Emily kissed his check then reached for her mother to kiss her as well. The instant the little girl's feet touched the floor, she ran off to her room.

Karida stared at him. "And what are you two doing all night?" Her eyes widened as if rethinking her question. She brought up both hands, palms facing him and Tosha. "Wait. No. Don't answer that. It's none of my business. I overstepped."

Zach chuckled and grasped Tosha's hand. "First, we go to dinner. Then, we'll see. I don't know how late we'll be, and I didn't want to drag Emily out into the night air after midnight. You're fine keeping her, right?"

"Yes, yes. Of course. It's just that…never mind."

"What?"

"Well, Tosha spent the night with us last time, and I liked having her over."

"Aahh. Tosha?"

"I can always stay over when he's on one of his many business trips," Tosha said.

"I'm going to hold you to that," Karida said. "Get going, you two, or you'll be late for dinner."

***

As soon as Zach stopped for a red light, Tosha turned her head to face him.

"Are we going to the same restaurant as last time?"

"Nope. We'll go back someday, but I wanted to take you to my second favorite place with Jamaican cuisine."

"Sounds delicious...and hot."

"Yep. Same qualities I like in my woman."

Tosha's cheeks heated, and Zach chuckled in response.

"You're a naughty boy, Zach Caldwell."

"I'll do my best to behave tonight, for your sake."

"You better."

Tosha stared out the side window as the car continued down the street and up a ramp. Where in the world is this place? Once he merged into traffic, she said, "I'm really glad you made it back in time for the prenatal visit."

"I enjoy going with you. I don't want to miss any of them." He paused during a lane change. "Be sure to tell me when I can feel the baby move. I've never had the opportunity before."

"I will."

"You don't mind."

"No. It's one of my favorite things about being pregnant, seeing those feet push my belly whenever the baby feels the urge. I used to turn it into a game. I'd touch a spot and giggle when the baby's foot pushed back. Chaz never wanted to…" She trailed off. "I'm sorry. I shouldn't bring up that man."

Zach glided toward the exit ramp. "It's fine. He participated in some of the memories you treasure most."

"I wouldn't say he 'participated.'" She shook her head. "Why didn't I see the signs?"

"Hey, don't let him steal this night away from us."

"I'm sorry."

"I'm here now, and I'll do right by you."

"Got it."

He pulled into a parking lot and found a spot not too far from the front door. "Here we are. Ready to go in?"

"You bet."

***

Zach paid the check and reached across the table to grasp Tosha's fingers.

"What do you think? Will you come back?"

"Oh, yes. The food here is filling and delicious." She patted her full lips with a napkin.

"Want to go dancing?"

"Dancing?" She placed the napkin next to her plate. "Where's there a club around here?"

"Up the street a few blocks. We'll drive. There's a lot across the street from the place. You up for it?"

She grinned. "Yes. I don't know the last time I went dancing. Don't laugh at me if I'm not up on the latest moves."

"Never." Zach stood and helped Tosha to her feet. "They play a cool mix of music, including Calypso. Tons of fun." He opened the door and let her walk past him.

"Zach?"

When he faced her, she landed a peck on his mouth which brought a sparkling grin to her lips.

"Thanks for tonight. I really needed this."

"But the night's not done yet."

"I know, but I wanted to tell you before I get too tired to remember."

He chuckled. "You're very welcome, sweetie."

Her heart felt light as she settled into the car.

***

Zach and Tosha headed into the crowded dance hall. He cleared a path through the gyrating crowd to prevent anyone from bumping into his pregnant girlfriend. He turned to face her once he found an open spot.

At first, she glanced around, her moves tentative. But after a few beats, she fell in step with him. She grooved to the music with swaying hips that mesmerized him. Waving her arms above her head, she closed her eyes and didn't step away when he closed the space between them. He placed one hand on the small of her back and slid the fingers of his other hand down the length of her raised arm. She opened her eyes and parted her lips…an invitation. His lips met hers, neither of them faltering in keeping up with the beat.

***

Two hours later, Zach wiped the sweat from his forehead with a handkerchief he kept in his back pocket. He motioned toward the exit with a jerk of his head. Tosha held on to his hand as he headed out the main door.

"Did you have fun?"

"Oh, Zach, thank you so much for bringing me here. I forgot how much I enjoyed this. Karida and I used to go before she met Tevin."

"Really? Did you hook up with anyone?"

"Never. We weren't looking for trouble, just a good time. Thanks for this."

"You know we can do this more often. Even after the baby."

"I know. I'd like that."

"Good."

"Where to now?"

"Hmm." He glanced at his watch. "It's after midnight. We could go to the harbor or if you're too tired…just head back to my place."

Tosha leaned her head toward her shoulder, something she did anytime what he said made her nervous.

"I thought you never took girls back to your place."

"You're not just any girl, Tosha. You are the only woman I want sleeping in my bed." He unlocked and opened her door. "I haven't forgotten what you told me when we first kissed. You can trust me."

She nodded and slipped into her seat. "Your place, then."

Neither of them spoke during the ride, but he could no longer resist her pouty mouth once he turned the key in the lock of his apartment. Refusing to break the rhythmically slow kiss, he had to feel around for the doorknob. He guided her inside and pressed her against the wall, still not halting the kiss as he fumbled to close and relock the door in the dark foyer. He slid his hand up the wall and flipped on the light. Only then did he back away. She panted.

"You want anything," he whispered.

"A little water. Not much or I'll have to get up before morning."

He led her to the sofa, strolled to the kitchen to get her what she asked for, then returned to her.

"Is that a shot glass? With water?"

"Sure. Why not?"

"Do you drink often?"

"Nope. But sometimes after an especially tough day, I'll throw down a glass of whiskey." He handed her the glass. "Interesting thing, though, I haven't needed one since that night we first kissed."

She placed the glass to her lips and drank in one gulp.

"Looks like you're familiar with how to use one," he said with a smile.

"I'm just thirsty," she said.

"Mmmhmm," he said and welcomed the glass in his open palm. "Where would you like to sleep, couch or bed?"

"Couch is fine."

"You want to change first?"

"No, let's just lie down."

He set the glass on the table and lay on his side with his head propped up on a pillow. She joined him, her back pressed against his front. Her hair smelled like berries. He kissed her neck. She groaned. Heat coursed through his groin.

"I have to get up," he said.

"Why? What's wrong?"

"A bit too cozy. Not that I don't like it, but if I'm going to keep my promise, we've got to sleep in the bed."

She turned to stare at him with wide eyes.

"I promise to be good."

He scooted off the sofa and helped her up.

"Shouldn't we shower first?"

"Why? Did you shower before we went out?"

"Yes, but we're all sweaty."

"And? We were just about to sleep in our clothes on the sofa."

"But in your bed?"

"I'll wash the sheets tomorrow." He entered his bedroom and opened a drawer. "I have a huge T-shirt you can borrow and elastic pajama pants that might fit you. You'll have to roll up the legs, though."

"Thanks."

"I'll be back in a few minutes." He grabbed a shirt and pants for himself and left the room to change. He knocked on the door when he returned.

"I'm all set," she said.

He opened the door to find her already under the covers with a silk cloth wrapped around her head. *Funny how a Black woman never forgets about her hair.* He walked to the other side of the bed and slipped under the covers as well. Scooting close to her, he pressed his lips to hers and revived the deep and slow kiss which began by the front door.

She eased away, and he leaned his forehead to hers.

"I thought you were going to be good," she said through breathy gasps.

"This *is* me being good. I love you so much." He pecked her lips and fell back onto his pillow.

"I love you, too." She laid her head on his chest and her hand on his other shoulder. "You okay with me like this?"

"Yeah."

He exhaled a long breath through his mouth and wrapped both arms around her body, her belly molding into his side. Soon, he drifted off to sleep, soothed by her warmth and soft snores.

***

Zach opened his eyes, a smile forming on his mouth at the sight of Tosha's backside facing him. He kissed her neck and shoulder.

"You up?"

"Mmmhmmm."

She rolled to face him, and he kissed her lips. She covered her mouth.

"Mm mm," she grunted, her tone a reprimand.

"I don't care that you haven't brushed your teeth." He pushed her hand away and kissed her again. The same slow and deep kiss from the previous night returned. He pulled away. "I want to wake up with you like this every morning." He kissed her again and moaned. "I have to get up or I won't keep my promise. I'll go make breakfast, but you stay in bed as long as you like."

"What about Emily?"

"She'll be fine for a while longer. Rest up. We had quite the night."

"You going to use this bathroom?"

"No way. I can't stay in here a moment longer with you and your alluring power. Resistance is becoming futile. Come on out when you're ready. I'm not going anywhere."

***

Zach wasn't joking when he said they had quite the night. Tosha's legs ached from not having danced that much in years. Even so, her heart pumped with vibrancy. He energized her. He underestimated the way he affected her whenever he kissed her the way he did last night…this morning. It scared her how much she wanted him.

A few minutes later, she rose, washed up, and dressed in the same outfit she had the night before. She opened the bedroom door and stepped into the hallway. Reaching the dining area, her jaw dropped as she saw a vase with four roses, an egg and sausage casserole, and a small black, velvety looking box.

"You made a casserole?"

"Yeah. I wanted this morning to be special."

"Is that why you got the roses?"

"Yep."

"Why four?"

"Two for us, one for Emily, and the last for our baby."

"And what's that?" Tosha nodded toward the box.

He snatched up the box and stepped toward her. "Well, remember what I said in bed about wanting to wake up with you every morning?"

She nodded and covered her mouth with both hands. Tears weighed down her lower eyelids.

"I really mean that… I want to be yours and you to be mine for the rest of our lives. I want Emily to be my daughter, your baby to be mine, and for us to be husband and wife." He knelt before her and opened the box to reveal a diamond surrounded by petite sapphires. "Tosha, will you marry me?"

Her left hand reached out to him before the words left her mouth. "Yes, Zach, I will marry you."

Chapter 14

Tosha had chicken fat smeared all over her hands but didn't dare remove her engagement ring for fear she'd drop it down the sink. A smile formed on her lips as she stared at stones. How had two weeks gone by so fast since he'd proposed to her? The connection they shared never failed to intensify ever since their first date nine weeks ago. This relationship, him, the way he doted on her little girl had to be a dream she'd crave to return to the moment she woke up.

A cute giggle drew Tosha's attention away from her ring. She glanced into the play area where Zach entertained Emily. He always arrived early to keep the girl busy while Tosha prepared dinner. Not one hour went by that day without her daughter asking when Daddy was coming. The toothy grin on his face proved he treasured these moments as well.

Tosha shook her head and returned her attention to the chicken.

"Whew, Emily! I think you just lit up the place."

Tosha glanced over to find Zach covering his nose.

"I sorry," said Emily with her hands hidden behind her back.

"Did you forget to go potty?" Zach asked.

"Yes, I was having fun," Emily added, peering up at him through her eyelashes.

"Sooo, next time we take a break from fun, okay? I promise not to play without you." He patted Emily on her shoulder. "C'mon, let's go get you cleaned up."

"I can take care of her, Zach," Tosha interjected. "Sometimes getting her spotless takes a while." She appreciated him trying to help, but she still felt nervous about her boyfriend changing her little girl's underwear.

"We'll be fine. I'm sure I'll survive the mess." He chuckled. "Besides, you're still cooking," he said, pointing at her greasy hands. Without delay, Zach ushered Emily into her bedroom.

Tosha sighed and returned to chopping the whole chicken for the stew she planned to make. She remained unsure why his willingness to accept child caring responsibilities still made her nervous. Tosha recalled the phone call to Karida after the first time Zach changed Emily's dirty pull-up.

"It just makes me nervous, Kar. She's not his daughter."

"Tosh, I know why you're concerned, but he'd never hurt her. Tevin and I thought about that before encouraging you to go out with him. He has a spotless track record when it comes to children and teens. He's never done anything suspicious even when he'd been in unexpected situations when he could have tried something. Believe me. He'll care for Emily like his own daughter," explained Karida.

"I know. You keep telling me he's the real deal. I just keep seeing all the stories about boyfriends and stepfathers with the kids in their lives. I just don't want to blindly go into a relationship that proves harmful for Emily."

"Tosha, he won't harm her, but your reaction will cause him to behave awkwardly around Emily. You need to talk to him about this before things blow up."

"I can't do that."

"You need to. He's already feeling self-conscious whenever you watch him play with Emily."

"He told you that?" asked Tosha, shocked and slightly upset.

"Like I said, you need to talk to him…and soon. You can't move forward until you rid yourself of these fears."

Tosha had still not brought up the topic to Zach, and the fact that Emily trusted him still bothered her. He never even closed the door to Emily's room.

I need to talk to him tonight. It has to be tonight.

Moments later, Emily dashed out of the bedroom giggling with Zach holding a bag not far behind her.

"I'm taking this out. It's really…something," he said.

"Thanks. I really appreciate you for dealing with that."

He didn't take too long throwing out her daughter's soiled pull-up. When he returned, Zach went straight to the bathroom. The sound of running water reached Tosha's ears. Moments later, he arrived in the kitchen where Tosha was stirring in the last of the spices before letting the meat simmer.

"Hey, Tosha, are you all right? You seem a bit…stiff," said Zach barely above a whisper.

She had hoped to bring up the subject, but…

"I'm sorry…I'm just nervous…"

"About me cleaning Emily?"

"Yes. I guess because she's not yours."

"You've got to believe I won't hurt her. I love that little girl, and I would never do anything to steal the joy she's rediscovering."

"I'm being silly."

"No," he dipped his head, causing her to meet his gaze, "you're right to feel the way you do. I've only known you for two months. However, I would hope that with all the time we've spent together eating and talking, you'd know me pretty well by now."

"I think I do. I have a question though. Why do you like kids? I mean, you're single, yet so comfortable with Emily."

"I worked in a local Kindergarten class as an aide before I graduated with my business degree. I was popular with the kids. Big Teddy Bear they called me because I'm so tall and gave everyone a bear hug when they entered the room and before they left for the day. My heart broke when I left to work at my current job."

"That makes sense. I wish I didn't have such a tough time with this."

"I love you, Tosha. I've told you over and over how much you mean to me. I won't betray your trust in me. You have my heart."

"Thanks, Zach. Thanks for not losing it over my fears. I love you, too."

Zach smiled and kissed her on the forehead.

"From now on, can you tell me what's on your mind, so I don't have to find out from our friends?" Zach asked.

"I'll try. It's so hard. They've always been there for me."

"I'm just as guilty and for the same reason. I've noticed for a while. I should have brought it up sooner."

"Growing pains."

"Yeah, but we're good now, right?"

"Yes, we're good."

"And it's okay if I change her clothes when you're too busy?"

"Yes, you can change her clothes. I trust you."

"Thanks," Zach said. He kissed Tosha on the cheek before returning to Emily to continue their game.

Once Tosha had finished dinner, Zach and Emily joined her at the dining table.

"Oh, I almost forgot." Zach rushed to the kitchen and returned with a bottle. "I stopped by the store today and picked up my favorite wine to go with dinner."

"With alcohol?"

A flash of regret flitted across his handsome features. "Oh, Tosha, I'm so sorry. I wasn't thinking. How stupid!"

"It's okay. I'll be able to drink again sometime after the baby is born."

"I'll put the bottle away. It can wait."

"No, don't do that. I can have one sip. I would love to have a taste," she said, hoping to soften an awkward moment.

"Are you sure? I'm okay with having something else."

"No, I want you to. I'll take a sip from your glass if you don't mind."

He grinned. "I don't. Thanks."

Zach poured wine for himself and sparkling cider Tosha kept in the refrigerator. She reached out for his glass and sipped the smooth, sweet red wine.

"Mmm. Very delicious. You definitely have to buy this one again." Tosha carefully returned Zach's stem glass to its place.

***

Tosha stood and began stacking the plates.

"Naw, I got this. You cooked dinner," Zach said, grabbing the pile and taking them to the kitchen.

"Okaaay." Tosha said the word half-way between a statement and a question. "Looks like Mommy will be getting baby bear ready for bed tonight. Let's go choose a bedtime story."

"No, Mommy. I want Daddy to read me the story. Pleeeease?"

Tosha peered into her daughter's now glistening eyes. When had this happened? Emily's preference for Teddy to read instead of her own mother. Tosha's chest seemed to squeeze in on itself just a bit for a moment.

She tapped his shoulder. "Zach. Change of plans. Emily wants you to read tonight."

"Really?" Soap covered his arms up to his elbows.

"Yeah, her pajamas are on the dresser. I'll finish up." She might as well start acting like she trusted him. Perhaps practice would make perfect.

Zach grabbed the towel, wiped his hands, and strolled past Tosha—pausing long enough to kiss her cheek—on his way to swooping up Emily into his arms.

"Yay," Emily said, clapping her hands.

His words, "So, what do you want me to read?" reached Tosha ears before her fiancé and daughter disappeared in the bathroom down the hall.

Tosha washed the rest of the plates, the glasses, Emily's cup, and the utensils while Zach helped her little girl brush her teeth, get changed, and settle in bed for the story of her choice. Tosha scrubbed at a pan in circles. Soap frothed up the sides before she rinsed it clean. A lullaby sung from a tenor voice as smooth as butter traveled from her daughter's room and washed over Tosha in warm waves. She stared at the running water until the silence jolted her out of her trance. She'd just finished placing the dish cloth near the sink when Zach's arms wrapped around her waist—well, what was left of it anyway. Her heart fluttered.

"Almost done?"

"Just about." She squeezed out the sponge. "Did she go down okay?"

"She zonked out before I finished singing."

Tosha rinsed the sink then turned off the faucet. "She likes when you come over."

Zach turned Tosha so she faced him. "I really want to spend some time with my big girl," he said, the smell of sweet wine on his breath.

"I know. I've been busy all afternoon."

"And dinner was great. It was worth all the effort you put into it."

Tosha snuggled into his arms.

"Come," he said and guided her toward the sofa.

He eased down first and tugged on her hand, encouraging her to join him. He gazed into her eyes and caressed her cheek. She leaned into his touch. The instant his fingers slid up toward her hair, the baby kicked her bellybutton.

"Ooh," she moaned.

"What?"

She smiled. "The baby just moved."

"May I?" His hand hovered over her now football-shaped belly.

"Sure," she said and placed his hand on the spot. She fought to keep her breathing even. Her baby jabbed her and Zach's palm with excited kicks.

A few seconds later, he said, "Wow. That's cool." Zach's gorgeous smile made her forget to breathe. "So strong."

"Yeah," she said, remembering how to speak. "If only he wouldn't hit my sensitive spots."

"He? Did you find out it's a boy?"

"No." She shook her head. "I just have a feeling. I didn't do any of those old wives' tests either. I used to refer to Emily as she. Maybe I'll get it right again."

Still caressing her abdomen, his gaze pierced her shield, knocked it down, and the world stopped. He didn't say anything. He didn't have to. Bringing her hand up to his lips, he kissed it. Waves of pleasure flowed up her arm and into her chest. Her hand floated in midair when he let it go. His fingertips blazed a deliberate trail across her cheek, past her ears, and down her neck. He leaned toward her and dipped his head. Heat flamed out from the spot where his lips grazed her neck.

This time, a quiet "Mmmm" escaped her. Unable to stop the sensations stirring a place of deep longing she'd kept under guard at her core, Tosha pressed close to him.

He eased away—cutting off the source of her euphoria—and locked her gaze. His eyes seemed to scan hers for some message seconds before his lips seized hers with intensifying fervor. Heat coursed down her back and radiated around her unborn child. His mouth massaged hers in a cyclic rhythm which matched the circles he traced on her neck with a fingertip. The hormones must be responsible for her inability to halt his advances.

No. She wanted this, him. Each move, the way he stroked her arms, the taste of sweet grapes on his mouth, urged her deeper into this nirvana. She liked it, never wanted the end of her skin warming under his fingertips and the…the fire ready to…to…

Her wayward hand that still lingered in midair found purchase, pressed against his chest, and slid up and over his shoulder. Her other hand clasped the first around his neck.

Zach paused long enough to stand and scoop her off the sofa up into his arms. With eyes closed, she allowed the clouds to lift her up and carry her wherever they floated. His lips never ceased to touch hers as he walked toward her bedroom. She opened her eyes seconds before he placed her onto the bed. She gaped at him like a starstruck girl when he stepped toward the door to close and lock it with a quick turn of the latch.

Returning to her on the bed, his eyes glazed over with dreaminess. His lips parted, but he didn't say a word. Only his shallow breathing reached her ears, lasting forever. With a gentle grasp of her shoulders, he guided her body back onto the pillows near the bed's headboard.

Ignoring silent alarms, her fingers found the bottom button on his shirt. It didn't matter much why she hadn't started at the top. Her unborn child—too smart for his own good—poked a limb against her belly whenever she undid another button, as if that child knew something was happening.

Like a muscle toned statue, he never moved until each button had embraced its newfound freedom. By the time she'd pushed Zach's shirt off his damp, broad shoulders, his muscles rippling when he shrugged it away, he'd tugged off her skirt. Tosha stared at his chest hair. She'd never thought much about it in the past, but now she realized she found a slightly hairy chest incredibly attractive, something she never encountered on bare-chested Chaz all the years she'd known him.

Why was she even thinking about that man?

Zach glided his palms down her back, crumpled the edge of her blouse, and pulled it over her head. She didn't resist as she threw her arms above her head to make it easier for him, exposing her royal-purple bra. He opened his hand to let the blouse fall onto the plush forest green carpet.

She failed at trapping a silent gasp when he unzipped and dropped his pants. The bulge in his navy plaid boxer-briefs proved he was more than ready for her. Knee first, he settled next to her on the covers, propped up on an elbow. Warm kisses lulled her into a euphoric haze. A moan escaped her lips when he nuzzled her neck again.

How is he doing this to me? I only had one sip.

Tosha's reason only returned the moment Zach's fingertips slid across her five-month-old baby bump toward the bra's clasp while he deepened the kiss, reminding her of too many broken promises by the man who fathered her baby. *Good Lawd, I can't do this again.* She turned her head with a jerk.

"Wait," she said, her breathing heavy. "Stop."

Zach furrowed his brows, but instead reclosed the distance she'd placed between them and kissed her neck with a bit more desperation.

Tosha shivered. Merciful heavens, she didn't want it to stop. She pressed her hand against his firm chest. "I'm so sorry, but we can't do this."

"What? Why?" he said, clearly puzzled by her behavior.

"I want you. I do, and we've come so far, but we can't."

He eased back. "Explain, Tosha. You're not making sense."

"Emily."

"The door's locked."

"I'm not ready."

"What just happened here? My shirt? You undressed me first."

She'd ruined the mood. "I'm scared."

He sat back on his heels. "Is it me?"

"No. It's just that I've done this before."

"I'm not him."

"I know. I'm so sorry. Besides…"

"What?"

"I need to be a good example for Emily."

"Emily?"

"Yes."

"She won't know."

"But I'll know."

He rubbed hard at his cheek, pushed off the bed, and stood facing her. "Stop it. Quit using your daughter as an excuse."

"I'm not. What am I teaching her if we do this?"

He sighed and shrugged. "That two people who really love each other can express that love in a most amazing way."

"I can't do this again…not like this. I'm so sorry, Zach. I know I just got you revved up." She paused, gauging him. "Are you upset?"

His angry gaze pierced her heart. "Just look at me." He gestured to his pelvis.

He didn't need to tell her that. She had a tough time stopping her eyes from gawking. She hated doing this to him.

"Please understand," she said.

"How, Tosha? How can I understand when one second we're steaming up the place and the next we're frozen over? Did I have so much wine that I misread you?"

"What? That I accepted your ring, so now you can have sex with me? Is doing it your main objective?"

He gaped seconds before a halted laugh escaped him. "No," he said in a gruff tone. "I was willing to wait. But this, tonight, you seem… Argh. I thought we were past that."

She glanced at the floor in search of her clothes. He stomped around the bed, grabbed up the clothing, and tossed her skirt and blouse onto her lap. She clutched both garments against her chest, trying to cover up her blimp of a body with only panties and a bra to cover the most intimate parts.

Tosha glanced across the room and sighted her robe. She hurried off the bed while Zach pulled and zipped up his pants. He'd just shoved his arms into his shirt, not bothering to button it, by the time she wrapped herself up in the robe. His still exposed chest called for her touch.

"Zach?"

"Tell me something, Tosha. Do you still love him?"

She shook her head. "No, not at all."

"Things went from hot to cold in an instant, and I doubt Emily's the reason for that. What happened that stopped you?"

"I don't know."

"Don't give me that crap, Tosha." He grimaced as if sorry the words came out so rash. "What popped up in your head when the baby jabbed against my hand?"

"That I...I've been here before. Believing promises that never came through."

He frowned and worked at his buttons. "I'm not that guy." He shook his head. "I won't break your heart." He finished with the buttons and looked up at her. "I'm crazy about you."

"I'm crazy about you too, but I can't do this right now. I'm sorry."

"I gotta get out of here." He unlocked the door.

"Don't drive. You had a few glasses of wine. Stay and sleep it off."

He huffed and glared at her. "Like I'm going to be able to sleep after what almost happened between us. This stinks, Tosha."

"I'm really sorry," she said but lacked the words to say anything more.

"I want you so much. I just don't know if I can stay here."

"You've always been good to me…and patient. I trust you. Please stay. I don't want to worry about you getting home."

Zach rubbed his forehead. "Fine. I'll stay." He opened the door and stepped out.

"I'll get the sheets."

"No, I know where they are. I'll get them myself." He shut the door behind him, triggering the tears that streamed down her cheeks.

***

"Daddy, Daddy," yelled Emily as she ran toward the sofa to a sleeping Zach.

"Hey, baby bear," answered Zach with open arms.

"You stayed. You stayed," she said.

"Yeah. I did, didn't I?"

"I went potty and washed hands all by myself."

"That's great. I'm so proud of you." He sat up and turned to find Tosha staring at them from her bedroom's open doorway. "Hey, baby bear. Would you go play for a bit? I need to talk to Mommy."

Emily nodded, pecked him on the cheek, and ran off toward her toys.

He stood and walked over to Tosha. "So what happens now?"

She shrugged. "Maybe we should slow things down, get some space."

"What are you talking about? We take things slow now," he said with an edge to his tone.

"I meant we probably shouldn't have dinner together every night."

"And how do I explain this to Emily? Dinner each night brought her some needed stability. I can be that for her. I want to be that for her...and you. Besides, she finally started going potty regularly."

"I know, but you don't have to do that. I'll explain it to her. Please don't come over tonight."

"Tosh."

"Zach, if you care about us as much as you say, you'll grant me this."

225

"Because of what happened last night?"

"I need time…to think. It's better if you leave."

"So this is how it ends. Fine. Where we go from here is your call." His throat tightened, but he ignored it and spit out, "Tell her I left." He turned on his heel and marched to the door.

"Zach, I'm sorry. I didn't mean—"

The door he slammed behind him cut her off.

Once outside, he glanced at his cell. *7 a.m.* He called Tevin the instant he sat in the car.

"Hey, man," Tevin said upon answering the phone. "Pretty early for a Saturday. What's up?"

"I don't know. I think… Things are messed up with Tosha right now."

"Wait. Are you still at her place?"

"No. She asked, no, *told* me to leave. I need to talk. Can you meet me at our regular coffee shop now? Please."

"Sure, man. Should I be worried?"

Zach's laugh came out manic. "I don't know. I feel like someone just ripped my heart out."

"I'll be there."

Zach ended the call and turned the key. The engine hummed to life. Leaning his head on the steering wheel, he shut his eyes and let the tears fall. How did he get here? Did he move too fast? How many times had she told him how much her ex hurt her?

"You doan know wha' she bin thru."

He lifted his head and gritted his teeth. How many times did he remind her he'd never hurt her like that? He wiped at the tears, cleared his throat, and checked the rearview mirror. He backed out slowly and turned left toward his and Tevin's favorite coffee shop.

By the time he entered the front door, Tevin had already been seated with two large coffees on the table.

"Hey, dude. Mind if we grab a table outside?" Zach asked.

"No problem." Tevin handed him one of the cups.

Zach returned outside and set the cup down. He couldn't sit.

Tevin frowned at him but didn't sit either. "Start at the beginning."

"Everything started out great, you know. We ate dinner. I put Emily to bed while Tosha did the dishes. She let me feel the baby kick. That was so cool. Then...it's like someone turned up the heat. Next thing I know, we're in her room, on her bed, clothes everywhere. Then, almost as quickly, the mood froze. She backed away. Asked me to stop."

227

"You were…naked?"

"Almost." Zach shook his head. "I wanted her…so much. I thought she wanted me too. How could I have misread that?"

"I don't think you did."

"Then what the heck happened last night? It grated me when she made her stopping things all about Emily. I yelled at her. It went downhill after that. I slept off the wine and tried talking to her this morning. She wasn't having it." Zach rubbed his cheeks with both hands and dragged them down until his fingers formed a steeple on his chin. He yanked the chair out from under the table, sat, and sipped the coffee. "I can't lose her, Tevin. I want to be with her, but I'm willing to wait, if that's what she wants. I just don't want it to be forever, you know?"

"She's had a tough go of it, man. I don't want to speak too much for her, but I know she's crazy about you. It's really hard for her to trust someone, especially after everything she's been through."

"But I've told her tons of times that I won't hurt her like that."

"I'm sure she heard you and her heart responds, but her mind hesitates. She just needs time."

"How much time?"

"She's the only one who knows that."

"I don't know. I'm committed to her and the chemistry between us is fantastic, but I don't know if I can do this. It's tearing me apart."

"Hang in there. I believe that the love you two have for each other will get you through this."

"I hope you're right. I really do."

***

Tosha sobbed the instant Zach left the apartment without even a goodbye kiss. Emily rushed over to her.

"Mommy, why you crying? Where's Teddy?"

"Not now, baby. Please go play."

"Is Daddy coming back?"

The pain of what just happened grated at her. "I said not now, Emily. Now go."

Her daughter's mouth quivered, making Tosha regret she'd been so cross. Entering her own room, Tosha closed the door and let the tears flow. A few minutes later, she wiped at her face and grabbed her cell.

No "hello" for a greeting from Karida. Just, "Tosha, what happened? I was just about to call you."

"What?'

"Tevin's talking to Zach right now. Speak to me."

"I sent him away, Karida. I messed up. He's the best thing that's ever happened to me, and, like an idiot, I pushed him away. I can't...I can't," she sobbed, "breathe." She coughed to clear the phlegm from her throat. "I don't know what to do."

"Okay. Back up a bit. What led to this? Why did you send him away?"

Tosha sucked in a deep breath to steady her emotions, frazzled as they were. "We were kissing on my bed. Things got heated really fast. It wasn't until we were stripped down to our underwear that I stopped him."

"Tosha, no."

"I know. I shouldn't have let it get so far. I wanted him so much."

"Then, why did you stop?"

"He touched my belly, caressed it actually, and I freaked. I didn't want to make the same mistake again. Then, I said I stopped because of Emily. That's when he got angry. He must hate me."

"So, you sent him away last night?"

"No. This morning. He had wine last night, and I didn't want him to drive angry. If he'd have died, I would never have forgiven myself. He tried to talk to me today, but I told him to leave."

"Girl, I'm so sorry."

"And the worst part is, I have to tell Emily why he left. That I pushed him away. She loves him so much. He's her dad, like her own father never existed. I can't..."

"Just tell her you had a disagreement and that adults have that sometimes. He'll be back."

"I don't know that. He really wanted to, you know. I still have his ring. Should I give it back?"

"Did he ask for it back?"

"No."

"Don't do anything rash. He loves you, Tosha. You're not some fling to him. Don't give up on him, okay?"

"You didn't see his face. Maybe I made a mistake opening up my heart to someone else so soon."

"No, Tosha."

A soft knock at the door reached Tosha's ears. "Mommy? I want you."

"I have to go. Emily's calling me. I'll talk to you soon."

Tosha ended the call and stared at the door, dreading responding to the girl yelling "Mommy" from the living room.

Upon opening the door, Tosha's heart broke into a thousand little pieces at the sight of her little girl's tear-drenched cheeks. *I caused this.* She knelt on the floor and pulled Emily close.

"Mommy? When's he coming back?"

"I don't know."

"Doesn't he love us anymore?"

"Of course he loves us, baby."

"Then why he leave?"

"Because...because I told him to."

Emily trembled. "But why? I love him."

"I need time to figure things out for both of us."

"Don't leave him too. I don't want him to disappear."

"Oh, baby" was all Tosha could say as Emily sobbed against her chest. She held her daughter for a long time.

Chapter 15

Tosha scrambled some eggs for breakfast. If this had been a workday, she'd have called out sick. Her whole body hurt. She stared at her phone each time she walked past, willing it to produce some message from Zach. But why would he call when she'd been the one to throw him out? No, she had to make the first move, but her pride just wouldn't let her.

Emily moved her eggs from one side of the bowl to the other.

"Try to eat something, baby."

"I don't want it."

"You not hungry?"

"No. Can I go lie down? I don't feel so good."

Tosha chewed on her lower lip but then stopped herself before she drew blood. "All right. Go lie down. I'll warm it up for you later."

Without a word, Emily trudged to her bedroom and crawled into her toddler bed.

Tosha stared at her own plate without much of an appetite either. She sighed and pushed back her chair. Taking both dishes to the kitchen, she wrapped them in foil paper and stuck them in the fridge. Against her better judgment, she picked up her cell and dialed Zach's number. Six rings later, his voicemail greeting spoke to her. The sound of his voice reached a place of deep longing. She ended the call, not bothering to leave a message.

***

Following the pain and anger of Saturday, Sunday passed like a blur with all its numbness. Zach had slept most of the day, almost not eating anything at all but managed to swallow down two slices of toast and a glass of milk.

As the alarm buzzed for the start of the work week, his energy failed him. He mustered up enough willpower to rise out of bed and place both feet on the rectangular area rug. He yawned and stretched out any lingering aches and pain, but the numbness remained.

He picked up his cell to shut off the noise and spotted six notifications, all stating Tosha had called. No messages, though. He returned the phone to the side table. He was in no way ready to talk to her yet.

In the bathroom, he stared at the guy in the mirror but hardly recognized him. His entire body drooped with weariness, worse than with previous breakups, and Tosha hadn't even officially broken things off. He sighed in an attempt to combat the stabbing in his gut.

Having showered and dressed, he left for work, grabbing a small breakfast bar as he walked past the kitchen. He arrived in the parking lot at work, not remembering how he got there. He exited the car, trudged through the main entrance of his office building, and rode the elevator to the tenth floor. Good mornings glossed over him on the way to his desk. A few minutes later, his boss, Carl Anders, stopped by.

"Wow, Zach. Rough weekend?"

"A bit. What do you need?" No way he wanted to get into why he looked and felt like crap.

"You up for an impromptu meeting in Seattle?"

At least it's not Honey's city, or Tosha would freak out. "When?"

"Tomorrow, so you'd leave tonight. But only if you're up for it."

"Yeah, I'm good. Fine if I leave around four to pack."

"Leave at three. The flight's at seven."

"Got it. For how long?"

"Two days."

Zach tapped his phone to open his schedule. *No OB appointments with Tosha.* His heart ached a bit. He didn't even know if she'd let him accompany her now.

"Still good to go?" Carl asked.

"Yes. Schedule's clear."

Halfway through the morning, his phone buzzed with a text from Tosha.

<Emily misses you and says hello.>

Did Tosha miss him, too? Even if she did, she may not say. He ignored his resistance to responding. He refused to ignore Emily.

<I miss her, too.>

The dreaded return text buzzed his cell. *<Can you talk?>*

His gut clenched. *<No.>* He just wasn't ready to deal with her at that moment. He'd fall apart at work.

<Okay.>

A memory of him kissing her flashed through his mind. He missed the taste of her lips. *Ugh. Why does it hurt so much?*

***

Zach dropped his briefcase on the floor and fell back onto the plush covers. He stared up at the unfamiliar ceiling with its stucco for decoration. It had been a long day at a non-stop meeting with a potential high-paying customer. His stomach grumbled. At least the admin ordered lunch, or he'd be doubling over. He glanced at his cell. Eight fifteen. *Room service it is, then.*

His phone buzzed. *Tosha.* He sighed.

<Emily's asking for you. Do you have time to stop by for a few minutes?> On East Coast time, Tosha would think he'd be getting off work just about now.

<Can't. Away.>

<To see Honey?>

A humor-filled huff escaped him. *<No. I'm in Seattle. Her office is in Chicago.>*

<Oh. Okay. Was this planned?>

<Last minute request.>

<Should I be worried?>

He sighed again. *<I'm not a slut, Tosha. I'm not the kind of guy who sleeps around after an argument. I'm still your guy unless…>*

<Things haven't changed between us.>

<Good, because I want…I hope we can get through this…if you want to.>

<I want to. I love you.>

<I love you. I'm beat. Been a long day.> He hated being so curt, but he didn't want to make up with her by texting over a phone. He wanted…needed to see her, look into her eyes, hear her explain why she kept pushing him away even though the attraction couldn't be any clearer.

<Ok. Let me know when you're back.>

<Sure thing.> He'd do so the instant the plane arrived at the gate Thursday morning before he headed in for work.

***

Thursday morning, Zach strolled onto the tenth floor of his office building with a lot more energy than on Monday even though he'd just finished flying for four hours. Sleeping during a red eye flight may not have seemed like much, but he'd slipped into the deepest sleep he'd had since before his heated connection, er, disagreement—whatever anyone looking at this objectively might call it—with Tosha. It sure didn't hurt being in first class.

He knocked on Carl's door and waited for his boss to wave him in. With a huge grin, Zach shook Carl's hand.

"The trip to Seattle was a success. We landed both contracts."

"Great to hear." Carl gestured for Zach to sit. "I knew you were the best one for the task. You've made us extremely profitable, and I haven't overlooked that. You'll see a sizable bonus in your next paycheck."

"Thanks, Carl."

"I'm in the midst of setting something up with Chicago next week. Will that work for you?"

"Actually, it won't. I have a doctor's appointment." He wasn't ready to divulge becoming a father when he didn't know where things stood.

"You all right?"

"Yes, I'm well. Regular checkup." *For my pregnant fiancée.*

"Good. Good. Just know you can always talk to me in confidence. You're my star employee."

"Wow. I didn't realize."

"You'll see just how much in the coming weeks." Carl paused and shuffled some papers. "All right, I'll push to a later date. I'm sure they'd have no problem working with the change."

"Thanks so much." Now the question remained whether Tosha'd let him join her on the appointment.

***

Tosha's heart leapt when three knocks echoed through the apartment. She rushed to the door, but her shoulders slumped a bit because Karida stood there instead of Zach.

"Girl, you okay?" Karida asked.

"Yes, we're fine. What are you doing here?"

"Checking up on the two of you."

Tosha stepped back to allow her friend to enter.

"Has he?"

Tosha shook her head, understanding the meaning behind her friend's cryptic question. "I texted him a few times, and he responded. It's not the same, though. He hasn't called or stopped by, and I don't know if he ever will again. He might be done with us. I should have never sent him away. What if things don't work out?"

Karida's eyes widened when she looked past Tosha who turned to find Emily standing close, lips quivering.

"Baby…?" Tosha began, but the rest of the words stuck in her throat when her stomach clenched.

Karida stepped to the girl and embraced her, but a few seconds later, Emily pushed away and ran back to her room. Karida faced Tosha with a frown. "I'm concerned, Tosha. I've never seen her like this."

"I know. What am I going to do?"

"Call him and ask him to stop by."

"What if he doesn't?"

"He'll come. That man called you for two weeks when you first met and stayed even after you told him about your babies. *You* told him to leave. He'll return when *you* ask him to come back. No hints. And don't use her as a pawn." Karida paused a moment and placed a gentle hand on Tosha's shoulder. "Do you want him?"

"Yes, of course."

"Then, tell him how much you want him. He knows how much Emily loves him. She never pushed him away."

Tosha stood there, speechless.

"I have to go. Tevin's taking me out tonight."

Tosha nodded and hugged her friend goodbye.

"Call him, Tosha. No more just texting. He's a grown man, not a teen."

"I called him like six times on Sunday, and he didn't call me back, not once."

"Did you leave messages?"

Tosha shook her head.

"Next time you call, and he doesn't answer, leave a message, telling him exactly what you want from him. He'll respond." Karida stepped into the hallway and waved goodbye.

Tosha stood in the foyer, her heart aching in additional places.

Chapter 16

Not feeling the urge to cook dinner, Zach sat on the recliner alone in his apartment, chewing milk-sodden cereal, still fuming over his argument with Tosha the last morning he saw her.

How illogical! How unreasonable!

He couldn't understand how not having dinner together every night helped the situation. They needed to talk this out, work through it...together. Why couldn't Tosha accept that he wanted her in his life...permanently?

Why can't she see that we want the same thing...a lasting, faithful relationship in which the children can thrive? I love her with my whole heart.

Zach finished his bowl of cereal and clicked off the television. He called Olivia to ask for some advice but got her voicemail instead.

"Hey, sis. I need you to pray for me and Tosha. We kinda had our first real fallout, and I'm scared I'll lose her. Please pray for God to help us work this out. I love you."

He collapsed into bed and lay there thinking about how far he'd come with this relationship compared to the others. He fought with Tosha sometimes, but he hoped at least it meant they wanted better out of their mutual connection. He couldn't see going on in life without her, something he'd never felt about anyone else.

A vibrating cell phone startled Zach awake. He rolled over and slapped at the bedside table until his fingers located the cause of the rumbling noise. He glanced at the screen.

Tosha? At 2 a.m.?

He clicked the answer button. "What's wrong?" His hoarse voice grated his ears.

"Zach, can you come over? Emily had a bad dream and screamed us both awake. She won't go back to sleep. She keeps asking for you...Teddy her daddy. She really missed you at dinner. I missed you, too," said Tosha, her voice shaking as she raced through her words.

Tiny sobs reached his ears over the phone, and he guessed Tosha was rocking Emily while she spoke to him. "Will she talk to me on the phone?"

Tosha asked the girl. "She's shaking her head. I can't do this. I need you. Please, will you come?"

"Sure. I'll be right there."

"And bring a change of clothes...so you don't have to go back home until she wakes up. I'll leave a key for you under the doormat."

Zach wondered if this was Emily's request…or Tosha's.

"All right. See you soon."

"Thanks."

Zach pushed himself out of bed and stripped to his underwear. He grabbed a T-shirt from the dresser and pulled it over his head. Yanking out sweatpants, he sat on his bed and shoved both legs in at the same time. He stood to pull up the pants and slipped his feet into leather loafers. Throwing a shirt, a tie, slacks, socks, and underwear into a leather garment bag, he headed into the master bathroom to grab his toothbrush. He hurried out his bedroom and picked up his keys without missing a step. Only after he began driving down the street did he think he should have splashed some water on his face.

He arrived at the apartment and found the key Tosha left for him. Zach opened the door to the outstretched arms of an almost three-year-old little girl.

"Daddy!"

He dropped his bag on the floor. "Hey, baby bear," he answered, wrapping her into his arms. "I missed you."

She sniffled into his neck. "Missed you, too, Daddy. You didn't come home."

He sighed, but only because he wished he could someday make a home with Emily and her mother...somewhere...anywhere. "I know. I'm here now. How 'bout we get you to bed."

"Okay," said Emily, yawning and rubbing her eyes.

"Are you sure this is okay? You look tired," Tosha said, her own eyes puffy and red from too much crying.

He snapped, "It's three in the morning. Of course, I'm tired. But it's okay. Emily's my daughter, too," with a bit of a jab.

Tosha tilted her head with slouched shoulders.

"Don't do that, Tosha. Nothing's changed for me." He regretted the harsh tone of his voice the instant the words rushed out his mouth.

Muffled sniffles vibrated against his neck as Emily's body tensed in his arms.

"We can talk more later. I got her," he said, but Tosha rushed ahead of him to the girl's room anyway. "What are you doing?"

"I'm going to help."

Zach carried Emily to her room and stopped in the doorway. He calmed himself before saying, "You look exhausted. I'm here. Go rest before you fall over. Please, Tosha."

She released the blanket and passed by him on her way out of Emily's room.

He sighed and laid the little girl onto her toddler bed. "Ready to go back to sleep?"

"Yes," she said and yawned again.

"Why were you so sad? Did you have a bad dream?"

"Yes, Daddy. I dreamed you never came back."

"But I'm here now, see?"

"Then, why you not come for dinner?"

His heart beat with pain in his chest. "It's hard to talk about right now."

"You not say bye to me last time."

"And I'm so sorry. I should have said I was leaving. I won't do that again, okay?"

"Promise?"

"Yeah, I promise. Now, go to sleep."

Emily stood in her bed and reached for him. "Daddy, Daddy, don't leave us."

"Baby bear, I'm not going anywhere. It's all right. I'm here now."

"Please, don't leave. Stay?"

"Tonight?"

"Yes. Please, Daddy."

"I'm planning on it. I'll be here when you wake up."

Emily yawned and nodded. He patted her back and tucked her in again. She rolled onto her side. He waited until her breathing fell into a steady, rhythmic pattern. Heading back to the living room where Tosha sat hugging herself on the sofa, he sat close enough to rest his arm against hers. Old habit. She eased away. He sighed.

"Why aren't you in bed?" He knew the answer but had to ask anyway.

"Is she asleep?"

"Yes."

Her shoulders hunched forward as she rested her face in her hands. He wanted so much to kiss away the pain from her heart and his, but since she sent him away, she'd have to invite him back into her arms. Now, though, her body language communicated anything else but that.

"You ought to go to bed. I have to get up in three hours, and I need the sofa."

She stood. "I'll get the sheets."

He rose to face her. "No need. I know where they are. Please…just go to bed." He fought the urge to raise his voice so she'd listen.

Although she frowned at him, she turned away and shuffled toward her room. She didn't close the door. Once he'd taken what he needed out of the linen closet and spread them on the sofa, he entered Tosha's room to check on her. She lay sniffling in bed with the covers up to her neck. He knelt close to her.

"You and the baby okay?"

She nodded.

"I'm sorry for being short with you earlier. It's been a long day with working right after flying back. But you already know that part."

"Yeah, I know," her voice cracked, "and I'm so sorry I had to ask you for help."

"Don't be. I want to be here when you need me, no matter what." He paused. "Want anything?"

"Tissues, please."

He reached behind the lamp, snatched out a couple tissues, and handed them to her. He stood and said, "Get some sleep," before turning off the lamp and leaving her room. He didn't bother closing the door.

***

A few hours later, to his surprise, despite an interrupted night's sleep, Zach woke before his phone buzzed. He reached over, grabbed his cell, and canceled the alarm. He peeked in Tosha's and Emily's rooms, finding them both still asleep. Not making any noise, he picked up his bag and tiptoed to the bathroom further down the hall.

He brushed his teeth, showered, and dressed in no more than a half hour. With some extra time before he needed to leave, he scrambled up some eggs, ate what he wanted, and left a heaping portion for Tosha and Emily to eat later.

In keeping with his promise, he entered Emily's room and knelt beside her toddler bed.

"Good morning, baby bear."

"Mmmm. Daddy?"

"Yeah. I have to go soon."

"I tired."

He chuckled. "No doubt. You stayed up pretty late last night. Probably best if you go back to sleep. Need to go potty?"

His little girl nodded and stretched her hands out to him. Cradling her in his arms, he carried her to the bathroom and steadied her as she pulled down her pull-up.

"Do you need a new one?"

"No, it's dry."

"Good job, baby bear."

She smiled.

When she finished, he helped her wash her hands and carried her back to her bed. He tucked her in and kissed her forehead.

"All set?"

"Yes, Daddy."

"Good. Going to work now."

"You come for dinner?"

He frowned and shook his head.

"Why?"

"Need to work things out with Mommy first."

Emily's mouth quivered.

"I'm sorry. I didn't want to upset you."

"I miss you. I want to play toys."

"I know, and we will. Just not tonight, all right? I love you."

"I love you too, Daddy."

"Be good for Mommy, okay? She's going to be really tired, so wait until she comes to get you."

She nodded and frowned.

"You want me to come back tonight, don't you?"

"Please. And stay again."

"Okay. I will. I promise."

"Why don't you stay here all the time?"

"Because I live somewhere else. But I do stay over when you have bad dreams," he said, tapping her on the nose.

"But you have no clothes in Mommy's closet. You really sleep over if you leave clothes."

He grinned. "I'll talk to Mommy about that sometime soon, okay?"

This time, she smiled up at him. It grew more difficult to deny her. "Okay," Emily answered before rolling over toward the wall.

He kissed her forehead again, stood, and left her room for Tosha's. His fiancée's head scarf covered one eye. The instant he reached the side of Tosha's bed, she blinked awake and pushed the offending scarf back up onto her forehead.

She peered up at him. "You going to be okay at work today?"

"Yeah, I'll be fine. What about you?"

"I feel like crap. I'm going to call out."

"That's probably a good idea. Emily's tuckered out, too."

Tosha pushed aside the covers. "I gotta get up so she can go potty."

"Already done. She held it all night."

"Oh," she said, falling back onto the pillows. "She knows you're leaving?"

"Yes, I told her."

"Can you come over tonight?"

"Sure, but not for dinner."

She frowned. "You need me to save food for you?"

His throat tightened. "Naw. Not ready to…"

"I understand." She rubbed her forehead.

"I'm heading out. I left some scrambled eggs for you both." He turned to leave.

"Zach?"

He faced her once more and waited, resisting the urge to rush over to her and kiss her. *No.* Since she hadn't said kissing was okay, he didn't want to ask and sound like he was begging. She'd halted everything. She'd have to give word to reinstate what they had before that night she chased him out of her bed.

"Thanks for helping with Emily and for cooking breakfast."

"You're welcome." He paused and stared at the round bump under the covers. "You still have that appointment next week?"

"Mmmhmm. Monday at three."

"I'll pick you up like I did last time."

"You still taking me?"

"Sure, unless you don't…"

"No, I want you to."

"Okay, then it's all set. Sleep as long as you need to. She'll be out for a while." He studied Tosha for a moment then turned around toward the open door, returning to the sofa to grab his phone and bag.

Chapter 17

Zach glanced at the clock on his computer screen. *7:55 p.m.*

"How late you staying, man?" his coworker, Doug, asked.

"One report left to compile."

"Well, don't work too late. There must be something more fun you could be doing on a Friday night."

Zach smiled. "Yeah, you'd think so. Have a good weekend."

"Sure thing. See you Monday."

Zach leaned back for a moment after Doug walked away. The distant ding-ding of the elevator reached Zach's ears. His phone buzzed. *Tosha.*

"Hey," he said in a low bass.

"Are you still coming?" Tosha asked

"Yeah, but I'm at work right now."

"This late?" The angst in her voice rattled his eardrum.

"Doesn't happen often, but yes. Sometimes 'til ten p.m."

"You had food?"

"I ate Chinese."

Her sigh irritated him. "So, what time can you be here?"

"Couple hours. I need to finish up and head home to change." He'd shower and dress in sweats and a T-shirt again.

"You're welcome to spend the night and maybe play toys with Emily tomorrow. She misses that."

"She told me. Sure. I'll pack a bag."

"We'll be up. She won't sleep until you're here."

"Oh. Okay." Looked like a Saturday workday was inevitable. No way he wanted his baby bear to stay up that late waiting for him. "I'll have to work some in the morning since I'm leaving here before I'd planned."

"Thank you, Zach. Really, I'm grateful for this."

"See you soon." Zach tapped the end-call button and touched the phone to his chin. *I can't keep living like this. I hate that they're both so miserable. I'm miserable. We should all be together.*

***

From the moment Zach entered Tosha's apartment, Emily wrapped her arms around his neck and wouldn't let go. He schlepped over to the sofa and dropped his duffle bag next to the coffee table.

"How about I tuck you in, baby bear?" Zach said.

"No. I stay with you." Emily sniffled and stuck her nose into the crook of his neck.

"You want my bed?" Tosha asked.

"I'll stay on the couch."

Tosha went to her room and returned with a pillow, sheets, and a blanket. Zach cradled the little girl in his arms as Tosha laid down the pillow and fitted the bottom sheet over the couch cushions. He sat, swung his legs onto the sofa, and reclined back on the pillow. Then, he repositioned Emily. Her head snuggled on his chest just under his chin. In seconds, Emily's breathing began a steady rhythm.

"You okay like that?" Tosha asked as she covered him and Emily with the top sheet and then the blanket.

"Yeah. I'll take her in when she's been asleep for a while."

"No need to get up. I can take her."

"Tosha," he said, lowering his tone. Why did she always have to micromanage everything?

"Okay. Sorry. I'm just trying to make things better since you have to work in the morning."

"I know. But I'm here because she wants me to put her to bed. If you take her, she might wake up, and we'll have to do this all over again."

"You're right. I'm going to bed."

Her frown and slumped shoulders gnawed at him. He hadn't wanted to hurt her feelings. He didn't want any of this mess to happen between them when they'd barely begun this journey, one he'd hoped would end with them together. Now...?

A half hour later, Zach pushed the sheet and blanket aside. He wrapped his arms around Emily's bottom and back with a hand cupping the back of her head. Avoiding sudden movements, he rose to his feet and tiptoed to the little girl's bedroom. He laid her in the toddler bed and gazed at her peaceful face for a couple minutes before heading back to the couch.

The screaming began in what seemed like seconds after he'd fallen asleep.

"Daddy!"

Zach sat up with a start.

Tosha rushed out of her bedroom and headed straight for Emily's.

As tired as he was, he sighed and arrived in the room to witness Tosha struggling to lift the girl out.

Emily batted Tosha's hands away. "No, Mommy. I want Daddy."

"I'll take you to Mommy's bed." Tosha's voice quivered with weariness.

"No!" Emily began to sob.

He placed a hand on Tosha's shoulder, but she shrugged away. "I'll take her back to the sofa," he said.

The girl scrambled up into his arms the instant he reached out to her.

"But she'll only wake up when you bring her back in here," Tosha said.

"Not my bed." Emily gathered up the collar of his shirt in her small fists. "I stay with Daddy. Please, Daddy."

He turned to Tosha. "I'll keep her with me this time."

"But how will you get to sleep?"

"I'll manage," he said as he strode into the living room. He plopped himself and Emily down on the couch and pulled the sheet and blanket over them.

"Zach." Tosha frowned. Her eyes glistened in the dim lighting.

Didn't she trust him yet? "She's safe with me."

"What if she falls off you?"

Emily cried, wetting his shirt with her tears. He wrapped his arms around her small frame.

"She won't. I got her."

Tosha lingered for a few shaky breaths.

"Go to bed before you fall down, and I have to explain that to Karida. You need sleep, too."

Tosha nodded and, with head bowed, returned to her room. There was no soft click to signal she'd closed her door.

"Don't leave," Emily mumbled into his chest.

Zach sighed again. "Go to sleep, baby bear. Daddy has you."

Only then did the little girl unfurl her fists, allowing herself to slip into slumber. He'd finally closed his eyes until chimes on his cell phone woke him the next morning. Exhaustion weighed down on him like a brick. He reached over to the coffee table and tapped on the phone to shut off the alarm. Emily heaved in a breath and let it out in jagged waves.

"Hey, baby bear, I have to go to work now."

"Noooo," she moaned and tensed.

"Oh, Emily." He patted her back to comfort her, and her body relaxed.

"Don't you want to be my daddy anymore?"

"Of course, I want to be your daddy. What makes you think that I don't?"

"You left. You stopped sleeping here. Are you angry with me?"

"No, I'm not."

"Then why?" Emily whined.

"Mommy and I had an argument. Do you know what that is?"

"You disagree?"

"Yeah, we disagreed, and I couldn't stay here."

"But why?"

"It's complicated, baby bear."

"You hate Mommy now?"

"No. I love your Mommy with all my heart."

"Me too?"

"Yes, I love you, too."

"Are you mad at her?"

"A little."

"For…give?"

"Not yet."

"Why take so long?" Emily whined again.

"Because adults can be silly," he wanted to say stupid, "sometimes." He let a few seconds tick by before saying, "Being away from her hurts."

"Then come back."

"It's not that simple." He sighed. "I'm sorry my leaving hurt you. I never wanted that."

"I miss you."

"I miss you, too." He kissed the top of her head, and she snuggled into his neck. Tears threatened to overflow. "Last night, you yelled at Mommy really loud. Are *you* mad at her?"

She nodded against his chest.

"Why?"

"Mommy sent you away."

"What makes you think that?"

"She said so. She told Auntie Karida. I don't want you to leave." Emily whimpered.

Zach huffed out a breath, his chest aching from sorrow. "Look at me."

Emily raised her head and peered up at him.

"I'm not going anywhere."

"You still be my daddy?"

"I'll always be your daddy."

"Promise?"

"I promise." He kissed her little forehead. "How about we both do our best to forgive Mommy real soon."

"Okay."

"You think it's a good idea to tell Mommy you're sorry for yelling at her?"

"Yes, Daddy."

"Good. That's my baby bear." Zach smiled and glanced at his cell. "Hey, uh, I need to get ready for work."

"Will you come back later?"

"You think you can sleep in your bed tonight?"

A fistful of shirt left no doubt as to her answer.

"You want to come over to my place and sleep in your bed there?"

She nodded on his chest. "I love you, Daddy."

This time he set the tears free. "I love you, baby bear." He pushed aside the covers and cradled her in his arms before standing. "You need to go potty?"

"Yes. I hold it like a big girl."

He smiled and peeked into Tosha's bedroom on the way to the bathroom. Her soft snore reached his ears. He set the girl down and waited until she finished. He then helped her wash and dry her hands.

"Mommy's still sleeping, so I need you to stay in bed until she gets up, all right?"

"Yes, Daddy."

"I'll come see you before I leave."

"And we see you at your home tonight, right?"

"Yes. That's right." He hoped Tosha agreed.

Zach grabbed his duffle bag, returned to the bathroom, and closed the door. The shirt, damp from saliva and tears, clung to his chest. He undressed and stepped into the shower. Warm water sprayed over his head and washed his tears down the drain. However, the deep ache in his chest remained.

Having showered and dressed, Zach returned to Tosha's room. She stirred, her scarf lopsided on her head.

Must've been a rough night. "You up, Tosha?"

"Barely." She rubbed her eyes and propped up on her elbows.

"I'm heading out."

"Did you sleep?"

"Yeah. Emily did, too."

Tosha sat up. "I'm so sorry about all this. She's really attached to you."

"I don't mind that. I hope… I want to be their father no matter what happens."

Tosha didn't react or respond. She merely stared at him.

"I'll always be here for her. I want you to know that."

"Thank you," she said.

"Here's the key to my apartment. Let's try having her sleep there. She might sleep through the night if she's sure I won't leave."

263

"I don't know."

"It's worth a try. We ought to do what we can to make what we brought about less painful for her."

"Okay." She offered him her palm to accept the key.

"Let me know if you won't be there by two. I can't get in if you're not there."

"We'll be there."

"You need anything?"

"No, I'm good." Her pouted lips tugged at him.

"I better go." He turned away before he broke down completely.

***

That afternoon, Zach knocked on the door to his apartment and waited. Tosha opened the door, but a blur of hair rushed toward his legs. He grasped the doorframe to keep from losing his footing.

Tosha glanced down. "She's been watching the door since we got here."

He patted the little girl's head. Emily stepped away giving him room to squat. "How about we go play toys?"

Emily nodded, her eyes glistening. He stood, took her hand, and led the way back into the foyer. Dropping his duffle next to the wall, he lifted his baby bear into his arms and strolled toward the dollhouse. He lost track of time as he focused on making Emily laugh. Tosha calling them to the table for dinner brought him back to his adult world. He frowned. He hadn't meant for her to cook.

As if Tosha read his mind, she said, "I didn't want you to say no if I asked permission. I miss this. I thought..."

He stood and sucked in a deep breath. "It's fine."

"Will you eat with us?"

He nodded. "Yes." He locked her gaze for a few seconds longer than was comfortable. "I'll get both of us washed up."

"Thank you," she said and continued setting the table.

Dinner conversation had lost the spice it once held. *I have to talk to her tonight, or we'll never make it.* As soon as Emily cleaned her plate of the last bit of broccoli, Tosha took the girl to the bathroom for a bath. Zach cleared the table and placed the dirty dishes into the dishwasher. Once finished with that, he paced the floor until Emily, all clean and giggling, returned to him.

"Will you read me a story?"

"Sure thing. Let's go pick out a book."

"Can you read two?"

"I'd be happy to read two stories for you. Does that mean you'll sleep in your own bed tonight?"

"Yes, Daddy."

He turned to Tosha. "Do you mind if I tuck her in?"

"I don't mind. I'll wait here on the couch."

"Go kiss Mommy good night, baby bear."

Emily scurried over to Tosha, hugged and kissed her mommy on the cheek, and hurried back to Zach, grasping his fingers.

"I'm ready to go to bed now, Daddy."

Zach let this precious angel tug him over to the bookshelf to grab two picture books before heading into the room she called her own. With the stories read and Emily covered with the blanket, he sat next to the toddler bed until his little girl fell sound asleep. A sigh escaped his lips. The conversation he dreaded most loomed foremost in his mind as he kissed Emily's forehead and exited the room. He plopped down on the opposite end of the sofa from Tosha.

"How is she?"

"Sleeping soundly. Feel free to check in on her if you like."

"No. I'd just jinx it."

"Can we talk?"

She sighed. "Sure."

He bowed his head and huffed through his mouth. "This morning, Emily reminded me that it's important to forgive those who hurt us." He turned to face Tosha. "You've said sorry many times, but I've found it hard to accept it because the pain ran deep. It was always more than just not being able to connect with you in that way. I felt...cut off from you." He heaved in a big breath. "Anyway, I want to say the words aloud. I forgive you."

"Thank you. I needed to hear that. Things have been such a mess since that night."

"Yeah, for me, too."

"Did you tell her to apologize to me? She said she was sorry for yelling at me and said she forgave me for telling you to leave."

"We had quite a heavy talk first thing this morning. She's quite a girl."

"Yes...she is."

"I want to adopt Emily."

***

Any response stuck in Tosha's throat. Zach had said as much the numerous times he'd said he wanted to be her daughter's daddy no matter what happened between them.

267

Still, she doubted he'd keep his word, considering how she'd treated him the past week.

"I want to be her father."

She stared at his frowning features.

"Tosha?"

"Why?"

"She thinks of me that way, and I will not break her heart. She's been through enough. It's up to us to give her what she needs. Let me be a part of her life."

"It's not just up to me."

"I know that. But this process, if it's going to happen, starts with you. Will you help me do this?"

"And you don't care…about how we'll end up?"

"I still have hope, but I don't want the timing of us working through our stuff to…leave her without a pillar to hold on to. Will you just think about it?"

Tosha nodded.

"Thanks. That's all I ask."

Tosha glanced past him toward her daughter's temporary room. "She's still sleeping in there."

"I think it's because she knows I won't leave my own place. Will you spend one more night?"

Tosha's muscles stiffened.

"Just so both of you can get some adequate sleep."

She relaxed and nodded.

"You can have my bed…as always," he added.

"All right. I'll stay one more night. You could use the sleep, too." She stood and walked to his room, grateful he didn't follow.

***

Zach blinked his eyes open to chase away the drowsiness. A movement across the room caught his attention. Emily opened her bedroom door and zipped toward the bathroom. Minutes passed before the toilet flushed and water gushed from the faucet. Seconds ticked by before she reappeared and scampered over to him. She jumped into his arms and gave him an I-love-you hug. Without hesitation, he wrapped his arms around her with a gentle squeeze. The scent of coconuts wafted through his nose from her braided hair, reminding him of St. Kitts. He so wanted to take Tosha and the kids there someday.

"Hey, baby bear."

"Good morning, Daddy. Why don't you ever sleep in Mommy's bed? Mommies and Daddies sleep in the same bed."

Tough question to wake up to. His memories flashed back to the time he almost did just that and much more. To honor Tosha's wish to be a good example for Emily, he said, "Well, I'm not married to Mommy yet. We wanted to wait until that happened."

"Why married take so long?"

At a loss for words, he shook his head in amazement.

"Then hurry up," she said before running off to her toys.

I have to fix things with Tosha somehow.

Chapter 18

Monday afternoon, Zach's car purred and hummed as Tosha stared out the window. He pulled into a parking spot just outside the front door of the medical office.

Why would he do this, especially after our fight and me avoiding getting close? I don't deserve him.

She glanced at him the instant he turned off the engine. "Thanks so much for bringing me. I know you didn't have to do this."

Zach bowed his head then looked at her. "Has no man ever loved you, Tosha?" He paused, but no words escaped her. He continued, "I'm not talking about sex. I mean, has no man ever showed you love by his actions? 'Cause that is what this is—me showing you that I love you, no matter what. This is who I am. This is what I do. In my opinion, if no one has ever been like this to you, then you've waited too long, and I hope you don't push it away because it's unfamiliar. You deserve better."

He shifted and stared out the windshield. His teeth clenched down on his bottom lip, and he chewed on it. A longing rose inside her core. Oh, how she missed kissing him.

Why am I doing this to him? Why can't I just accept his love for me?

"Let's get in there before you lose your spot," he said seconds before he eased out of the car.

She placed her hand in his and let him help her up out of the bucket seat. Not wanting to give up the warmth that radiated into her fingers and palm, she fell in step while continuing to maintain her grasp. His grip tightened just a bit and then relaxed as if in thanks for this reprieve from their separation.

Having checked in and filled out the necessary paperwork, Tosha followed an ultrasound tech to one of the rooms in the back. She climbed onto the bed in the center of the room and leaned back into it. Zach stood next to her while the technician sat near the monitor. Minutes later, following the slathering of the goop on her abdomen and the positioning of the wand on her lower belly, Tosha smiled as she studied the fuzzy dancing movie of her unborn child.

"Wow," Zach said. "This is cool."

He reached out to grasp her hand again and smiled at her when she glanced at him. Such an unexpected but welcomed surprise. This is how it should be...what she wanted—Zach enjoying every moment with her. She didn't look away until he peered up at the monitor. She followed his gaze and relished in all the good news of her baby's measurements.

"Do you want to know the sex?"

"No," Tosha said, and Zach echoed her sentiment.

"That's it then. I'll wipe you off. Take your time. Just check out at the front desk."

"Thank you," Tosha said and, once again, accepted Zach's help to a sitting position. She'd forgotten how much the extra weight hindered getting up from lying on her back without help.

Once she'd checked out, she missed the warmth of his hand as they strolled back to his car.

"Ready to get Emily?" Zach asked.

"Sure."

Her daughter's squeals at seeing Zach brought Tosha both happiness and consternation. He hadn't planned on staying over that night and spent the ride back to her apartment explaining this to Emily.

"I want you to stay."

"I know, baby bear, and I will again, just not tonight, okay?"

"Why?"

"I have to work late and get up super early. I need you to try and fall asleep in your bed. I will come back."

"Promise?"

"I promise."

"Tomorrow?"

"Yes, tomorrow."

They entered Tosha's apartment, then Zach sent Emily off to play for a bit while he remained close to the door.

"May I talk to you for a sec?" Zach asked in a low tone.

Tosha nodded and dreaded what might come next, something he didn't want Emily to overhear.

He shoved both hands in his pant pockets. "Are you ready to be straight with me?"

"What do you mean?" Tosha asked.

"When you're ready to empty your closet of all its luggage and open each one so I can see what's inside."

She shook her head. "I don't think I'm ready for that."

"It's okay. I'm a patient man."

She folded her arms.

"Good night, Tosha."

He walked over to the play area to hug and kiss Emily then made his exit.

Tosha locked the door determined not to cry this time.

***

Zach parked outside of his best friends' place and tapped on his steering wheel, his mind a whirlwind from all the questions. *What will it take for Tosha to trust me?*

He pulled out his phone and searched for local private investigators in the area. Grabbing a pen and pad from the glove compartment, he jotted down a couple with five-star reviews. He tore off the sheet, returned the pen and pad to their spot, and exited the car. With a shake of his head and a sigh, he knocked on the door.

Karida's greeting smile turned into a frown. "Everything all right?"

Zach chuckled. "Now, that's bad when your friend's first words aren't 'hello' or 'how are you?,' but a question that implies misery surrounds me."

"I didn't mean... Sorry. You're right. Come in."

"Who's at the door, Kar?" Tevin yelled from a room Zach couldn't see.

"Your best pal."

Tevin entered the living room in a rush. "What's wrong?"

Zach raised his eyebrows at Karida.

"What's going on?" Tevin asked. "Something I said?"

275

"We both greeted Zach, assuming the worst. Some friends we are," she said.

"Oh. Sorry, man. It's just…"

"I know. We're still working through some things, and Emily's having nightmares about me not sticking around. I've been sleeping on Tosha's couch or mine, a lot. I asked her over to my place for the weekend. Emily slept like a champ. I'm hoping she'll be fine tonight. I just need to sleep in my bed, you know?"

"Yeah, I get it," Tevin said. "What's up?"

"I need you to give this to Tosha," Zach said, giving Karida the paper.

She widened her eyes as she read it over. "Why are you doing this?"

Tevin read the note over her shoulder. "Wow! Now, that's love, man."

"Well, I got to thinking that maybe it'll help if Tosha knows about me, my background, who I am."

"We've told her all that," Karida said.

"But that's just it. You're both our friends who see mostly the good in us. I kinda feel she needs an objective point of view."

"We told her the truth. We know she loves you. I just don't understand. Why a private investigator?" Karida asked.

"Because Tosha won't relax with me around Emily until she's convinced I won't hurt her daughter. Tosha has the power to keep herself, Emily, and the baby away from me if we don't work out, and there's nothing I can do, no legal standing, to show the world I'm their father, although in my heart and mind, I already am. I can't lose those kids, not after seeing the baby on the ultrasound today. That would tear me apart. I want to adopt them."

Karida placed a hand on his shoulder. "What do you want us to do?"

"Give her those numbers. It doesn't matter which one she chooses. I'll pay the fee. I just want her to know I'm the real deal. Could you convince her to do this?"

"Sure. I'll try to visit with her in a couple days. Will that work?" Karida said.

"Yeah, that'll be great. I'll drop off the cash payment tomorrow." He sighed. "Thanks for supporting us through all this."

"Anytime, Zach. You're like family to us, and we'd like to see all of you happy."

Zach hugged them both and returned to his car for the ride home and a good night's sleep.

***

Following another long day at work on Tuesday, Zach schlepped into his apartment around eight-thirty. He dropped his keys and phone on the coffee table and continued walking to the bathroom. He stared into the mirror, wishing he hadn't promised to return to Tosha's place tonight. Having taken a shower, he zipped up the leather garment bag when a vibrating noise reached his ears. With bag in hand, he hurried into the living room to pick up his cell and swipe the screen. *Nine o'clock.*

"Hey, Tosha," he said, mid-yawn.

"You sound tired. Maybe…"

"No, I'm good. She waiting up for me?"

"I tried to get her down like last night. She didn't wake until six this morning, but tonight…"

"The nightmares are back."

"Yes. Can you still come over?"

"I'm leaving now."

She sighed into the phone. "Thank you," she whispered.

"I know this is hard. We'll get through this."

"I hope so. See you soon."

He pocketed his phone then grabbed his keys on the way to the door.

***

Emily flew into Zach's arms the instant Tosha opened the door. Tears streamed down Emily's face. He gazed at Tosha who seemed close to crying herself.

With the I'm-so-glad-you're-here-Daddy hug out of the way, Zach settled on the sofa and set Emily on his lap. She leaned against his chest and rubbed at her eyes. Her body shivered in silent whimpering waves.

"I'll be in my room. Let me know if you need anything," Tosha said.

He nodded understanding and wrapped his arms around his baby bear. "I'm sorry the bad dreams came back. I'd hoped to be here earlier. I'm sad when you hurt."

She snuggled into him. "Can you read me a story, Daddy?"

"Sure. Ready to go to your bed?"

"No. In Mommy's bed."

"But."

Emily wriggled out of his arms. "Come, she's still awake."

Zach grabbed a book and followed. He knocked on Tosha's bedroom door, but Emily opened the door and ran ahead. She climbed up next to her mother before he or Tosha had a chance to speak.

"Are you all right with this?" Zach asked.

Tosha sat up and smiled toward Emily. "I guess I better be. It's fine. Come in."

He climbed onto Tosha's bed. Things had been a lot different the last time he got in this bed. His skin warmed as he recalled what led up to the almost first time. He sat on the comforter and opened to the first page of the story. A few minutes later, the little girl yawned while he read the last sentence in her picture book.

"Ready for bed?"

She yawned again. "Yes, Daddy. Sleep here. I say you married now."

He wanted to say it didn't work that way but thought better of doing that.

Emily lay between them. In minutes, her even breathing indicated she was fast asleep. He began pushing up from the bed, but his name in Tosha's silky tone gave him pause. He faced her.

"Stay. It's all right. She'll fuss if she doesn't see you. *I* want you to stay."

Without a word, he lay back down and closed his eyes. Her last sentence warmed his heart.

***

Zach opened his eyes in the dark room and panic gripped him. He'd forgotten to set the alarm on his phone which he left in the living room the previous night. Soft breathing sounds from Emily calmed him.

What time is it?

He rolled a bit toward Tosha's side of the bed to catch a glimpse of the time on the bedside clock. Her dark form propped up on her elbow and gave him a start.

"You're up, too?" Zach asked.

"Yes. It's five to six. I took the alarm off. Figured I'd wake you myself so she didn't have to get up yet, but it looks like I don't have to."

"I thought I'd overslept. Glad I didn't. I better get ready."

"Um."

"Yeah?"

"What was that about us being married?"

"Uh… I may have been the cause of her saying that. She asked why we aren't sleeping in the same bed. I told her we needed to be married to do that. I said what I thought you'd want me to say. Did I overstep?"

"No. I was surprised." Tosha sighed and her form relaxed onto the pillow. "She asks so many questions."

"Emily's a smart girl. We'll figure this out...together."

"Thanks for sticking around."

"No place I'd rather be."

***

Tosha pulled on a robe and tied the belt around her bulging waist. She left Emily in her bed and walked into the living room to wait until Zach finished getting ready for work. She wanted to make eggs for him, but he'd said he was in a hurry and wouldn't have time to eat. She sighed. He always loved her cooking.

Why did he stop?

She leaned against the back of the sofa. A thought flashed through her mind. What if his eating with her and Emily reminded him of what he doesn't have since she pushed him away? Ever since their first date, food had been a part of the fun connection they'd experienced. Well, not food, but the mood surrounding spending time together over a meal.

I have to fix this.

From the moment Zach exited the bathroom, his firm and tall form captured Tosha's gaze.

What am I doing with this gorgeous man?

She stood. Her gut clenched as she took in the frown planted on his lips. She missed his smile, the way his laugh excited her.

"You leaving now?" Tosha asked.

"Yeah, but I wanted to say something."

"Go ahead."

"He's got a hold on you."

"What are you talking about?"

"Your ex has got a hold on your heart."

His words offended her, raised the hairs on the back of her neck. "No, he doesn't."

"Then explain to me why his baby girl has pushed *him* to the curb and calls *me* Daddy while you *push* me away every time you think about him."

"I don't *think* about him."

"All right. Crosses your mind. Little kids are as loyal as they come no matter how messed up the parents are. So, if she can move on, why can't you?"

She opened her mouth to answer.

He raised a hand, palm toward her, to stop her. "No. Wait. You need to really think it over before you respond. Do some soul searching if you have to, because our relationship, if it's going to last a lifetime, depends on that answer."

She pressed her lips together and nodded.

"I better go, or I'll be late for work." He stepped toward the foyer.

She followed. "Will you be back later?"

Facing her, he said, "Yes, I'll spend the night."

"Dinner?"

"Sure. I'll be a little late."

"That's fine. We'll wait."

He smiled, opened the door, and left her standing in the foyer without as much as a peck.

As soon as he crossed the threshold, she rushed out and grabbed his hand. "Wait," she said and tiptoed to kiss him. He leaned into her and nibbled her lower lip. Butterflies swirled in her abdomen, maybe a little lower. She eased away and licked her lips. "I missed that."

"So have I." He pulled out of her arms, locked her gaze for a couple too-brief seconds, then strode away down the hall with his fine self.

Chapter 19

Tosha hurried to the door in response to a knock that vibrated to her core. She looked through the peephole hoping Zach had come back for more of what they had when she'd kissed him a half hour ago. But it wasn't him. Disappointed, she opened the door.

"Good morning, Karida."

"Someone looks a little disappointed to see her bestie."

"I'm sorry. It's just…"

"You hoped it was him."

"Yeah. Come in. I only have a couple minutes, though."

"I know. I'm on my way to work myself, but I have something for you."

Tosha stared at the piece of paper Karida handed her. "What's this?"

"Zach asked me to convince you to hire a P.I. He'll cover the cost."

"Why?"

"He wants you to trust him, Tosha."

"But I *do* trust him."

"Really? Then why are you so nervous when he changes Emily's pull-up? And why won't you open up to him about the real reason you're having trouble being intimate with him? He loves you and wants you to know everything about him, so you'll trust him."

"I don't need this." Tosha offered it back to Karida. "I won't call."

"I'm not taking it back. You're going to call one of those numbers and give them the information they need to dig up Zach's history."

Tosha nodded, but tears streamed down her cheeks. "I didn't mean to hurt him."

"My dearest friend." Karida pulled Tosha into a firm hug. "I really think that if you tell him you want to wait until you're married, he'll accept that. I'm all for waiting. You know that's what I did."

"I know. I should have done that, too."

"And miss out on your beautiful babies? Listen. You chose a different path and with the wrong guy. But Zach loves you tons. He won't treat you the same."

"I know, but I'm scared."

"Then, explain it to him. Don't make it sound like you're waiting in order to be a good example for her. Although admirable, that's not the real story. We both know that."

Tosha nodded again.

"Here's the payment." Karida handed over a stuffed envelope.

Tosha's hand shook as she took it. "He trusts me with this?"

"Of course. He's trying to show you just how much he does."

This time, Tosha cried into her friend's shoulder. "I'll call the P.I. I'll call him today."

***

Zach halted reading an email when his phone vibrated on his desk. *Tosha.* He sighed and answered.

"Hey."

"I'm so sorry to bother you at work. I just wanted to make sure you're still coming over tonight."

"Yeah, I'll come over."

"For dinner?"

"Yes. Is Emily all right?"

"She's fine. She misses you." A few seconds ticked by. "I miss you. Dinner's not the same without you." A breath later, she added, "I just wanted to hear your voice."

"Uh, Zach," said his boss from the aisle.

"Tosha, hold on a sec." He turned to his manager. "Sorry, personal call."

"That's fine. Would you stop in my office after you're done?"

"Sure thing." Zach waited until the man had walked away. "I'm back," he said to Tosha.

"Did I get you in trouble?"

"No, he just wants to see me. I'll stop by after work…for dinner, okay?"

"Okay," she said without the bright tone she'd had before everything came crashing down around them. Was he asking for too much? "Do you have any special request?"

"Surprise me." He ended the call, strolled to his boss's office, and walked through the wide-open door.

"Close that, will you, Zach?"

Zach complied and sat in the chair across the desk from concerned eyes.

"Is everything all right on the home front?"

"My fiancée and I are working through some things." He didn't want to get into it. "What did you need?"

"You're my best salesman, Zach, but you've lost your usual spark. I need to know if you're going to be okay on this next assignment."

"Sure, I won't disappoint you."

"That's good to hear. It's a two-week assignment. Two cities. Ten companies. Your first meeting is at seven Monday morning. You leave on Sunday."

"Two weeks?" *Tosha's not gonna like this.* How in the world was he going to patch things up with Tosha while away for two whole weeks? *Emily's not even sleeping without me yet.*

"Is that a problem?"

"No." Zach shook his head. "I wonder...well, would it be all right if I brought my fiancée and our daughter out for the weekend?"

"Not at all. I didn't know you had a child."

"Well, she's not my biological daughter, but I'd like to adopt her. We've sort of adopted each other already." *Might as well give him a bit more.* "She hasn't been sleeping well unless I'm there to tuck her in."

"I see."

"Also, I really enjoy traveling for this company, but now I'm thinking I'd like to stick around more often."

"Hmm. Well...like I said, you're the best one I got for the job, but...if you hire someone to take your place—and I mean imitate your ethic and your success—I'll give you the corner office. It's not public knowledge, but Jim's retiring in a few months. If you find someone with your drive, I'll give you a promotion *and* the corner office. Will that work?"

Zach smiled. "Thanks, boss. I really appreciate that."

***

Emily screamed out ten minutes after Zach had tucked her in. He moaned. Dinner went better than he expected. Must have been that kiss Tosha gave him this morning. He'd hoped for the end of the nightmares. But…

"I got this," he said to Tosha, leaving her in the kitchen to finish cleaning up. He strolled into Emily's room and knelt beside the toddler bed. "Hey, baby bear. Daddy's here."

She sniffled and rubbed at her eyes. "I want you. I want to stay with you."

"I know. Look at me." When he locked Emily's glossy gaze, he said, "I need you to try and sleep in your bed, okay?"

"No," she whimpered.

"I will be here when you wake up in the morning."

"You promise?"

"I promise. Have I ever broken a promise?"

"No."

"And I don't intend to start now."

Emily pouted but didn't object.

He sighed. "I want to explain something to you."

"What?"

"I know you want me and Mommy together. I do too, but even though you want us to be married, we're not there yet. We have to work through some things first."

"But you'll visit?"

"Yes."

"And call me?"

"Of course. I will. I won't abandon you. You believe me?

"Yes."

"You trust me?"

"Yes, Daddy."

"And I will fight my hardest not to damage that trust, okay?"

The girl nodded.

"I'm not perfect, but I will fight to be here for you."

"I know you will."

"So, sleep, understanding no one can make me stop loving you."

"Dream of us a family?"

"Yeah, because I will be doing that, too."

"Okay, I go sleep in my own bed."

"Good, baby bear. I love you."

"I love you, Daddy. Nite nite," the girl said and closed her eyes.

"Nite nite." He smiled and kissed her on the forehead. Standing, he stepped back from the bed and returned to Tosha who now sat on the sofa in the living room.

"She went back to sleep?"

"Yeah. I think she'll make it to morning." He plopped down on the sofa a couple feet from Tosha, the one woman he'd rather share close space with, and leaned back into the pillows. Uncomfortable silence hung thick in the air. He resisted the urge to reach out and pull her to him.

"Karida gave me the number for the P.I. Did you want to learn about my past, too?"

"No need. There's nothing I can't learn from you."

"Can I ask you something?"

"Sure. Anything."

"Did you and Karida date?"

"No," he said, shaking his head. "Not at all."

"Did you ever want to?"

He sucked in a breath. "No. Karida knows what I want. She knows me better than anyone, but she's always been more like a sister. We laughed about it once or twice, how it was weird not to want more, but we agreed we just didn't feel that way about each other. You okay with us being close friends?"

"Yes. I just wondered."

"She'd promised to find my perfect match. I'd like to think she did when she set me up with you. Any reason this bothers you?"

Tosha blew an audible breath out her mouth. "Did you call her when we…?"

"No. I called Tevin. I won't risk us by calling another woman, no matter how close she is to me. Is that okay?"

Tosha nodded.

"We good with this?"

"Yeah, we're good with this."

Zach exhaled, not just for wading through this particular topic without ending up in another argument, but also that Emily remained asleep.

He stared at Tosha for a moment longer than he dared, intensifying his longing for her. *Why is this so hard?* "I better go," he said as he stood. "I'll come back before Emily wakes up."

"Zach." Her gentle tone hammered at the shield he'd put up.

"What, Tosha?"

"I spent the day thinking over what you asked me this morning. It was hard to hear. I didn't...don't mean to push you away. I'm sorry."

He hesitated, not wanting to hurt her. "So am I."

"I'm not good enough for you. I—"

"Stop." He grimaced. "Don't say that. If I put you in the same room as the other women I've dated, you'd outshine them, and I'd pick you every time. But I wouldn't dare take you there. They don't deserve to be in your presence."

"But I'm broken. I feel like I'm losing pieces of myself every day."

"I'll pick up your pieces, and you may pick up mine."

"I'd like that."

"Then stop pushing me away."

Her mouth turned down at the corners and quivered. "You deserve better."

No way to avoid this. "You're wrong about that. You captured my interest the first night we met. The fun and flirty way we bantered back and forth. That you cared how much dinner cost, not because you wanted the most expensive thing, but because you didn't. I avoided taking others there because all they wanted was to be wined and dined no matter the cost. You wanted to connect to me.

"I liked the cute way you hid your face after you moaned through the steak. And the swans. I fell in love with you that night. I'd wait as long as you needed. But don't get me wrong. I'm crazy attracted to you, and I want to experience the culmination of all we've said to each other, the way we've kissed. I want—I can't believe I'm saying this—I want to climax with you. But once I do, there's no going back, so I'm willing to wait until we're married if that's what you want.

"But as much as I adore that little girl, us waiting can't be driven by her. That choice is just between the two of us."

He turned to leave. A tentative grasp of his elbow made him pause. She stepped around to face him and grasped both of his hands.

"Don't go," she said, her eyes glistening. "I'm having a tough time trusting again. I gave myself to him, thinking we'd be together for life. I didn't hold back, and he stepped all over my heart. I want to be with you more than anything, and that scares me. I don't want to be in the same place I've been before—broken and alone but for the two babies I carried. I need you. I'm frightened how much. I need you to be patient with me." She paused for two breaths. "Stay." She snuggled into his chest. "Just hold me."

"I trust you with my heart," Zach said.

"My problem is I'm having trouble trusting you with mine. Em's father hurt me."

"I'm not that guy."

She eased out of his embrace. "I know, but I gave that guy my love and my body. I have two babies I love dearly but no man to love and commit to me for a lifetime. I'm scared of making another bad decision."

"I stink at this relationship thing, too, but we didn't do this. Our friends brought us together."

"For which I'm eternally grateful. I just wish I met you first. I'd go anywhere with you, even on those business trips, meet this Honey."

He laughed. "I like that even in the midst of this conversation you can still remind me that I'm yours. Believe me, Honey is no threat."

Tosha smiled and her eyes watered. "Let me finish before I can't. I want us to work out." She sighed and stroked his wrists.

He pulled her close and breathed her in. "Where do we go from here?"

"My heart is yours, and I wish I could say I'm ready, but I'm not. I want you in my bed, but I can't give myself to you yet. I..." She peered up into his eyes. "He broke me."

"I'm so sorry." He tightened his embrace. "I love you, Tosha. I get it."

She eased away, this time curving her fingers into his. "Will you come to bed?"

He nodded.

"Just to sleep?" Tosha asked.

"Yeah. Just to sleep."

"Thank you," she said.

"Try not to undress me this time."

She giggled and pressed her lips against his.

Chapter 20

Zach woke to soft kisses planted on his forehead, his cheeks, and lastly on his lips. On instinct, his arms wrapped around Tosha and pulled her close. The kiss deepened, but he didn't stop her. Moments later, she pushed away with hesitation and rolled back onto her pillow. Tears dampened her cheeks. When she sat up, he did as well.

"Tosha, sweetie, talk to me."

"I'm so sorry."

"It's all right. I forgive you."

She faced him, shifting into a kneeling position, and leaned her forehead against his. Her fingertips caressed his shoulders and arms. She placed a palm against his cheek.

"Zach, I want you with every fiber of my being."

"Then, what's holding you back?"

"I loved him, Chaz, with everything I had. I sacrificed my future for him. My heart...my life shattered the day I caught him with that woman. I was so angry. I hate him so much. I *hate* my daughter's father." Her tears fell onto the sheet.

"Do you hate me, too?"

"No."

"Then why push me away?"

"I love you with my whole heart, and I'm…I'm scared that you'd hurt me like he did. I know, you said you're not him, but…"

"Listen to me carefully. I will *never* betray your trust in me. I promise to love you for the rest of my life. I won't abandon you. Do you believe that?"

"I want to. I don't want to lose you."

"You won't." He sucked in a deep breath. "Let's get married."

"You already asked, and I said yes, remember?"

"I mean, let's plan it now."

She eased away and sat back on her heels. "While I'm pregnant?"

"Why not? It doesn't need to be big. Just closest family and friends. I think this engagement needs to culminate into our connection, or you'll continue to feel like you're in limbo."

"For when?"

"As soon as we can pull it off. In my heart and mind, I'm already committed to you. I don't have to or want to wait long." He struggled to interpret her intense gaze.

"Oh…okay. I'm in."

"Would you move some of your things to my place? That way, you won't have to pack a bag every time you and Emily stay over. I'll give you a key so you can stop by whenever you like, even when I'm away."

She nodded. "You want to bring some of your things to this apartment, too?"

"I'd like that." He caressed her cheek. "We good?"

"Better than good," she said and kissed him.

***

Tosha backed off the bed and stood, the gravity of what she'd just confessed hitting her like a whirlwind. And Zach still wanted her. A wedding. Soon. She turned toward the bathroom and froze.

"What's the matter?" Zach laid a gentle hand on the small of her back.

"I am a mess without you," she said. "I haven't been myself. Can't think straight. I almost forgot about Emily's birthday."

"When is it?"

"Sunday."

"Shoot."

She turned to face him. "Zach?"

"Remember when my boss interrupted our call yesterday?"

"Yes. What happened? He got upset with you, didn't he?"

"No. Nothing like that. It's just that…"

"Zach, just tell me."

He signed. "I have to go away for two weeks, and I leave on Sunday."

The world fell out from under her feet. Hollowness filled her gut. "Two weeks? I can't. I'm not ready for that. She just started sleeping in her bed again. Zach."

"I know. The timing stinks, but I'll talk to her. She'll understand. It's just… I hate leaving on her birthday. I didn't know."

"Not your fault. I should have told you sooner, but with us fighting…"

"Don't blame yourself either. It's been a tough couple weeks."

"Is Honey going to be there?"

"For one of the visits, yes. Are you worried?"

"Of course. We've been fighting for two weeks. I…"

"Hey. I'm in love with you. Nobody else, okay?"

"Okay."

"I wish I could take you with me. Can you take off work?"

"I can't, especially not with maternity leave coming up."

"You don't have to work."

"What?"

"I can take care of you both, if that's what you want."

"I…"

"You don't have to decide now. I just wanted you to know."

She laughed. "Your job pays you that much?"

"Yeah, it does."

She studied him. "I've always taken care of me."

"I know. And I'm not asking you to change anything you've always done. Just wanted to put it out there that you don't have to go it alone anymore. If you choose to stay home after the baby, I can take care of everything. Are you doing all right paying the rent?"

"Yes, we're fine."

"Good, because if you're ever strapped, I can help you out. How much is it?"

"Like two grand."

"Yeah, I can handle that."

"What? Are you made of money?"

He smirked. "I kind of am, not an extreme amount, but plenty. It's what made finding my 'one' so difficult."

"Wow. Thanks, but we are fine."

He tilted head, expecting her to say more.

"I had ten thousand saved before I met her dad. I never told him. We had a joint account, but I'd take a hundred out of my weekly pay and put it into my account. I told him I spent it. He never found out."

"Shrewd."

"I don't even know why I'm telling you."

"You have nothing to fear from me. Your account can remain yours as long as you like. So, back to the trip. If you can't take off the two weeks, can you and Emily travel out to meet me the following weekend? My boss said it'd be fine."

She grinned. "I'd like that."

"And...if you land early enough on Friday, I'll even introduce you to Honey."

"Really? She won't mind?"

"Not at all. She's dying to see the woman who won my heart."

Tosha grinned. "I look forward to meeting her."

"Great," he said, smiling. "We'll tell Emily when she gets up."

***

Zach stood next to the taxi at Chicago O'Hare, panning the area until he sighted Tosha holding onto Emily with one hand while pulling a carry-on and car seat with the other. A smile spread across Tosha's face the instant she saw him.

Emily hugged a stuffed panda bear to her chest, reminding him of her words, "You remembered my favorite animal, Daddy. I take care of him for you," when he'd given it to her on her birthday, hours before his flight to Florida. Since Emily had been sleeping well with her new pal, Tosha chose to travel for an extended weekend, so she'd only miss two days of work.

His chest filled with warmth as he hugged and kissed them in turn. "I missed you both so much."

The taxi driver took the carry-on and belted the car seat in the back.

"What's this car?" Emily asked. "It's not yours."

"That's right. It's a taxi. He's going to drop us off at a huge building in the city. Then, later we'll get another one to the hotel."

"Are we staying with you?"

"Yes, baby bear. My boss got me a suite with enough space for you to play."

Emily climbed into the car, but Zach grasped Tosha's elbow for a brief smooch before she got into the backseat following their little girl.

***

Tosha stared out the window, admiring the architectural beauty in this city she'd never visited. Soon, the taxi stopped, and some trepidation crept up into her gut at the pending meet and greet between her and Honey.

Zach helped her and Emily out of the taxi. Once the driver handed him the carry-on and Emily's car seat, Zach paid the guy and picked up the bag and seat. He strolled toward a tall building with two glass doors.

"How was your trip?"

"Uneventful."

"The best kind. Emily did all right?"

"She loved it. Never stopped talking about getting to see you in Chicago. We both missed you a ton."

"I've been dreaming of today ever since I left you two on her birthday."

He pulled open one door to allow her and Emily to enter then followed them in.

"The meeting is upstairs." He approached a waiting elevator and entered.

Tosha adjusted the purse hung over her shoulder and made sure her daughter stepped on without tripping. "Where do you want us to wait?"

"Honey set up a conference room for you with lunch and some toys for Emily."

"She did that for us?"

"Yes. I'm sort of a big deal around here. My company strives to keep our business relationship healthy, and this company does the same. I'm the glue that strengthens the bond. Everyone knows who I am and wants to keep me happy, so I have nothing negative to report."

"Wow. I'm so proud of you."

"Thanks." The door opened. "Here we are. Honey's straight ahead."

The woman smiled and moved from behind her desk to greet them. Her complexion held the same hue as her name, and her dark brown tresses hung past her shoulders. She wore three-inch heels like she was born in them.

"Hello, Tosha. It's such a pleasure to finally meet you," Honey said.

Tosha wanted to be jealous, but the woman seemed so genuine and friendly, and Zach paid Honey no attention at the moment with his gaze fully on Tosha and their little girl. "I'm pleased to meet you as well."

"And this must be Emily. How cute as a button you are."

"Tank you," Emily said.

"Come. Let me show you where you'll stay until Zach's meeting is over." Honey turned to Zach. "You failed to tell me how beautiful your family is. I'm so happy for you."

"Thanks so much for setting everything up. I didn't want them to be alone their first day here."

"Our pleasure." Honey pushed open a glass door. "Here you go. Tosha, if you need anything, press ten on the phone to call my desk."

"I will. Thanks."

With new toys, tasty pastries, sandwiches, and fruit, three hours passed like mere minutes before Zach entered the spacious room.

"Ready?"

"Daddy!" Emily hurried toward him and hugged his legs.

"Yes," Tosha said. "Just give me a minute to pack up."

"I'll help," he said.

"Everything turn out well?"

"Very. We signed a five-year contract which added three more sites."

"You have to travel to those, too?"

"Not if I find someone to take my place."

"What?"

"With everything that's happened, I never got to tell you about a possible promotion. I won't have to travel as much."

Tosha pecked Zach on the lips and grinned. "That makes me very happy."

He grinned and kissed her, this time a bit longer.

***

Tosha got Emily cleaned and tucked into the comfy queen size bed then turned and grabbed a brown envelope out of her purse. She gestured for Zach to follow. Once seated on the sofa in the second room, she placed the envelope on her lap.

"Is that what I think it is?"

"Yes. I got it yesterday but wanted to go through it with you, you know, just in case I have questions."

"Fair enough. Open it up."

She opened the package and pulled out a stack of papers. Her eyes scanned the first page. "Good Lawd."

"What?"

"Zacharias Tiberius Caldwell?"

"Yeah." He chuckled. "My Bible-toting father was a big fan of Star Trek. I thought of changing my middle name to Teddy many times."

"Why didn't you?"

"I love my dad and, after he passed, I wanted to keep the one thing he chose for me—my name. He was a wonderful father."

Tosha patted Zach's hand. "I wish I could've met him."

"He would've loved you."

She smiled and returned her attention to the papers on her lap. Zach scooted closer.

"Bachelors in Accounting. Masters in Business Administration. Graduated top of your class at Columbia University." She gazed at him. "Isn't that school super expensive?"

"I got a full scholarship."

"Handsome *and* smart."

"My father stood for nothing less than excellence. I worked hard to please him. To make him proud of me. To be proud of myself. After I graduated with the B.A., my current boss paid for the master's degree."

"That's great." She turned the page. "No record. Great citizen. A volunteer."

"Did my best to stay clean. Didn't want to become another black man statistic in and out of jail."

She leafed through the pages. "The names of all your girlfriends. Same number you said. Everything else matches what you told me." She stopped at the finances and closed the packet.

"Aren't you curious?"

"You've already told me you can take care of us. That's all I need to know. Anything more will only mess with my head." She adjusted and patted the stack of papers on her lap. "One phrase keeps repeating itself in my head."

"Which is?"

"And this man loves me."

He positioned two fingers under her chin and turned her head to face him. "This man adores you." He smiled. "So, you still want to marry me?"

She nodded. "Yes. I do. I want you, Zach. Sending you away because I had trust issues created chaos for me and Emily. My thoughts, my emotions, my whole being points to you."

He kissed her forehead. "Do you have a date in mind?"

"Not yet. You?"

"What do you think of three weeks before your due date?"

"Wow, that's fourteen weeks away."

"Practically four months."

"Three and a half."

"I think we can make it happen. Worst case, my company can host the reception in their ballroom-sized conference room. You in?"

"Absolutely." She brushed her lips against his. "And are you game for Lamaze class with me?"

"Of course, beautiful lady. Wouldn't miss 'em. When do they start?"

She giggled. "In about a month or so."

"Tell me when you've signed up, and I'll make sure I'm not on travel." He leaned in and kissed her.

"You got it," she mumbled against his lips.

Zach took the papers off her lap and dropped them on the floor. He pulled her close and eased her back onto the sofa. Her body trembled as the kiss deepened. She placed a hand on his chest and hated having to slow things down.

He stopped and sat up. "Sorry."

"Don't be. You didn't do anything wrong. I missed all of that. I just…have some unfinished business with Chaz."

Zach frowned.

"Not my feelings for him. I couldn't care less about that man." She pecked Zach on the lips. "I need to talk to him about releasing Emily so you can adopt her."

"Really? You're ready?"

311

"Yes. I don't see any reason to wait. Do you mind giving me a few minutes? Then we can continue where we left off."

"Sure. You want me to stay or give you some space?"

She sucked in a deep breath. "Stay close. My conversations with that man never end well."

"I'm here."

She smiled then stood and strolled to the desk to grab her cell. Releasing pent up air, she exhaled through her mouth.

The phone rang once. "Wha' you want?" Chaz asked.

"I won't keep you long, but I have a request. I'm getting married in a few months to a great guy. Emily likes him, too."

"You shacking up with him?"

"None of your business."

"Emily's my business."

"Since when? He's very attentive to her and wants to adopt her—"

"Hell, no. It'll be a cold day in hell before I sign over my daughter to some guy you sleepin' with. You just had to get some, didn't you? Now, he's marrying you. Did he knock you up, or is it true love?"

"Chaz, just listen to me. He's a good man."

"Naw. I ain't got to listen to no slut. Only call me when you're ready to give me back my daughter."

The phone went silent, and Tosha moved it from her ear. She stared at the screen in disbelief. Then, the tears brimmed over her eyelids and streamed down her cheeks.

***

Zach took the phone from Tosha's hand and laid it on the desk. He wiped at her tears with his thumb and kissed her forehead.

"He said no?"

She nodded. "He said I'm a slut."

He pulled her close when her body jerked as she cried again.

"I want to shove what he said back in his face," she said.

"You plan to tell him the baby is his? 'Cause once the baby is born, he'll think he's right."

She groaned. "No, I don't ever want him to find out that he's the father."

"Why do you care so much what he thinks?"

She eased out of his arms and peered up into his eyes. She shook her head. "I don't. I wish I'd done better with my life, but then I wouldn't have had Emily." She sighed.

"You're starting over with me. No one else matters."

A shrug followed another nod. He needed to convince her.

"It's time a man makes you feel like the woman you are." He caressed her face. "Beautiful." He grasped both hands, pulling her close again. "Sexy."

"Sexy?"

He smiled. "You have no idea what you do to me, Tosha. I adore every single one of your curves." He intertwined his fingers with hers and stepped until their bodies met. "And sensual." He dipped his head and brushed his lips against her neck.

She giggled. "How...how am I sensual?"

"Have you forgotten the way you washed my hands? Long after the dirt had been scrubbed off, you kept going until my private parts responded."

She gasped. "Zach."

"Just keeping it real, sweetie." He pressed his lips to hers, inhaled, and eased away. "It's happening again."

"Stop it. You're so...so..." Her breathing staggered.

"You sure you want me to stop?"

"I..."

He locked her gaze. "My promise stands. I won't go that far."

"Okay. Don't stop."

He grinned. "Lie on the sofa with me."

"What about Emily?"

He glanced at the bedroom. "She's still sleeping. We'll join her later. I want to hold you for a while before we go in there."

She didn't resist as he guided her toward the plush couch a few feet away. He got settled first, his back to the pillows, and tugged her down so she'd lean her back against his chest, her head snuggled next to his cheek.

He wrapped his arms around her rounded abdomen and grasped her hands. "You comfortable?"

"Very. This sofa is wider than ours."

"Yep." He pecked at her ear. "Close your eyes." He waited a few seconds. "Ready?"

"They're closed."

"Picture me in your mind."

"Okay."

"Only me," he whispered in her ear.

"You got it."

He nibbled her ear. "Well, maybe you should think about that piece of filet, too."

She cackled and clasped a hand over her mouth. "Did I wake her?"

He chuckled softly. "I think she's still asleep."

Her body relaxed back against his. "Why did you bring that up?"

"Are you kidding? I'm *never* letting you forget your sexy moans when you ate that piece of meat."

She gasped. "You said it wasn't that bad."

"I said no such thing. I believe I used words like 'moving experience' and 'wishing I were that piece of meat.' In fact, I'm thinking that's what I'll order for room service for our first time on our wedding night. Should keep things rather…exciting, don't you think?"

"You're incorrigible, Zacharias Tiberius Caldwell."

"Ha. And I'll remain this way if only to see you this happy always."

"I'm sorry about earlier."

"You have nothing to feel sorry about. He's a brute, and we'll keep pressing him until he gets tired of us and just gives us what we want."

"He's stubborn."

"So am I when what I'm fighting for has filled my heart. You can take him to court. Make him pay child support. When the money is taken before he sees it, he'll break. You can save it in that special account of yours. Emily doesn't need his cash. I can take care of her."

"I know you can."

A few minutes later, he sighed and kissed her temple. "I want more times like these, the sensual makeups following unavoidable disagreements. No matter what happens, this is how I hope we always end up."

"I want that too."

"Stay with me, Tosha."

"I will. 'Til death parts us. But you better live until you're ripe with old age. I'm not starting over with anyone else."

"I'll do my best."

He gave her a little squeeze and closed his eyes.

***

Tosha closed her eyes. Zach's arms felt like home. Oh, how she'd missed them. She tried to relax, but Chaz's face flashing through her mind caused her muscles to tense.

"Tell me about your baggage to keep my mind off me and my issues. That kind of thing wasn't in the P.I.'s package."

He sighed. "And it wouldn't be because I never let that side of me out."

"What side?"

"The overachiever me, which on the surface doesn't seem so bad. It helped me do great in school and fast track at my job. My father taught me to be my best, and I fought hard never to disappoint."

"So, what's the baggage part?"

"That characteristic doesn't work too well in relationships. Women have found me overbearing, one prone to explaining how things work instead of just enjoying discovering what's there. You reading about my successes actually made it seem less like I was boasting. Many told me as much. I'm proud of what I accomplished. I pursue what is right and, in effect, make others feel like they're not good enough. Not worthy of me. I never want you to feel that way."

"I do, but not because of you. You always made me feel special…loved."

"Good. Because I failed at that with the others, and I worked hard not to mess things up with you. Agreeing to pursue a relationship with you meant jumping into fatherhood, something I had no experience doing and couldn't really learn from a textbook. Emily was my biggest challenge. At least, that's what I thought at first. My being successful in a relationship is tied to my manhood, so when you sent me away…"

"I made you feel like less than a man."

"Yeah, something like that."

"I'm so sorry."

"I know you are, but you don't need to apologize for that anymore. We've grown a lot since that night. I'm glad it happened." He paused for a breath. "Don't get me wrong. It hurt like heck, but it led me to understanding who I am and can be with you." He kissed the back of her neck and adjusted to press his lips to hers. "I love you."

"And I love you." She smiled up at him. "Ready to go to bed?"

"Let's stay here for a while longer."

As soon as he repositioned himself against the pillows, she pressed into him and secured his arms around the moving mounds of her kicking baby.

"Wow. Think he'll settle down?"

"After a bit." She closed her eyes again and thought of the happy family she'd make with Zach. "By the way, you're a great father. I must admit you being younger than me had me worried, but you've been wonderful."

"Thanks. You saying that means a ton."

She smiled and snuggled into his arms. Once the baby stopped its kicking, she released the lingering pent-up tension, and her mind quieted down.

"Mommy? Daddy? Where are you?"

319

"We're here, baby girl." Tosha's eyes fluttered open. Daylight seeped through the curtains. "Did we sleep out here all night?"

"Mmmhmm." Zach said.

"Why didn't you wake me?"

"Too perfect."

She couldn't disagree. She wiggled out of his arms and wobbled onto her feet. "Baby? We have something to tell you."

Grasping Zach's hand, she led the way into the bedroom where they plopped on the bed with Emily in the middle.

***

Tosha dialed her best friend's cell phone and enabled the speaker. As soon as Karida answered, Tosha prompted Emily to start talking about what they'd rehearsed just moments before.

"Aunt Karida and Uncle Tevin."

"Oh, hi, little one. Give me a sec to put this phone on speaker so he can hear you." After a short pause, Tevin said, "Hey, Emily."

"Mommy and Daddy have something to tell you."

"We're getting married," Tosha and Zach said in unison.

Tevin guffawed. "Come on now. It's about doggone time."

"Watch your mouth, Tev. Little ears are listening," Tosha said.

"I kept it clean."

"We're so happy for you," Karida said. "Did you set a date?"

Zach spoke this time. "In fourteen weeks."

"Hoowee. That's quick, man."

Tosha smiled. "Three weeks before the due date."

"Wow. Let us know how we can help," Karida said.

"Why so soon?" Tevin asked.

"We want to get this done before the baby arrives. You understand, right, buddy?"

"I hear ya, brother. These women of ours keep us waiting until we say 'I do.'"

"Stop," Karida said in a playful tone.

"And so worth the wait," Tevin said.

Kissing sounds came over the phone.

"Hm. Looks like we started something." Tosha turned to Emily. "We better let Uncle and Auntie go."

"Where, Mommy? What they doin'?"

"Something husbands and wives do," Zach said with a grin. "We'll catch you two later."

"And, Zach, don't forget to tell Olivia. She'd want to be here for your wedding," Karida said.

"I'll call her right now."

Tosha ended the call and wrapped her arms around Zach and Emily, her new family unit. *Fourteen weeks. Wow.*

Chapter 21

"What are you two up to today?" Zach asked. He craved time with Tosha and Emily now that he'd returned from his two-week trip, even though it had only been four days since he'd seen them.

"We're going to the park."

"Cool, I'm on my way." Excitement revved him up. Without bothering to unpack, he returned to his car. His phone vibrated just as he pushed the key into the ignition. Olivia's phone number showed up on the dashboard screen.

He hadn't even finished saying "Hey, sis," when a loud squeal filled the car.

"Praise de Lawd. Me beerbee brudder getting married." She'd laid heavy on the Kittitian dialect. He'd forgotten how much he enjoyed hearing her speak like that.

"Yeah. Sorry I left a message. I wasn't sure when I'd be able to catch you."

"Dat aw right. I see the pictcha you sen' me. She pretty-pretty, eh? Ah whey you find she?"

"Karida and Tevin introduced us."

"Dey good friend. Always bin so."

323

"The best. Like family. So, are you able to make it back for the wedding? I'd really love for you to be a part of it."

"Wouldn't miss it for da worle. Only de two ah we left in we family now." A slight twinge of painful remembrance hammered at his chest. Her husband and daughter, their only child, had been killed in a highway pileup ten years ago.

"Well, this marriage will add two with one on the way."

"She hav' eh be something fe you to jump into farderhood so fast."

"She is, Olivia. I can't see a future without the three of them in it."

"I look forward to seein' she."

"Speaking of my new family, I'm on my way to take them to the park. I hate to cut this short, but…"

"No, you go to dem. I'll catch you later. Luv you tons."

"Love you more." Zach ended the call, started the car, and drove over to Tosha's place.

Fallen leaves crunched under the car tires as he pulled into a parking spot. He glanced toward the building. Tosha stood waving with Emily seated in a stroller. They wore jackets, and Zach grabbed his before exiting his car.

He jogged over and greeted Tosha with a hug and lingering kiss. Oh, how he'd missed her.

"Hey, baby bear," he said and kissed the girl's forehead.

"Hi, Daddy. I'm so glad you're home."

"Me too." He stood. "Ready to go?"

"Yes." Tosha began walking. "I brought the stroller. Figured you'd be tired after your trip. Hope you don't mind."

He smiled at her. "I don't. Thanks. It was a long flight."

Once they arrived at the park, he undid Emily's straps and helped her out. The little girl ran to the sandbox as soon as Tosha handed her a ball.

Zach kept a watch over Emily as he talked to Tosha.

"So, you really think your job will let us hold the reception there?" Tosha asked.

"Sure thing. I just have to book a date with the admin. Have you thought of any specific day?"

A boy walked over and pushed Emily onto her bottom before running away. Zach stood.

"Be right back." Zach strolled a few paces to his little girl. Sand from the sandbox covered her legs. He brushed off the sand and placed his hands under her arms to help her up. "You all right?"

"Yes, Daddy. Tank you," she said with a smile and began kicking her ball.

He returned and sat next to Tosha who leaned her head against his shoulder. He clasped her fingers.

"Three Saturdays before the due date good?" Tosha asked.

The boy approached Emily again and began pulling her ball away.

"Hold on, Tosha," Zach said and stepped briskly toward his daughter and the boy who taunted her.

"Hey! Back off!"

"You can't talk to him like that," said a woman in a sweatshirt and Capri pants.

"Is he your son?"

"Yes."

"Then tell him to stop picking on other kids. He's harassing my daughter."

"You stay away from him, or I'll call the cops."

"Fine. I have no problem telling them what he did."

She huffed. "You should take your girl and leave."

"No. *You* leave. She's done nothing wrong. Bullies are not allowed."

The woman took hold of her boy's arm and stomped away. She glanced back, sending dart-like glares his way. She said something to her boy.

Zach stooped next to Emily, all the while still following the woman and her son with his gaze. Beyond them, Zach spotted the same guy he'd seen before in a green-camouflaged baseball cap getting into a black pickup truck. Uneasiness rushed over Zach as he knelt on one knee.

"You okay?"

Emily nodded, her lips quivering. She wrapped her arms around his neck. He grabbed the ball and rose with her in his arms. She cried into the crook of his neck.

"Don't ever stand for that, baby bear. If anyone ever treats you badly, you tell me, okay?"

"Okay."

"You deserve to be treated with respect. I'll let you know who the good boys are. Some of us can make a mess of things. So, what are you?"

"Someone who deserves to be treated with respect."

"And who will help you choose the best guy?"

"Daddy."

"Good girl." When he reached Tosha, he said, "Let's go."

Tosha stood and held the stroller steady as he strapped Emily back in. "Where do you want to stay tonight?"

"Is my place okay? I don't have any clothes with me. We can order out."

"Sounds like a plan. Should I bring extra clothes to leave there?"

"Yeah," he stood, "and I'll bring some of mine to your place next time I stay over there."

Her smile warmed every part of him.

***

"All right, moms. We're going to practice faster breathing. The kind you'll need when the pain has kicked up a few notches, cluing you in that your baby's arrival isn't too much longer," said the Lamaze instructor.

"Mmm," Tosha groaned.

"What is it?" Zach asked.

"A Braxton Hicks contraction."

"You sure? Or will we be doing this breathing thing for real?"

Tosha blew out a soothing breath. "It's passed. I'm good."

"So, here's what I want you to do," continued the instructor. "Partners, shimmy up behind and make a V with your legs so your radiant moms can lean back against you. And, moms? Lean back and release all that tension. Your partner will support your weight. Bend your knees to the ceiling and spread those legs to give your bundle of joy a little room. Feel free to support your abdomen weight. Or, if you prefer, your partner can do that for you."

"Not sure if this is really Lamaze class or one-on-one foreplay," Zach said in Tosha's ear.

She trembled and slapped the hand that had already found its place under her rounded belly. "Stop, Zach."

He chuckled. "I'm just saying. Spread legs. Supporting your weight."

"You're making it harder for me."

"To do the breathing thing?"

"No. To keep you in my bed."

"Ahh. Sorry," he said. A few seconds later, her abdomen wobbled. "Wow. That baby has a strong kick."

"He likes you."

"Cool, 'cause I was afraid he was sending me a different message."

"Quick huffs for fifteen seconds starting…now."

Tosha complied, and Zach kept time with her.

"Okay, stop. How'd that feel?"

Mumbles and groans reached Tosha's ears. "Yep, that just about sums it up."

"Tiring work, huh?" Zach asked.

"Yes, and when the pain hits and the baby's coming, the whole breathing thing happens on auto pilot. It's as if the body knows what it needs," Tosha said.

"Again," said the instructor.

A few minutes later, during a break, Zach helped Tosha up. "So, you serious about the bed thing?"

"I hate saying this, but I need you to sleep on the sofa again."

"I'm cool with that. Now or after Thanksgiving in a couple weeks."

"After what you said during this class, I need you to start now."

He smirked. "Anything for my love."

The touch of his lips on hers sent warmth to all the right places.

"Break's over," said the instructor. "Let's continue before something else happens to speed up delivery. And yes, intercourse has been known to cause the onset of labor, so if the baby lingers past your due date, feel free to have some fun."

"Hmm," Zach said.

Tosha flashed him a stern glance. "Don't even say it."

His grin said more than words ever could.

***

The urgency Tosha felt for Zach refused to be quenched. His kisses shot hot waves through her. She barely remembered her three-year-old slumbering in the room nearby. Zach eased away just when she thought she might rethink waiting until they were hitched.

Who cared anyway?

He sat facing her, his panting matching hers.

"I should go," he said and slid his hand out of hers.

She stared at him as he walked toward the door, but then she turned away. She could not watch him leave. She wanted him too much. Minutes passed before she realized she never heard the door open and close, didn't hear the latch click when he turned the key.

Tosha turned slightly to see why when she found Zach rushing toward her, his eyes filled with hunger. Kneeling between her knees, he kissed her lightly.

"I can't leave," he said and kissed her again, this time a bit more eager.

"Mommy," called a little voice from the dark behind a closed door.

Tosha hesitated but instantly gave into her urges.

"Mommy," came the voice again.

"I have to check on her," Tosha said, her gut hurting from the delay.

"Go to her," he said.

Tosha woke on sweat-dampened sheets. She turned to look at the clock. Only two in the morning. She squeezed her eyes shut and patted the sheets. She was alone. Only a dream, but what a dream. She grappled the sheets and sighed, unsure whether in relief or disappointment. She drew a hand to her clammy forehead. She longed for him, knowing full well the risk hidden in that longing.

Her mouth felt dry, but she feared to satisfy her thirst. Zach slept on the sofa. She couldn't guarantee her self-control in this state. After fifteen minutes of toggling between closing her eyes and glancing at the time, Tosha sat up. She pushed off the bed, the baby kicking vigorously, awakened by her jostling, and waddled over to her bedroom door. Her belly wobbled slightly. In addition to being thirsty, she needed to pee. She placed an ear to the door but heard nothing. Perhaps he'd sleep through her visit to the kitchen. She eased open the door and stepped into the living room. She tiptoed toward the sink and exhaled relief.

"Tosha?" he said softly.

Oh, no.

"Why are you up? Is it the baby?"

"No," she responded, hoping he'd remain on the sofa. Instead, he stood by her side in seconds. His gentle touch shot waves of warmth through her, no doubt enhanced by the dream. Not a good sign. She fought not to think of the one thing she didn't want to do just yet. She shrugged away. "I'm fine. The baby's fine."

"What's wrong?"

She didn't want to say. She shook her head.

"Tell me." He turned her to face him, but she couldn't look him in the eye. "Tosha, did you dream about me?"

Her gut clenched. She nodded.

He smiled. "That good, huh?"

"Yes," she whispered, her voice quivering.

"I've dreamed about you every night since I met you," he said, surprising her but making her feel better at the same time. He kissed her forehead. "It'll be all right." He sighed. "Our wedding date is not too far away. Get some sleep before Emily gets up to open her Christmas presents."

"Will you join me?"

He cupped her cheeks and pecked her on the lips. "Between your dreams and mine, that won't be such a good idea. It's just a few more weeks. We can do this."

333

She sighed.

He released her face and stepped back. "You know you'll stop things the second it gets too hot, and I'll end up on the couch anyway." He smiled again before returning to the sofa.

He wasn't wrong. She filled a glass with water, drank her fill, and stopped for a visit to the bathroom before returning promptly to her room.

Chapter 22

"Today is your special day, Tosha," Karida said. "You look absolutely beautiful."

Tosha stared at her side profile in the mirror. "The dress doesn't make me look too big?"

"Not at all. The A-line is perfect for showing off your motherhood without exposing all your curves. Besides, Zach didn't want you trying to hide your pregnancy, remember?"

"I know. It's just messing with my head wearing white when I'm—"

"That's why you chose off-white. Stop downplaying the dress. You're messing up your radiance."

Tosha grinned. "I can't wait to be with him."

"I'll know where the fireworks are coming from."

"I hope Emily will be all right."

"Girl? She's already planned our week together."

A knock sounded through the door.

"You ladies decent?"

"Come on in, Tev," Karida said.

He peeked in his head. "Someone wants to meet Tosha." He opened up the door and let in a woman with features similar to Zach's.

"Ah just had to meet ma beerbee brudder's beautiful bride before the ceremony. I flew in too late last night to visit."

Tosha embraced and pecked Olivia's cheeks. "I'm so glad you stopped in. I look forward to catching up during the reception."

"Definitely." Oliva stepped back. "You sure looking good, Tosha. He pick well. I knew when he lef me a message to pray for two ah you that he'd done good. Ah met Emily. She's such a little angel."

"Thank you. How long are you staying?"

"Four weeks. It's bin too lang since ah set me eyes on Zach. It only right ah spen' some time before ah go back. You all ah me only family now."

"Zach told me. I'm so sorry."

"Let's not harp on that today. These are times to celebrate, and you could only cry happy tears."

Tosha nodded.

"Well, ah betta go back to Zach." Olivia paused for two breaths. "Tank you for meking him the happiest man on dis planet." She kissed Tosha's cheek one more time before exiting and closing the door.

Karida adjusted Tosha's veil. "You want us to decorate your new place while you're away?"

"No. Everything's happening so fast. Us buying a house the day before the wedding. Who does that?"

"Zach."

"Yes, so true. I think he wants us to do that together. Make it our own. We have the apartments for another month, so it'll be fine."

Another knock sounded at the door. "You two ready?" Tev asked without opening the door this time.

"Yes," Karida said.

"The music will start in five minutes."

"We won't be late."

"Emily's itching to go spread those petals."

"Mm mm," Tosha groaned.

"You okay?" Karida asked.

Tosha straightened and blew out a breath. "Braxton."

"You sure?"

"Yes."

"How often?"

"They've been happening more lately, but then they stop." Tosha rubbed her belly. "I'm good now. Let's get out there. This baby is not stopping this wedding."

"Great. Let's go."

***

Zach smiled as Emily stepped toward him while spreading red rose petals on the white runner. She trotted over to him and hugged his leg once she'd dropped the last petal on the floor just a few inches from where he stood. But when Tosha came into view in the open doorway, his breathing halted and his heart beat faster. Her radiance reached out to him and filled him with warmth all at once.

The minister said a few words, but Zach barely heard them.

"I do," she said.

"I do," he repeated.

Her vows, although nothing new, stirred his spirit. He repeated words he'd said before regarding his steadfast love for her. Tears streamed down her cheeks.

When the words "I pronounce you husband and wife" filled the air, he pulled her close and locked her lips with his. *'Til death do us part, my love. May God grant us long lives together.*

He looked down toward the little girl who tugged at his pant leg while everyone in the room cheered for them.

"Are you and Mommy married now?"

He lifted Emily up into his arms. "Yes, baby bear, we're a family now."

He took Tosha's hand and walked out of the room with his new wife by his side and his daughter on his arm.

***

Tosha swayed as she peered up into Zach's eyes. She finally had what she'd always dreamed. No. Better than her dreams. She had a man who loved her so much he gave up his bachelor lifestyle to become a husband and father all at once. She loved him with her entire self and couldn't wait to show him how much.

He spun her out and back again. Leaning close, he nibbled her ear.

"Ready for a change of scenery?"

"Mmmhmm."

He eased back and grinned. "Great." Taking her hand, he led her over to where Karida and Tevin chatted with Olivia.

"Hey, newlyweds, what's up?" Tevin asked.

"We're heading out. You okay taking care of everything?"

"Certainly. We got this. The gifts. The cake. Everything. You two go have some private time," Karida said.

"Is Mommy and Daddy going on the honeymoon now?"

Zach picked Emily up and kissed her cheek. "Yes, baby bear. You'll be staying at Aunt Karida's and Uncle Tevin's for a few days. You have panda, right?"

"Yes, and pony too."

"Good girl. Give Mommy a kiss."

Tosha hugged her little girl. "I'm going to miss you."

"I miss you too, Mommy. Nite nite."

"Hey, sis."

"Yes, beerbee brudder. Wait, you a big man now, all married and ting."

Zach hugged Oliva. "I love you. I'm so glad you're staying a while."

"Ha' fun. Don't tink 'bout us."

"Won't be a problem. Ready, Tosha?"

"So ready."

Zach placed his hand on her lower back and guided her out of the ballroom-sized conference room. They walked past the reorganized board room where they said their vows and stopped at the elevator.

With all the kissing and caressing, she barely remembered getting in the limo or the ride to the hotel where they'd spend the week. Her pregnancy was too far along to risk traveling long distance.

Zach helped her out of the car. She bit down a moan when her uterus tightened for a brief moment.

Not too bad. Another Braxton, right? It better be just another Braxton.

"You all right?" Zach's gaze held concern. She hadn't hid the discomfort well enough. "You want to go to the room first or get our bags?"

"Let's get the overnight bags, then you won't have to leave me alone."

"You got it."

When they reached Zach's Lexus, he opened the trunk and pulled out two bags.

Tosha glanced into the trunk and gasped. "You have my hospital bag?"

"Yeah. After what the Lamaze instructor said in class, I wanted to be prepared. It's been a looong time since you've been with anyone. Us doing it might actually start something."

"I see."

Zach smiled. "C'mon, let's go to our room."

Once they arrived on their floor, Zach unlocked the door with the electronic key and propped it open with both bags. Tosha stepped forward.

"Wait. I got to take you over the threshold."

She stared at her new husband. "You better not drop me."

He chuckled. "I won't. Trust me, sweetie."

"I do," she said and let him lift her up into his arms.

She wrapped her arms around his neck and kissed him as he stepped through the doorway. With careful motions, he set her feet back on the ground, his lips never leaving hers. A few moments later, he eased away.

"I better get our bags and close the door before someone gets an eyeful."

She giggled and rubbed her achy abdomen. *Why won't these pains just go away?* She walked over to the mirror and stared at her reflection then at her new ring. *I'm married. I'm a wife, and I have a husband.* She grinned and leaned into him when he approached her from behind.

"What are you thinking about?" Zach asked.

"Us. I'm so happy right na-ow."

A kiss on her neck radiated warmth down to her fingertips. His lips traced a path down her back as he pulled her zipper open. A gentle shove at the shoulder straps allowed her wedding gown to fall around her legs. She turned to face him and pressed her lips to his. Nimble fingers sought to let out each button on his shirt while he worked on his pants.

She ignored the slight pain radiating from her lower back to just under her navel. *That's different.* She didn't want to say what she feared might be happening. *Please wait until after.*

Zach guided her back onto the bed. She welcomed the touch of his fingertips from her shoulder to the palm of her hand. He'd just deepened the kiss when a sharper pain radiated from her back to lower abdomen.

"Ugh."

He paused, staring at her.

"Give me a minute." She blew out a breath.

He sat back on his heels, concern in his eyes. "Braxton Hicks?"

Another jolt of pain made her eyes water. "No. Too powerful."

"Bummer. A guy can't catch a break."

"Just give me a moment. Maybe it'll pass."

"Did I jinx us by packing your bag?"

"No." She huffed through the pain. When she thought it might be over, warm fluid gushed through her panties and down her legs. "Sugar Honey Iced Tea."

"You took the word right out of my mouth. Just a bit cleaner."

"I'm so sorry."

"Nothing to be sorry about. I'd just hoped it would happen after we…"

"Yeah, me too. Ugh."

"So, from what I read, once the water breaks, you need to go to the hospital. I'm calling Tevin."

"Zach?"

"I'm crazy about you, Tosha, and we're about to have a baby."

"But now you'll have to wait six weeks."

"They'll go like a flash, or maybe I'll be so tired from taking care of a newborn, I won't notice the time." He winked at her and pressed a few buttons on his cell. "The call's on speaker," Zach said during the first ring.

"Hey, man, shouldn't you be a bit busy just about now?"

"We were getting there until Tosha's water broke."

"Oh, snap."

"Yeah, I'll call you once the baby is born."

"Got it. Good luck. I'll tell everyone."

Zach ended the call and rushed to the bathroom. He returned with towels and began wiping down her legs.

"I wet the bed."

"They'll clean it up. I'll call the front desk while I grab our bags."

Tosha huffed through the call, being redressed in casual clothes by Zach, and a difficult walk down the hall and to the car from the elevator. "Your car."

"Will survive. I grabbed some extra towels. But don't worry about it. It's just a car. You are my new bride who is about to give birth to a precious little baby. Just think about that."

Her heart swelled at his words. Once they arrived at the hospital, Tosha signed paperwork while Zach hurried back out to park the car. He returned, panting, just as they began to wheel her to the delivery room.

He held her hand as the nurse checked how far along she was.

"We've got a bit of time yet. I'll call your doctor to let her know you're here."

"Thanks," Tosha said.

"Need anything?" Zach asked.

"Ice chips. Thirsty." He'd just returned with a cup when another contraction hit. "Zach." His name floated on a breathy huff.

"Yeah?"

"Press against my lower back. It hurts."

He complied, and the pain, although still present, didn't seem so overwhelming. In between contractions, she sucked on ice chips. Moments later, she felt the urge to push, but she sped up the rhythm of her breathing to keep from pushing until the nurse said she'd effaced and dilated enough.

In the middle of the next contraction, the nurse checked again.

"Oh my, your cervix is ten centimeters and fully effaced. Have you felt the urge to push?"

"Yeh-eeh-es, but I didn't know if I should, so I did my breathing."

"Oh dear. I'll get the doctor. You may start pushing now."

The nurse hurried to a phone while another approached the bed.

"I need you to push when I tell you. You'll push three times and then rest."

Tosha nodded, unable to speak for all the huffing she was doing. On signal, Tosha pushed and rested as instructed.

"You're doing great, sweetie."

"The doctor is almost here," said one of the nurses.

Tosha squeezed Zach's hand when the next contraction hit. Weariness washed over her.

"Bear down. Almost there. Push," said the nurse.

Tosha did so with all her might.

"Rest. The baby's head has crowned. A couple more pushes should do it."

Sweat streamed off her forehead, but Zach wiped it off for her. He even kissed her sweaty brow.

I love him.

The doctor entered the room and rushed over to the end of the bed. "I'm here. Give me a few good pushes, Tosha."

At the conclusion of the last push, the healthy wail of a baby reached Tosha's ears. She cried for joy as the doctor placed the baby on her chest. *What a precious gift from God on our wedding day.*

"What is it? Boy or girl?" Zach asked.

The medical staff glanced at each other. No one knew. The doctor turned the baby over on Tosha's chest.

"Boy. It's a boy. See if he'll latch on for you."

Zach smiled at her. "He's just like a little cub. This...this is incredible. Thanks for letting me be a part of it."

"I'm going to give the baby your last name."

"Really?"

She nodded. "You've been a father to him long before he was born. I want this."

"Thanks."

The doctor returned. "If he's all done, we need to take him for measurements."

"Sure, doc," Tosha said and handed over the boy.

She gazed at Zach. "Sorry about the honeymoon."

His lips formed a playful smirk. "Not a problem. We have the room for a week. I'm sure we'll figure something out."

"You're right. Intercourse isn't the only way to have sex."

"Teach me, oh wise one."

"Are you pulling younger guy rank on me?"

"For this? Absolutely."

She pouted at him.

"Does it help that I think you possess amazing strength for just doing what you did without an epidural?"

"A little," she said.

"Good, because your steel grip almost crushed my hand during one of those contractions." He chuckled just as the nurse returned with the baby and placed him on Tosha's chest.

"All the numbers look great. Take some time to bond with him while we clean you up. Did you choose a name?"

"We haven't had a chance to talk, but I thought Alexander would be nice."

"Yeah. That's cool. Do you mind if his middle name is T.J. for Teddy Junior?"

"I like it. Emily will too."

Zach grinned and pressed his lips to hers.

Chapter 23

Zach hugged his sister and let tears wet his cheeks.

"Thanks for *everything* you've done for us these last four weeks. We couldn't have made our new house a home without you."

"Anyting for me beerbee brudder. You have me heart, and I'm so very proud of the man you've become. Congrats on your new life as a married man and the promise of a promotion."

"I'm going to miss you too, Olivia."

"Oh, Tosha, you ah sweet and kind woman. Tank you for giving Zach you heart and you pickney. They sooo precious." Olivia knelt on the floor. "Come ya, Emily, gi' your Auntie Olivia a big hug and kiss."

The little girl rushed into his sister's arms and stayed there for many seconds.

"You sure you don't want me to take you to the airport?" Zach asked.

"Ah sure. You know how ah be 'bout good-byes. Be safe and stay as sweet as ever."

"We will. Call me when you arrive no matter the time."

"You bet."

Olivia smiled and kissed everyone again, ending with a small peck on the little baby boy's forehead.

She hugged the four of them as she prayed, "Loving Farder, please watch over dis new family. Keep dem safe and mek it possible for Zach to adopt Emily. In Jesus name ah pray. Amen."

A pang ached in Zach's chest as he watched his sister enter the taxicab. She waved as the taxi pulled away from the curb.

***

"You want to go to the mall?" Tosha asked. "I still need a few things for the baby."

"Sure. Give me a few minutes to refill the baby bag, and we'll be ready to go."

Tosha forgot how many things a tiny baby required for a simple shopping trip: car seat with handle that fit snug in a stroller, baby bag with bottles, burp cloths, diapers, and an extra outfit or two. She put a snuggly, warm body coat on Alexander and a girl's pant coat on Emily. Tosha didn't bother to button her own coat. *Too hot for that.*

Zach, dressed in a warm leather jacket, packed everything into the car without missing a beat and still wore his gorgeous grin as he drove to their destination.

"Where to first?" Zach asked.

"A store on the first level, but you can park outside the second level like we did before and take the elevator down."

"You got it."

Tosha smiled as she gazed at Emily whose eyes and mouth rounded with amazement at all the pretty New Year decorations in the store display windows.

"Dat's the store with the giraffe, right, Daddy?" Emily pointed to the children's store where she'd given Tosha a fright when she hid under the clothes.

"That's right, baby bear."

"Only hide when in danger."

"You remembered."

Tosha sighed in relief. No way she wanted to experience that again. A few minutes later, she stepped off the elevator and led the way to the store with the items she needed for her precious baby boy. He slept quietly having just been fed right before Olivia left for the airport.

"One elevator trip, and I'm already sweating," Tosha said.

"I get what you're saying." Zach nodded. "Having the baby is less work than the everyday care. Makes me admire my parents and others who have little ones."

Tosha unzipped Emily's coat, parked the stroller next to a tall shelving unit, and set to picking up some needed baby accessories.

"I'll be right back," Zach said.

Tosha hummed to herself and cooed to Alexander as his eyes flittered open. He had a drowsy haze. "Sleep, little one. This will take a while."

"Look what I found," Zach said as he held up a baby floor gym.

Tosha glanced around Zach's legs. "Where's Emily?"

Zach looked down and turned around. He gazed at her with eyes wide with alarm. "I thought she was with you."

"She stayed by me for a second, but then she walked toward you. I saw her." Tosha's gut dropped out and sank beneath her feet. "Oh, God. Zach, I can't lose her."

"She couldn't have gone far."

"She never wanders off."

"And she wouldn't hide again like she did."

Anguish washed over Zach's features an instant before he rushed for the store's exit. Tosha unlatched Alexander and followed with the baby cuddled close to her breast.

"What?" Tosha asked.

Zach glanced about the mall's walkways. "I don't see her. We need to tell security."

"How can you be so calm? I'm hurting here."

"And you think I'm not?"

"She's *my* daughter."

***

Tosha's words wounded him.

"So what? I can't love her as much?"

Tears welled up on her lower eyelids. His tone had been too harsh.

He spoke past the lump forming in his throat. "That little girl stole my heart from the first moment I met her. I'd be devastated if we don't find her. Don't think I love her less than you do because I didn't have a part in her existence."

"I'm sorry." The baby fussed in her arms.

Zach huffed out a breath. "I think I saw that guy with the camouflaged baseball cap. I'm scared *he* took her. Tell the cashier to call security. I'm going to look for her."

"I want to help find her." The baby's fussing grew into an agitated cry.

"It's too much with T.J. You're still healing. Please. I'll text you when I know something."

She nodded and backed into the store.

He sucked in a shaky breath and prayed, "Jesus, help me find her." Panning the immediate area, he sprinted past many stores in search of his little girl or that man he kept seeing.

An image of the painted giraffe flashed in Zach's mind. He found an escalator and bounded up the moving steps, never stopping his search for his girl or her possible kidnapper.

If she isn't there, I'll check every store until I find her.

He found the children's store and rushed in. He squatted and scanned under the first set of racks. No Emily. *Where is she? No, she wouldn't hide so close to the entrance. Where is that giraffe?*

Fear gripped him. *What if they painted over it?* He kept moving toward the back of the store. The clerk glowered at him.

"I'm looking for my daughter. She's missing."

Concern flashed over the clerk's face just as screams from somewhere outside the store reached Zach's ears. Panic jolted him. *Tosha.*

He turned to the store's rear and spotted the door with the giraffe painted on it. Squatting again, he saw little feet.

"Emily," he said softly, "is that you?"

The feet shuffled. Then a little voice came forth.

"Daddy?" Emily's voice.

"Yes, I'm here, baby bear. Come out."

She rushed out from the clothes and wrapped her arms around his neck. "Daddy! The bad man took me when I tried to find you. I did what you said. I smashed his foot. He said bad words."

"So glad I found you." He texted Tosha. *<I found her.>*

"Where's Mommy?"

"Let's go find her. She'll be so happy to see you."

A gunshot rang out, followed by more screams and people running for cover. He had to find Tosha and Alexander.

He lifted Emily and dashed to the exit that the clerk had begun to close.

"Wait. Let me out."

"Sir, it's not safe," the clerk said. "The shooter's out there."

"I have to find my wife and baby."

Zach glanced at his phone. Still no return text from Tosha. *Where are you?*

He ducked and rushed back to where he'd left Tosha.

"I'm scared, Daddy."

"I know. Just hold on to me."

Peering over the railing, Zach spotted the top of the camouflaged baseball cap. He slowed his pace and studied the man's gait. The guy lifted his gun and pointed it in the direction where Zach had left Tosha. *Please, God, no. Don't let him hurt her and the baby.*

Zach hurried past shoppers ducking into shops or heading for the exits. He reached the escalator and let it carry him down as he said reassuring words to Emily. As soon as the guy spotted him, the barrel of the gun moved from Tosha to Zach. Slow steps brought Zach next to a frozen Tosha.

Emily gasped. "There he is. The man who took me." She began to whimper.

Zach drew the girl's pointing finger back and placed her arm on his shoulder. He patted her back. "Look at baby brother in Mommy's arms." He didn't want the guy's grimace to instill fear into her mind and heart.

"I want the little girl," the man said.

By instinct, Zach tightened his embrace around Emily.

"Don't," Tosha whispered.

"I won't," Zach whispered back. "What do you want with her?"

"Chaz wants his daughter back."

"Chaz did this?" Tosha asked. "How could he do this to his own flesh and blood?"

"Hand her over, and there won't be any trouble."

"Well, we don't know you. We'll work this out with Chaz face-to-face."

"That's not the deal."

"Zach, be careful."

He turned to Tosha. "He won't hurt the one person he came for. Back up into the store."

She shook her head.

"Please," he said and faced the man once again. "Call Chaz."

The man hesitated, and Zach hoped he'd given the cops enough time to approach unnoticed.

"Ah, forget this," the man said and leveled the barrel to Zach's head.

"No," Tosha cried out from some distance behind.

Zach's mouth went dry as he focused on the gun so that he wouldn't give away those approaching from the man's rear. *His trigger finger is twitching. I don't know if...*

"Drop it."

The man grimaced and shook his head.

"Don't make me shoot you," the cop said. "Drop the gun now."

The guy's body tensed seconds before he lowered his arms and let the gun fall to the floor. Only when the cops threw the kidnapper down on the floor did Zach exhale and turn in search of Tosha.

Tears streamed down her cheeks.

Without hesitation, Zach dashed to his wife and wrapped his arm around her.

"Daddy? We safe now?"

"Yes, baby bear."

Without conscious thought, Zach pulled out his phone and called Olivia. He spoke the instant he heard her voice. "Getting ready to board, sis?" His voice quivered.

"I just sid down in de plane. I hav a little time. What de matter?"

"Your prayers kept us safe today."

"Wha' happen?" She gasped when he told her.

"Tosha's ex hired a man." He dared not refer to the brute as Emily's dad. She wouldn't want that.

"Dear Jesus. Ah so glad you all alive. Wahn me to stay?"

"No. We'll be fine. Shaken up, but okay. Love you tons."

"Luv you more, beerbee brudder. Perhaps, eh time to go back to chuch."

"I think you're right." He ended the call and looked up to find one cop approaching.

Zach spoke first, followed by Tosha and Emily. The police officer took notes and frowned when Emily told him how the man pulled her out the store.

"He told me not to say anything or he'd hurt Mommy. I remember what Daddy said about the giraffe store. I stomp his toes and ran to hide."

The cop peered up at Zach who pointed out the store Emily talked about.

"That was very brave." The officer smiled at Emily. "Thank you for your statements. We'll need you to come down to the station once we have Chaz in custody."

Tosha stepped away to retrieve the stroller from the store they'd been shopping in when all this horror started.

"I love you, Daddy." Emily snuggled her head into the crook of his neck. "You're da best Daddy in the whole world."

Her words cast out the fear that almost paralyzed him moments earlier. "I love you, too, baby bear. Let's go home."

***

Zach snuggled with Tosha and Emily in the master bedroom's queen bed that night, too traumatized to sleep apart. He read stories until Emily fell asleep.

Suddenly, Tosha dashed out of bed. Zach followed. She threw up in the toilet then went to the sink to wash out her mouth.

"Tosha?"

She walked past him into the living room, head bowed, and slumped to the floor near the sofa. He flew to her side, wrapped his arms around her, and pulled her up to her knees.

"I'm so sorry," she said.

"For what?"

"For the things I said today. I know you adore her. I shouldn't have implied… When he pointed the gun at you, all I could think was I didn't want those words about her being my daughter to be my last to you. I was so scared."

"I was scared, too. But remember, they weren't your last words. We were both frightened we'd lost her. I forgive you. Please forgive yourself."

"She chose the right man to call Daddy. I don't want to lose you."

"And you never will."

He kissed her, and her muscles relaxed in his arms.

Chapter 24

Tosha gathered her papers and her nerve as she stood to follow the police officer down the hall. She glanced back once at the two children she birthed and their daddy, dreading the upcoming conversation with the man who supplied the genetic material that fathered them. That's the only thing she ever wanted from him. That and his squirmy signature on the papers she carried.

Zach had offered to join her, but she must do this alone—face Chaz and be done with him once and forevermore. The cop turned around a corner and stopped at the closest door.

"Ready?"

She nodded and entered through the door he held open for her. Chaz sat in a small room with white walls, handcuffed to a metal table. He snarled at her.

"Wha' you want?"

"You know what I want." She placed the stack of papers on the table and shoved them toward him.

"I ain't signing that."

She snuck in a cleansing breath. "Either you sign these papers releasing Emily, or I will take you to court for child neglect and child support."

"Ha. Like you're going to get anything from me in here."

"You got savings. Plus, indecent exposure to a minor."

"What now?"

"Did you forget the orgy you had the day I left? She was with me when I walked in on you with everything hanging out. So, if you think kidnapping isn't enough of a charge, I'd be happy to add some more." She stopped talking and waited for some response. When he rolled his eyes at her and sucked his teeth, she leaned over the table to gather back up her documents.

"Wait."

She paused and stared at him.

"He'll take care of her?"

She straightened and clasped her hands in front of her slightly enlarged abdomen. "Yes, he's already started."

"Fine then." Chaz grabbed the stack of sheets and took the pen she offered him. In silence, he signed all the pages with the highlighted X on them. When he finished, he shoved the papers and pen toward her.

"Thank you. It'll be as if you never had her. See you at court for the other mess you caused for yourself." She picked up her papers and pen. "Looks like there's a blizzard in hell today."

"What?" Chad asked, a bewildered look on his face.

"Goodbye, Chaz." Tosha turned and exited the room. *Good riddance.* She couldn't leave fast enough.

"Did he sign them?" Zach asked as soon as she reached him and the children.

"Yes. He released her. You can adopt Emily now."

He looked down at Alexander asleep in his arms. "What about the baby? When will we tell him and how?"

Emily tugged on Zach's pants and said, "I'll tell him you're the only daddy he'll *ever* need."

***

Tosha nursed Alexander while Zach read Emily a story and tucked her into her bed. Tosha yawned. It had been a long day of checkups—the baby's and her six-week examination.

"You are cleared for intercourse," the doctor had said.

Tosha pretended not to notice Zach's grin, but the same happiness coursed through her body.

Once Alex burped, Tosha placed him into his bassinet in a second bedroom. The house they bought had four bedrooms and a den, doubling as a playroom for Emily. The fact that Zach could afford such a huge place still amazed her.

With the baby sleeping soundly, she returned to bed where Zach waited for her. He moaned and kissed her shoulder.

"So where were we before T.J. interrupted us to make an entrance?"

Tosha giggled.

"That's right. An attempt at our first time," he said.

She rolled on her back. "And?"

"You know what today is?"

"Let me guess."

"No. I'll just tell you. Six weeks plus one day."

"I see."

"So…"

She bit her lower lip. "So…"

"You ready?"

"So ready."

The End

Epilogue

(15 years later)

"Ready for your prom, baby bear?" Zach asked.

"Yes, Dad."

"Remember what I told you?"

"Of course. I memorized all my self-defense moves. And no sex."

"That's my girl."

Emily turned toward Alex who'd just peaked out the window. She stared at him, and he grinned at her.

"Relax, Em, he's not there yet."

"So, T.J., what do you think? Do I need makeup?"

"Naw. Lip gloss's good enough. I think the guy will find it hard not kissing you. You're beautiful."

Yeah, because she inherited her mom's amazing features. Zach frowned. *She's grown up so fast. Where have the years gone?*

Tosha entered the room, followed by the younger two, Zachary and Olivia. "Nobody's kissing anybody," Tosha said.

"That's going to be tricky since Dad's going to be there."

Just a precaution. "I'm sorry I have to chaperone you tonight, but we got news that your...father...did indeed get released from prison today. Your mom insisted. Although we moved soon after Chaz went to jail so he couldn't easily find us, we can't take chances."

"I know, and I don't mind," Emily said. "You're my real father now, and I'm glad you get to tag along. You've warned me about the other losers I liked. But you think this one's okay?"

"Yeah. He'll do."

"Good, then maybe my first kiss *will* happen tonight." Emily smirked.

"Don't push it, baby bear," he said and playfully jabbed her shoulder.

She laughed. "I trust you, Dad. I chose you, remember?"

"Yes, and I chose you, too. I love you. Have fun tonight."

"I will. I love you, too, Teddy Bear."

***

A few days later, with the kids hanging out with Karida and Tevin, Tosha took advantage of the time to spend some alone time with the love of her life. Snuggle time on the sofa followed lunch and a movie. He nibbled her ear and kissed the nape of her neck. *I love when he does this.*

"Shower?" Zach asked.

"But I'm not dirty yet," Tosha said and kissed his chin.

"I can change that. You got flour, right?

She eased away from him and studied his face. "Boy, you better behave."

He chuckled and stood. "It's more fun being naughty." He held his hand out to her. "Coming?"

"You bet," she said and cackled like a school-aged girl.

ೆಖ

<u>BONUS POEM</u>

I Can't Forget

ଔ

Special Note: This poem was first published in "A Love Gift" by Cassandra Skelton.

Cassandra Ulrich

෯

I Can't Forget

I can't forget those strong arms

that keep me from harm

Or those eyes that pierce through my

inner being.

Your strong stature of body and mind and soul

Makes my love for you stronger day by day.

I could never love anyone else the way

I do love you now.

I can never forget what my love means to you

Or your love for me. I love you.

AVAILABLE FROM

Cassandra Ulrich

A BEAUTIFUL GIRL

છ

Attempting to survive a horrible secret – abuse by her step-father, Sara meets the one person she dare not make friends with. Rick's friendly nature draws Sara into a relationship that helps her heal but also threatens her safety and that of her family. How will she escape the man who also holds her mother and siblings hostage?

Buy on Amazon

Buy Print on Amazon

Buy on Barnes and Noble

Buy on iTunes

Cassandra Ulrich

Love's Intensity

Brad loves fast horses, cars, and bikes. Life would be perfect if his stepmother could only mind her own business. Instead, his father hired a longtime friend and her family to work in their home, turning his world into a feudal mess.

He wants to hate the new arrivals and it doesn't help that Kressa, daughter of the newcomers, is the most gorgeous girl he'd ever laid eyes on. With a scent that draws him to her, Kressa causes him more internal conflict than he ever dreamed possible. He falls for her so deeply, he tells her a secret he'd never even told his best friends – that he's training to be a ninja warrior.

Kressa adores her country and loves hanging out with her many cousins. News of the move to Massachusetts comes as a shock to her. She refuses to be happy in this new place working as a servant for a rich man and his mean son, who had the nerve to be cute. And why does her skin tingle every time her hand brushes against his?

Despite her efforts, she finds herself desperately longing for a friendship with the one boy who scowls at her. Matters are only made more complicated when his family and hers clash. When he goes on a dangerous mission, she wonders, will he return so she can tell him he's won her heart or will their families manage to keep them apart?

Buy on Amazon

Buy Print on Amazon

Cassandra Ulrich

Billiard Buddies

An avid pool table player, Gina has yet to meet her match among her billiard pals. Pete O'Reily, one of the guys she plays against at a local bar, finds someone he thinks will finally give her a challenging game.

Gina was thrilled she could finally compete with someone who sharpened her skills, but Sean Savage became much more to her after a few games. She started falling in love with Sean who remained loyal to his career-focused girlfriend, Cindy. Gina, having been hurt by a cheating ex-boyfriend, is determined not to cause the same pain to any woman. Because of this, she keeps her feelings for Sean a secret from everyone except her flamboyant cousin Gene and a girlfriend on the other side of the city.

Without realization, Sean stretches her ability to do this whenever he visits her like she's one of the guys. Conflict occurs on many fronts: Gina avoids her ex, Hank, who wants to get back together; Sean longs to marry Cindy who spends more time at work than with him; and Gina has a falling out with Sean when he tries to set her up with a friend of his.

Will true love prevail?

Buy on Amazon

Buy Print on Amazon

Cassandra Ulrich

ADELLE AND BRANDON
Friends for Life

Adelle answered yet another phone call from Brandon about his latest breakup. After all, what're friends for, right? During their last stint at Coney Island, they'd pinky sworn to be friends for life. At twelve, that's great, but at twenty-four, not so much. Will Adelle succeed at keeping her true feelings for Brandon hidden...again?

<u>Buy on Amazon</u>

<u>Buy Print on Amazon</u>

Cassandra Ulrich

If It *Kills* Me

Recent breakup. Layoff. What else could go wrong for Jaeson Rhodes? He just couldn't catch a break. That is, until he met Jessica Stewart.

After losing a promising accounting job, Jaeson secures a position at a coffee shop where he first meets Jessica. He instantly falls for her, but weeks later, he is shocked to find out his playboy-turned-suddenly-serious roommate, Rick Springer, is her new boyfriend. Jaeson, thrown into the middle of this mismatched pairing, is left tormented that he cannot have what he wants most. He's determined to let her know how much he loves her... even if he dies trying.

Buy on Amazon

Buy Print on Amazon

Cassandra Ulrich

DANNY R.O.S.S.

A blast during a covert operation destroyed a Navy SEAL's eyes and killed his best friend. He woke up six months later in darkness, his eyes wrapped. His only contact with the world a soft voice. When the wraps were removed, the world took on a different hue. His ruined eyes had been replaced with mechanical eyes. His new mission: Defend the defenseless on the home front with a young female prodigy scientist as his only lifeline during dangerous missions.

Buy on Amazon

Buy Print on Amazon

ABOUT THE AUTHOR

~

Cassandra Ulrich was born on the beautiful island of St. Croix, United States Virgin Islands, located east of Puerto Rico. Living in the tropics allowed her imagination and daydreams to flourish. For years, she wrote poetry and entered competitions. However, only many years later did she discover joy in writing stories longer than a few pages.

She published her first young adult novel, "A Beautiful Girl", in April 2011. The inspirational novel has already touched many hearts ranging from teens to adults.

Her second novel, "Love's Intensity", is a teen paranormal romance and was released on July 11, 2013.

Her third, "Billiard Buddies", a New Adult romance novella, was released on May 24, 2014.

On June 25, 2014, she published/released "Real Purpose: You Are Special", poetry written while in high school and college. She released "Life Experienced" later that summer.

On June 25, 2016, she published/released two more poetic compilations: "Encouraging Through Sharing: A Christian's Perspective" and "A Love Gift".

"I Exist. Hear Me." won first place in the South Jersey Writers' Group 2018 Poetry Contest, short story, "Adelle and Brandon" was released on August 29, 2018, short story Zale's Tale won a spot in "Beach Fun" released by Cat & Mouse Press in October 2018, and short story Battle at Kitee made it to the semi-finals in the Mad Scientist 2019 Science Fiction Writing contest.

New Adult novella, "If It Kills Me", was released on September 21, 2020. Young Adult SciFi Adventure and NaNoWriMo2011 winner, "Danny R.O.S.S.", was released on November 1, 2020.

In 2021, two non-fiction stories made it into two Chicken Soup for the Soul books: "I'm Speaking Now" and "Tough Times Won't Last But Tough People Will."

CONNECT WITH ME ONLINE

Web: Cassandra Ulrich, Author Official Mobile Friendly Site

Facebook Fan Page: Cassandra Ulrich, Author

Facebook Group: Cassandra Ulrich's Journey as an Author

My Blog: Cassandra's Journey

Twitter: @CassandraUlric1

Instagram: cassandra_ulrich

Do What's Write Writer's Group & Podcast: dwwpodcast

Made in the USA
Middletown, DE
22 January 2022

59398665R00219